Finding Hour Way

RANDALL ANDREWS

iUniverse®

FINDING HOUR WAY

iUniverse books may be ordered through booksellers or by contacting:

iUniverse
1663 Liberty Drive
Bloomington, IN 47403
www.iuniverse.com
1-800-Authors (1-800-288-4677)

ISBN: 978-1-4917-7193-8 (sc)
ISBN: 978-1-4917-7194-5 (e)

Library of Congress Control Number: 2015910999

Print information available on the last page.

iUniverse rev. date: 08/13/2015

Contents

HALF-FULL

MULLIGAN

The Lab and the Lavatory

It's funny now, in retrospect, to think back to how that day started. I went to my nine o'clock class that morning, organic chemistry, found out I'd failed my midterm, and just about had a nervous breakdown. I'd never been a 4.0 student, but I'd never failed anything either, which was good because I couldn't afford any retakes. What's funny is it honestly seemed like the end of the world, or at least a catastrophic derailing of my life. I'd failed the test, which meant I'd flunk the class, which meant I wouldn't graduate on time, my student loans would run out, and I'd be condemned to a lifetime of regret and minimum wage. I thought it was *sooo* important. But not for long.

Holding someone's life in your hands tends to give you a little perspective. It certainly did for me.

My next class was physics at noon, another subject that was kicking my butt, though not as bad as organic. Physics also had one major redeeming factor, a cute TA named Wendy Octover. She was a math whiz, and a total fox, but too timid to make an effective instructor. I always looked forward to seeing her, but she wasn't helping my GPA any.

It was the same as always that day, a bunch of scribbled equations and mumbled lecturing, little of which was comprehensible to me, until the very end of class, when Wendy announced that she had an opportunity for someone to pick up some extra credit. She was offering ten bonus points to anyone who could find a green and black camouflage wristwatch, which had been lost somewhere in or around the science building. This was a strange enough offer to start with, but then she pushed it way out there by adding that if someone did find it, they were to leave it where it was. Under no circumstances was anyone to move, or even touch, the watch. She only wanted to know its location.

I had no idea what to think about that, except that I could definitely use those ten bonus points. I'd keep my eyes open, just in case.

As it turned out, finding the watch was about as hard as finding a tattoo at a Metallica concert. About thirty seconds after I walked out of the lecture hall, I stepped into the men's room to take a leak, and there it was, waiting for me on the floor just below the urinal. I bent over without thinking, reaching for it, but remembered at the last second to let it be. I was surprised to see it was really just a cheap, plastic piece of junk, the kind of watch you could buy in the toy aisle at the dollar store. What value it could hold for my favorite physics nerd, I couldn't imagine, but whatever, ten points were ten points, and that's all I really cared about.

Still, I was curious.

I relieved myself first, because I really did have to go, and then I headed back to the lecture hall, where Wendy was still erasing her notes from the whiteboard.

"Miss Octover," I said when I was almost to the front desk. Apparently she hadn't heard me coming, because she just about jumped right out of her shoes at the sound of my voice. "Oh, sorry. My name's Brody Wyoming. I was in your last lecture. I found your watch."

She made Kermit the Frog eyes for a second, like I'd just given her the winning lottery numbers, and then she bolted past me, up the aisle, and right out the door. I followed after her, *walking*, and found her waiting for me in the hallway.

"You'll need to show me where it is," she said, looking suddenly embarrassed. "I forgot."

From the mouth of a math genius. Seriously.

I led her to the men's room, checked to make sure no one was inside, and then held the door for her.

"You're sure no one's in there?" she asked, hesitating. "And you're sure *it* is?"

"I'm sure," I answered, "about both."

She took a deep breath, building up her courage I guess, and then marched inside. She spotted the watch before I could point it out to her and immediately rushed to it, kneeling down on the tile floor so she could read its digital face.

"Do you know what time it is?" she asked without turning toward me. Her voice was jumpy with barely contained excitement.

I reached automatically to my pocket, remembered I still hadn't come up with the money to replace my broken cell phone, and shrugged. "It's got to be about ten after two."

She made the Kermit eyes again and then bolted away, just like before.

I was about to chase after her, to remind her I had ten bonus points coming, but she reappeared at the door.

"Could you watch that for a minute?" she asked. "But don't touch it." And then she was gone again, zipping away without waiting to hear my response.

When she returned, she was accompanied by another woman, whom she introduced as Dean Flannigan, the head of the physics department. *Doctor* Flannigan was a sixtyish woman whose short gray hair was still tinted faintly with its former reddish hue. She had sharp, green eyes and an all-business handshake.

"Well, Mr. Wyoming," the dean said as she released my hand, "I'm very grateful for your assistance in this matter. I understand Miss Octover has promised you some bonus points toward your physics grade. She also tells me you could use them. Good, they're well earned. You can go now."

I was a little put off at being so abruptly dismissed, and at having my scholastic failings discussed with the department head, but whatever. Besides, I was starving, and my next class was at three on the other side of campus.

As I started to leave, the two women knelt down before the urinal in a position that struck me as almost reverential. I had a feeling that despite her extended college career, Wendy Octover had never prayed to the porcelain god.

I backed into the doorway, but hesitated when I realized I could see the ladies' reflections in the mirrors that hung on the wall opposite them, above the sinks. Dr. Flannigan had opened a black, plastic case I'd noticed her carrying, and from it she extracted what appeared to be a G.P.S. unit.

"Do you see what time it says?" I heard Wendy ask. "This means it really happened. I mean it really worked. I can't believe it!" Her voice was hushed but urgent, and her words spilled out so quickly I could barely understand them.

"Yes, it worked," Dr. Flannigan agreed, sounding much less surprised, "but it's not time to celebrate yet. We need to conduct another test right away and see if we can adjust the settings to compensate for this geographic drift. We'll use as precise coordinates as we can, but remember, we can't be sure Mr. Wyoming, or anyone else for that matter, didn't move the watch from its original arrival position. In fact, we can't even be sure it didn't materialize some distance above the floor and fall down to where it ended up."

In the mirror I saw the two women get back up to their feet, so I ducked out into the hallway and melted into the sparse but steady flow of students passing by.

What I should have done next was go power down a burrito in the dining hall and head to my three o'clock botany lab. But *nooo*, I let my curiosity get the best of me instead. I couldn't resist.

I shadowed the two women through the building, being way more cautious than was necessary. They were so engrossed in their own whispered conversation I probably could have done cartwheels down the hallway behind them and they wouldn't have noticed.

They made their way to the lowest level of the building, which was uncharted territory for me. I knew there were several labs down there as well as the professors' offices. After creeping down the stairs behind them, I leaned out around the corner just in time to see the nearest door swinging slowly closed. I rushed forward and barely managed to keep it ajar with the toe of my shoe.

Nobody else was around, not even Jim Fitz, the building's custodian, who was a seriously crotchety old dude who sold "homegrown" out of the back of his VW microbus to supplement his income. He was like an old hippie who'd lost the *make peace* mindset of his counterculture youth, but held on to the big hair and the pot habit. He was only supposed to clean and do maintenance work, but he was notorious for giving students a hard time when he wasn't giving them a fair price. If he showed up and caught me spying on a dean, I'd be in deep crap for sure.

Careful to keep the door from slipping closed, I leaned in and held my ear to the gap. I could hear the two women continuing their conversation inside.

"So once we've programmed in the shift coordinates, we'll try it again?" I heard Wendy ask. "The watch again?"

"We'll try again," Dr. Flannigan answered, "but not with the watch. We'll try to confirm the results of the first test with a different method, as a double check. I was thinking of an ice cube. As hot as they keep it down here it won't be hard to tell whether or not it's worked."

A door directly across the hallway opened right then, and out through it stepped a very scholarly looking, silver haired man in—no kidding—a tweed jacket. The man paused, looked at me, started to say something, looked at the clock on the wall, and then continued on his way. Apparently he was too crunched for time to report my spying and bring an end to my academic career, which he could have, I was certain, which prompted me to wonder just what in the world I thought I was doing? Sure, I was curious about Wendy's strange behavior and about her mysterious conversation with Dr. Flannigan, and yes, about how that two dollar watch ended up under the third floor tinkler, too, but was I *that* curious? Was it worth risking three-quarters of a bachelor's degree over? Probably not. Then again, if I flunked organic it'd be a moot point anyway.

I'd nearly talked myself into leaving when a strange, mechanical hum began to emanate from the room. It sounded like someone had hit the start button on a turbo-charged microwave, and for all I knew someone might have. Who knew what they tinkered with down in the dungeons of Southern Michigan University? Dr. Flannigan could have been some mad scientist with tenure and a grant (and a cute TA), conducting all sorts of bizarre experiments right there beneath all those classrooms full of naïve and overcharged students, like myself.

I eased the door open a little further and poked my head inside. Wendy and Dr. Flannigan were both bent over computer terminals on the far side of what turned out to be a spacious laboratory. As was the case in the hallway earlier, they seemed much too preoccupied to take note of my presence.

In the center of the room a dozen or so metallic spheres were arranged in a six-foot wide circle on the floor. Each shimmering globe was about the size of a grapefruit and sat perched atop a short pedestal, four or five inches tall. Heavy electrical cable connected their ring, and the current flowing through it filled the room with the humming sound that had piqued my curiosity. I couldn't even hazard a guess at what the contraption was meant to do, but my finely honed instincts told me it was *not* for speed-cooking frozen burritos.

There's one other thing. As crazy as it sounds, the spheres were sort of . . . hard to see? No, that's not quite it. Maybe it's more like they were . . . hard to *look at*. I don't know. It's hard to describe. I mean they were right in front of me, and the room was certainly well lit, but I couldn't quite manage to bring them into focus. It was like trying to make out the wings of a hovering humming bird. I rubbed my eyes, but it didn't help. Since everything else still looked normal, that hardly surprised me.

"We're getting close," Dr. Flannigan said as the steady hum progressed into a pulsing rhythm. "Go ahead. Put it right in the center of the ring."

Wendy straightened up, spun toward me, and froze. Busted. Her eyes locked with mine, and a look of sheer panic came over her face. In fact, she looked terrified, like *she* was the one caught with her hand in the cookie jar. I was the one who was going to be in trouble, right? I was pretty sure.

"Have you got it? Are we ready?" Dr. Flannigan called out, still without turning away from her computer.

Wendy held my stare for another fraction of a second and then hurried across the room to a gleaming stainless refrigerator. She jerked open the appliance's top door and dug a single cube out of the ice-maker reservoir. By the time she slid it into the middle of the spheres, the thrumming of the machine's voice had quickened to a pace that almost matched my racing heartbeat.

As she stepped cautiously back from the apparatus, Wendy's eyes shifted quickly from Dr. Flannigan to the ice cube to me. She finally settled her attention in my direction and mouthed a few words I didn't catch. I pointed at my ear and made the *no comprendo* face.

"I said you should leave!" she hollered back, her voice echoing across the room, which had fallen suddenly, and perfectly, silent.

Maybe I should have—left, that is. Maybe I should have turned around and sprinted right back out the door. And maybe I would have—if it hadn't been for that stupid ice cube. At the exact moment when the machine fell silent, I glanced over and saw it become a tiny puddle of water.

Now I'm not saying it melted. I knew right away that's not what had happened. Even if you'd thrown it into a furnace, there still would have been a split-second when you could've seen it changing phase, and this happened instantaneously. None of it turned into steam, and none of it trickled across the floor. It was a still chunk of ice, and then it was a still pool of water. There was nothing, including time, in between.

"What was that?" I asked, stepping into the room, drawn to the edge of the ring. "What just happened there? How—"

"Wendy, would you go make sure the door is closed, please, and *locked*," Dr. Flannigan said, cutting me off. I was surprised at how calm she sounded. I was not feeling calm.

Wendy went and rattled the doorknob a few times. I could hear her mumbling, but could only make out a few words. "Too excited . . . more careful . . . complicates thing . . ."

"Is this some kind of turbo-charged microwave?" I asked, looking back and forth between the two women. I really did. And, of course, they both looked back at me like I was an idiot. *Like* I was an idiot, not *because* I was an idiot.

"Why don't both of you come have a seat," Dr. Flannigan suggested, pulling out two chairs from the table beside her. "Don't worry, Mr. Wyoming, you're not in trouble. In fact, I might have some more extra credit work to offer you."

She said this so innocently, like it was no big deal. She didn't give away the slightest hint that she was about to ask me to risk my life.

Dr. Flannigan didn't bother starting at the beginning. In retrospect, I imagine she skipped over most of it because she knew it would be way over my head anyway. I was, after all, struggling to master basic physics concepts that were 200 years old, and what she was doing was literally revolutionary. She was way . . . ahead of her time. So to speak.

At the Dean's request Wendy retrieved a familiar camouflage watch from the pocket of her corduroys and laid it on the table. It read 3:25.

Dr. Flannigan reached across the table, showing me that her own watch, which was a gold-banded beauty that definitely did not come from the dollar store, read 2:25.

"It's an hour ahead," I noted uncomprehendingly.

"And so is the ice cube," Wendy added. She had an expectant look on her face as she said this, but her expression quickly changed to one of disappointment. I still didn't get it.

Dr. Flannigan picked up the plastic watch and held if before me. "This doesn't merely read an hour fast, it actually is ahead of us. Of everything. It spent an extra hour *yesterday* that we didn't."

That certainly didn't clear things up for me, but it did get me thinking along the right line. And what thoughts!

"Are you trying to tell me . . . Did you build a time machine?" I felt ridiculous even saying the words.

Dr. Flannigan and Wendy shared a long, meaningful look, and then, in almost perfect unison, nodded together in confirmation.

"Moldy crap." What else was there to say?

Dr. Flannigan moved the watch closer to my face, forcing me to focus. "I had Wendy pick this up on her way to campus this morning," she said. "As far as I know, it hung there on the rack where she found it all day yesterday, probably without ever moving an inch. From ten to eleven yesterday morning it was *also* sitting on the floor of the men's room above us, right where you found it this morning."

"And it was there all night?" I asked, struggling to concentrate.

"No, it spent the whole night in the store," she corrected. "Wendy didn't pick it up until this morning, and we only sent it back to yesterday for one hour, from ten to eleven. It spent that hour in both places, in the store and in the bathroom. At eleven, the *older* watch was pulled back here, and it returned to the exact same moment when it left. I just miscalculated slightly, which is why it ended up in the bathroom. Our intention was that it would move back and forth through time, but stay right in the same physical place, right in this room. There was a little drift we didn't anticipate."

"But as you saw with the ice cube," Wendy added, "we've already corrected for that. It would appear the machine worked perfectly on the second try."

"So the ice cube did melt," I thought aloud, "but it melted *yesterday*. You sent it back for an hour, it melted, and then it came back here to the same moment it left—as a puddle of water. Moldy crap."

The three of us sat quietly for a moment while I processed.

"So you can only send something one day into the past?" I asked and then waited for the double-nod reply. "And it can only stay there, *then*, for one hour? And then it comes right back?"

Nod, nod.

They let me be for another minute. I tried to think through the implications and applications of the technology they were describing. A new thought occurred to me, a really *out there* one.

"Were you in here yesterday between . . .?"

"Between 2:22 and 3:22 in the afternoon?" Dr. Flannigan finished for me. "We sent the ice cube back at right about 2:22, and so it would have spent the next corresponding hour here yesterday. And no, I wasn't in here during that part of the day. No one was."

"Would you remember seeing the ice cube if you had been?"

She stared at me blankly for several seconds, taking way too long to answer. Finally, and quite unconvincingly, she said, "Yes."

"Could you send anything back? Anything that would fit inside the ring?"

She hesitated again before answering, "Or anyone."

Extra credit work?

Moldy crap!

Yesterday's Hero

In a feeble effort at subtlety, Dr. Flannigan followed up her earth-shattering revelation by asking me to deliver some paperwork to one of her other TAs on the third floor. She could have just asked me to step out of the room for a minute so she and Wendy could talk in private. I'd have been happy to get out of there and catch my breath anyway. I needed to.

I made it about five steps from the door before I heard the knob rattling behind me, and I had to smile. No one else was likely to be walking in uninvited any time soon.

I took my time delivering the papers and barely noticed the people I passed by. Believe it or not, I didn't even consider telling any of them there was a time machine in the basement. Like they'd have believed me.

I knocked when I returned from my errand, but didn't have to wait to be let in. Wendy flung open the door as soon as I touched it, grabbed a handful of the sleeve of my shirt and pulled me inside.

"Come on," she urged. "We have to hurry." She looked frantic.

We rushed back over to the table, where Dr. Flannigan was still seated. A newspaper was opened out before her.

"Have you read the new Campus Bugle?" she asked. She spun the paper around so it was right-side-up for me and flipped it back to the front page.

I shook my head and started tracing my fingertips down from the top, taking note of each article. I wasn't surprised to see the top story was the basketball game. We'd played our biggest rival the previous evening and pulled out a miraculous win at the buzzer.

The headline read, *It's the Woodsmen by O'Hare!* Grady O'Hare was our star guard, and he'd made the last shot of the game, a three from the corner, that had sealed the deal.

"Had you already heard?" Dr. Flannigan asked.

I looked up from the paper and nodded. "I was there. I saw it."

"You were there?" Wendy asked. She sounded shocked, and I didn't understand why. "You just . . . happened to be there?"

"Everybody was there. There wasn't an empty seat."

Dr. Flannigan looked at me quizzically, then rolled her eyes and said, "I'm not talking about the game. I couldn't care less about basketball. I'm talking about this." She stabbed her index finger into the paper. The headline she was pointing at read, *Pit Attack Results in Tragedy.*

The incident, it read, occurred at the corner of Main Street and Erie Avenue in full view of mid-afternoon traffic. Witnesses said the attack was unprovoked. The dog, a 16-month old pit bull, had been reported twice before for aggressive behavior. The victim, who died en route to the hospital, was a four-year-old girl who'd been walking home from the East Branch Library with her mother.

I flipped the page and scanned the rest. The author recalled several other dog-related incidents from the past year and briefly summarized the state and local leash laws and the potential penalties for violating them. He also mentioned that Sara, the little girl, had recently begun dance lessons and frequently told friends and relatives she was going to be a ballerina when she grew up.

The story was so gut-wrenching that for those few moments I completely forgot about everything else. I didn't even pause to think about why they might be having me read it.

"She was only four years old," Dr. Flannigan whispered. "Her whole life was ahead of her. It still could be."

My stomach clenched and all the air rushed out of my lungs. After several seconds my chest began to burn. When I was finally able to pull in a breath, I used it to say, "I'll do it. I'll go."

"It'll have to be right away," Wendy said. She still looked frantic, and now I understood why.

I glanced back to the camo watch, which was still lying on the table, but couldn't think clearly enough to remember if it was ahead or behind or what. "What time is it? When did it happen?"

"It's almost two-forty," Dr. Flannigan said. She still looked impossibly calm. "The girl was attacked at right around three o'clock yesterday afternoon, about a mile from here, Main St. and Erie Ave. You know how to get there?"

"Yes."

"And you're sure about this?"

I couldn't answer. Of course I wasn't sure, but there was no time to mull it over. It had to be yes or no right then. And it couldn't be no.

"Go on, stand inside the ring," the dean told me before turning back to her computer and typing in a quick sequence on the keyboard. "I need Wendy monitoring the second workstation, and you might as well be our third since you're now the only other person who knows."

I just nodded. I couldn't talk. As I stepped into the ring I noticed one of them had mopped up the little puddle of water while I was gone.

"Like I said," the doctor went on, "no one was down here yesterday afternoon, so the room will be empty when you arrive. The door will be locked, but you don't need a key to unlock it from the inside. Just flip the button."

"And then you'll only have twenty minutes to get there in time," Wendy added. "And then forty minutes after that you'll be pulled back here to the present."

"And you'll still be here?" I asked, finding my voice. "Both of you?"

"For us, it'll be like you never left."

Another insane thought I could barely wrap my mind around. I had a dozen more questions, but it was impossible to prioritize them. I ended up asking none.

Both women were seated at their workstations now, and the machine started to hum. It seemed like the pulsing, and then the acceleration of its rhythm, came quicker than before. It probably just seemed that way.

"Wait," I yelled when I was struck by what should have been an obvious thought. "I need a watch. Or a cell phone. I need to be able to keep track of my time."

Without looking away from her monitor, Dr. Flannigan slipped off her watch and handed it to Wendy, who rushed it across the room. She pulled up just outside of the ring, and then tossed it to me rather than reaching it across.

"This is so brave of you," she whispered so softly I had to half-read her lips. "You'll be a hero." Then she dashed back to her computer.

I won't say I felt fine about things after hearing that, but I have to admit it did bolster my courage some. *Hero* is a hard word to resist, especially when someone's aiming it at you. Especially when that someone is a pretty brunette you've had a crush on all semester.

I pictured myself standing atop a podium in a yellow jersey, like I'd just won a stage in the Tour de France. Wendy stepped up beside me in a tiny skirt I'm sure she'd never really wear and kissed me on each cheek, Euro style. The crowd cheered. Then a giant, white pit bull appeared from nowhere, clamped its jaws over my ankle and dragged me, kicking and screaming, away down the street.

I shook my head and chased the images away.

The pulsing of the machine was racing, sounding like an out of round tire at highway speed. I knew there could only be seconds left. Fear and an overpowering sense of doubt gripped me. What was I thinking? I was risking my life!

I almost jumped back out of the ring, but I couldn't quite bring myself to do it. I'd like to say it was the little girl's story that kept me where I was, or even Wendy's pep talk, but I can't. At that moment I'd forgotten all about them both. What I was thinking about was what might happen if I was halfway out of the ring when it . . . did . . . whatever it did.

I heard a banging sound, like somebody knocking at the door, and then . . . nothing. I never felt dizzy or disoriented. I never felt anything except a little startled when the room went dark and silent—instantly.

"Dr. Flannigan?" I whispered. I didn't really expect her to answer. Wherever and whenever I was, it seemed more than likely that I was alone. It was pitch black and dead quiet. I couldn't even see the ring of spheres, if I was still standing inside them.

I dropped down to one knee and ended up setting the palm of my hand right on top of something cold and wet. A partially melted ice cube, I realized. Moldy crap.

I reached over and found part of the cable that connected the spheres. Very carefully, I stepped over the ring and started tip-toeing across the room in what I thought was the direction of the door. I ran into the white board instead, probably smeared some of Dr. Flannigan's notes, and then followed the wall to the door from there.

I tried the knob and found it locked. Surprise, surprise. It took me a second to figure out the button in the dark. I cracked open the door, letting in a blinding stream of fluorescent light, and listened for any activity in the hallway. As far as I could tell, no one was around.

I made it down the hall and up the first flight of stairs without running into anyone, but the ground level was packed. I felt like an intruder as I waded into the crowd, like the only one at a party who hadn't been invited, but no one paid me any attention.

And then there she was, stepping out from one of the lecture halls just thirty feet ahead of me. "Wendy," I called out, rushing toward her.

"Yes? Brody, is it? What can I do for you?"

And then it hit me. My mouth fell open, but nothing came out because I suddenly had no idea what to say. None of the things between us that were worth talking about had happened yet.

I improvised. "I . . . just wanted to tell you how much I enjoyed your lecture last week." Lame!

A look that was equal parts confusion and suspicion spread over her face. "Okay. Thank you."

Then came the awkward silence. I had no idea what to say, and obviously she didn't either.

"You'll have to excuse me," she said finally, but I have a meeting at three up on the third floor. I need to hurry."

She needed to hurry? I needed to hurry! What was I doing? The clock was ticking!

The urgency of the situation came crashing back over me like a tidal wave of responsibility, jarring me into action. I literally sprinted away down the hall, dodging in and out of traffic, oblivious to what Wendy or anyone else must have thought. I jetted past Mr. Fitz, accidentally kicked his push broom right out of his hands and heard him yell that this was *not the Indy 500!* Whatever.

I plowed into about four different people where the crowd was bottlenecked at the doorway and sent a curly-haired blonde's books and papers flying. I yelled *sorry* over my shoulder but kept going. She yelled something back I'm choosing not to repeat. Something really not nice.

I didn't slow down until I was three blocks off campus, and I wouldn't have slowed down then if I hadn't been run over by the bus. Well, run *into*, I guess, not *over*. Regardless, it hit me.

I was hurrying, and winded, and I wasn't being careful. I saw the bus ahead of me, just starting to pull away from its stop where one of the side streets met Main. I thought I could slip in front of it real quick. I stumbled on the curb. *Bam!* Pancaked by public transportation.

I literally bounced off the bus's grill and slammed into the side of a parked, and occupied, police car hard enough to put a big Brody-shaped dent right in his driver's side door. When my head hit the window it made a frighteningly loud *crack*, but it didn't actually break. My head, that is. The window didn't break either, but I was talking about my head. I'm surprised they didn't both shatter to be honest.

My final pinball maneuver was from the police car out into the middle of Main Street. I was teetering like a drunk and so stunned from the double impact I didn't even realize I was headed into serious traffic. The sounds of blaring horns and screeching tires assaulted me from every direction. The brief but wildly intense ruckus ended with a final, terrible note. My jiggled brain was barely functioning, but I did manage to come up with two words to go with the sound: *car crash.*

The next thing I knew I was sitting in the middle of the street with people all around me, asking if I was okay. I don't even know if I sat down on my own or if someone coaxed me off my feet. As my vision started to clear I realized the extent of the mayhem I'd caused. I could see at least a dozen cars jammed together all around me.

The police officer from the cruiser I'd hockey checked was leaning in through the window of an eighties Firebird right in front of me, shouting instructions. When he stepped back a moment later I saw a young man about my age seated behind the wheel. There was a trickle of blood running down the side of his face. I thought he looked familiar, but in my frazzled state I couldn't think from where. Probably a classmate of mine whose car and day I'd just ruined. At least.

It seemed like only seconds later the sirens started wailing from down the street.

"Well I hope it was pretty damn important," spoke a voice beside me, louder than the others, "whatever you were in such a big damn hurry for." I realized it was the police officer now addressing me. "I hope it was worth this disaster you just caused."

Why was I in such a hurry? For a second I couldn't remember. When I did I was immediately back on my feet and back in motion. I had to scramble over the hood of the Firebird in order to find enough clear pavement to start running again, and then I loped away down Main Street—in the wrong direction, away from Erie Ave. There was a throbbing pain behind both of my eyes that was making it awfully hard to think.

I could hear several different voices yelling at me and could pick the officer's out from the bunch: *stop right there, don't you dare, etc.*

I had to go back past the whole mess after I turned around and got headed in the right direction, which further infuriated the policeman, but he only continued to yell—he didn't come after me. He was a little busy.

My mind started to clear a little as I ran, but I still had to focus on every step so as not to trip and fall. My equilibrium was totally shot. I glanced down at Dr. Flannigan's watch, which was still around my left wrist, but the face had shattered, making it impossible to read. How long I'd set there after the accident, I had no idea. It was a blur. For all I knew I might already be ten minutes too late for poor Sara, the aspiring ballerina.

I reached the intersection of Erie and Main a minute later and found . . . nothing. No girl, no dog, nothing. Did that mean I was early, and it hadn't happened yet? Or was I so late that the aftermath had already cleared out? Was little Sara still at the library or already at the morgue? I didn't know. I couldn't think.

A powerful surge of nausea bloomed in my stomach, and I was so dizzy I had to sit down to keep from falling. I closed my eyes, took a few deep breaths, and tried to swallow down the sour taste of bile that was suddenly strong in my mouth.

When I opened my eyes again there was still nothing to see, which struck me as odd. It seemed like I must've been delayed long enough for my cushion of time to have expired, and yet it didn't seem like the attack could already have happened and every trace of it been removed. Unless . . .

It suddenly occurred to me that I couldn't really even be sure of what *day* it was, let alone what specific time. I'd just been sent into the past by a machine that had only been tested twice on inanimate objects, and that junky watch had only shown the time, not the date. Dr. Flannigan's calculations had been off once, and maybe they were off again. Maybe the watch and the ice cube and I had all been shot back a week instead of a day, or a month. What kind of temporary insanity had come over me anyway, making me agree to this crazy mad science experiment?

"Are you okay? Hey, do you need help?"

I looked behind me and found a concerned looking woman holding hands with a little girl.

"Were you involved in the accident down there?"

My heart, which had finally started to slow a bit, kicked right back up into high gear. I stood up too quickly and my head swam. The lava in my stomach climbed toward the surface again, threatening to erupt.

"I think maybe you should stay sitting," Sara's mother said, taking hold of my arm in an attempt to steady me.

I wobbled, windmilled my free arm a couple times, and ended up resting my hand right on top of the little girl's head, using her tiny frame for support.

She screamed.

"Sorry," I apologized, pulling my hand away.

She screamed again, and this time I knew it wasn't because of me.

I spun around and there it was, the pit, galloping toward us from the other side of Erie Ave. with its tongue flopping out the side of its mouth. Sara screamed again, but there was nothing to do, no shelter to reach quickly enough, no makeshift weapons close at hand. The dog would certainly reach us before we could reach safety, and I *knew* what it would do then.

The woman grabbed her daughter and dragged her away toward I don't know where. I kept my eyes on the dog. The stoplight changed and several cars accelerated into the intersection. *Hit him, hit him,* I prayed, but they weren't going to. I knew they weren't.

The dog charged to within ten feet and then leapt at me through the air. Somehow, by good reaction or good luck, I don't know, I wound up with my forearm in its mouth instead of my throat. We rolled and thrashed across the ground, and I could feel the skin of my arm tearing further with every shift in our struggle. I could tell I was hurt bad.

I could hear the screaming voices of both Sara and her mother, and the ferocious growling of the dog, just inches from my face. I punched at it everywhere I could with my free hand, but few of the blows landed solidly, and those that did seemed to have little or no effect. As we rolled back and forth I glimpsed a terrifying amount of blood spattered across the sidewalk and absently realized it was mine. I was in trouble.

The pain was incredible, way beyond anything I'd experienced before. It was so intense that when something hit me in the back with enough force to knock my shoulder out of socket, I barely even felt it. The sound of the blow, however, registered with me with perfect clarity. *Whump!*

Over and over the dog and I rolled, each struggling to get on top of the other and stay there. I couldn't believe how strong it was.

Whump!

This time I definitely felt something—I felt the dog let go. Suddenly I was free, lying there on my back, gasping like a caught fish that's been tossed to the bank.

"Get out of here!" screamed a woman's shrill voice. "Go on! Get!"

I lifted my head enough to see the little girl's mother standing between me and the stiff-legged pit, which was still growling and showing its teeth, now stained with my blood. Over the woman's shoulder, cocked like a big leaguer's bat, was a fat, hardcover edition of *The Once and Future King*. I realized it was the source of the *whumps* I'd heard, and the reason I was no longer being chewed on. She'd hit it with her library book.

The dog lowered its head and inched forward, ready to lunge. I knew there was no way the woman could hold it at bay, and as soon as it got its teeth on her she'd be just as helpless as I'd been. I tried to pick myself up, but found that neither of my arms was obeying my commands. I rolled to my belly, put my forehead to the pavement, and lurched up to my knees and then to my feet. I didn't know what I was going to do, but I knew I had to do something, *anything,* to try and help.

"Get out of here!" I yelled, echoing the woman.

As the dog turned toward the sound of my voice I could see its shoulder muscles tensing. It was about to spring.

A gunshot exploded right beside me, painfully loud in my ear. I stumbled back, tripped over my own feet and landed hard on my tailbone. I barely felt it.

Two more gunshots rang out in rapid succession. I desperately wanted to cover my ears, but my hands just lay there, unresponsive.

Into my narrowing peripheral vision stepped the police officer whose car door I'd dented, his pistol still trained on the still form of the dog.

"Mommy!" screamed a little girl's voice from behind me. I turned to see Sara on her hands and knees on the roof of a Cadillac that was parked at the curb, not thirty feet away. Apparently her mother had stuck her up there for safe-keeping before rushing to my aid with her deadly Arthurian legend.

My vision swung up, and I found myself looking into the concerned face of the policeman. I think he'd pushed me down onto my back, but I'm not really sure. The lights were almost out by then.

Sara's mother appeared beside the officer, and I was vaguely aware that they were doing something with my arm, wrapping it up in a cloth of some sort. I picked up my head for a better view, but could only hold it there for a second, just long enough to realize it was the woman's shirt they were using to bind my torn limb. I remember feeling embarrassed, which, in retrospect, seems pretty ridiculous. I was bleeding like crazy, hovering around the threshold of consciousness, probably concussed and possibly under arrest, and I was worried about some strange woman having to go down to her bra in public. *Seriously!*

"You're having quite a day," the officer said as he checked my scalp for damage. There were probably paint flecks from the door of his squad car. "Just take it easy. Help's on the way."

I tried to say *thank you*, managed something more like, "ay-oo," and then turned my head to the side and threw up across his shoes. The massive head rush that followed carried me into unconsciousness. Mercifully.

Unsung

I woke up about thirty-eight minutes later, give or take, in the hospital, which was, fortunately, only a couple blocks farther down Main St. from the site of my mauling. Of course I didn't immediately know how long I'd been out, but I know now, pretty close. I know because I only stayed in the hospital a couple more minutes after waking up. Then I came (dare I say it?) . . . *back to the future*. Or . . . to the present, really, but it seemed like the future when I was in the past. I mean it was the present when I left it an hour earlier, but . . .

Anyway, my left arm was laid across a stainless steel table, and there were about a thousand stitches in it. My right arm moved when I told it to, to my great relief, and seemed okay except for a dull, throbbing pain in the shoulder. My head felt like a mushy apple. It felt like there were worms in there crawling around and messing stuff up as they went. My mouth was watering dangerously, and I was pretty sure I was going to puke again.

"Oh, no you don't," said a woman's voice from so near it startled me. I realized there was a nurse standing right next to my bed, but I hadn't noticed her until she spoke. That's how out of it I was.

"Just close your eyes and concentrate on taking slow, deep breaths. You are *not* going to throw up. You hear me? You're fine. Just take slow, deep breaths."

I followed her instructions, and after a moment the nausea passed. I glanced back down at my arm and couldn't help but cringe at the sight. It looked like they'd done my repairs at a baseball factory.

"What'd you do, try to play dentist to a hungry crocodile," the nurse asked. "It could be worse, though. We had a guy in here last week who got three fingers cut off with a weed-whacker. Right off! This is nothing compared to that."

I tasted bile again. Gosh, I wish I could remember that nurse's name so I could send her a thank you note for her excellent care. Such a fine bedside manner.

She must have seen the look on my face and been afraid for her shoes, because she slowly backed out of the room, smiling all the way. "I'll go tell the doctor you're awake," she said when she reached the door. "He's right in the next room checking on the other boy, the one with the concussion that's not quite as bad as yours."

I took a better look around after she was gone and noticed Dr. Flannigan's ruined watch and my pocket knife lying on a tray, just out of the reach of my good arm. Make that my *better* arm. I shifted in the bed, scooting myself over inch by inch, and let me tell you, I earned every one of those inches. It felt like somebody had turned gravity up to three times its normal strength, boosting my weight to about five-hundred pounds.

Seeing the little flip-blade knife, an heirloom from my grandfather, certainly didn't boost my morale. I'd only been carrying it around in my pocket for about a decade, and though it wouldn't have been much to try to defend myself with against the dog, it would've been better than nothing. If only I'd remembered it was there.

I stretched my arm toward the watch, just brushed its cracked face with my fingertip, and then I was back in the lab, lying on the floor, surrounded by the ring of spheres.

The machine was silent. Wendy and Dr. Flannigan, both seated at their workstations, twisted around to face my direction. Expressions of shock bloomed across both their faces—at the sight of me, I assumed. Wrong.

"Mr. Fitz," Dr. Flannigan practically shouted from her seat, "I will not tell you again. The next time you enter this laboratory without authorization it will mean the end of your employment by this university. Now leave. Now!"

I glanced over my shoulder to see the smug face of the world's grumpiest building custodian peering in through the door. Apparently I really had heard someone knocking just before the machine sent me back. Fitz's gigantic ring of keys was dangling from the knob, and he was pointing the handle of a broom before him, giving the impression of both janitor and jouster. He eyeballed me for another moment where I lay within the circle of spheres, prompting Dr. Flannigan to shout out his name again, which finally sent him scampering away.

"What happened to your shirt?" Wendy asked, rising from her chair and striding toward me.

I was topless, I realized, and my shirt was lying next to me, bloody and torn. Actually it wasn't torn, I decided, but cut. Dr. Flannigan's broken watch and my pocket knife lay beside it.

"They must have cut it off me at the hospital," I answered. "I got bit." I held up my arm for show and cringed at the resultant surge of pain. Blood was seeping from the wound, which was, to my shock, *un*stitched. The jagged laceration was lined with neat needle marks, but there was no thread. It had disappeared.

"Oh my God!" Wendy cried out as she rushed to my side. "Bit by what? A Tyrannosaur?"

"By the dog," I said, unsure why this wasn't obvious. "I barely got there in time. There was nothing I could do but get in between it and the girl. What happened to my stitches?"

"Your stitches? You barely got where in time? What girl? Brody, what happened to you?"

I didn't even know what to say. Was she messing with me? No way. No way she'd be goofing around while I was lying there on the ground, bleeding. I looked to Dr. Flannigan for help.

"I think you'd better tell us everything that's happened to you, Mr. Wyoming," she said very slowly. "Start with this morning."

"But Doctor, look at his arm," Wendy interjected. "That needs taken care of before anything else. Whatever happened, he's hurt bad, and he needs to go to the hospital. Everything else can wait."

Dr. Flannigan continued to scrutinize me for a moment, and then said, "You're right, of course, but I don't know about taking him to the hospital if he just came from there. If he was just there yesterday, that is. They'd surely recognize him, his wound. How could we explain things? I know someone who works at the campus fitness complex who could help, and he'd be discrete. We'll take you there, Brody, get your arm treated, and then we'll figure everything else out after that."

I nodded my approval of her plan. As we headed out of the room I noticed the white board, still smeared by the clumsy swipe of my fingers. I assumed it had been that way for a day now, even though I remembered having done it only an hour before.

With the arrival of that most recent revelation came a wave of disorientation. All the evidence pointed toward my being back in what was to me the right time, where I belonged, but my connection to the present moment now felt fragile beyond belief. I was like a replanted tree whose roots were yet to take hold in their new soil. The slightest breeze, I felt, would topple me right over, send me crashing down into the past, or the present, or who knew when?

At Dr. Flannigan's suggestion, we rode to the fitness complex in Wendy's dilapidated Le Sabre, which was a rusting, late-eighties boat with a voice like a Harley. I guessed the dean probably had a car just as fancy as her watch, and she didn't want me trashing it, too, bleeding all over the upholstery.

We rode in silence. There were a hundred questions I wanted to ask, but something told me I should hold off. Dr. Flannigan's face was a mask of such deep consternation I felt like I'd be interrupting if I so much as cleared my throat. Plus, my arm was really starting to hurt a lot. Whatever pain meds they'd given me at the hospital were wearing off. Or maybe they'd disappeared right out of my bloodstream at the same moment I lost my stitches.

We parked at the back of the building, in the employee lot, and after asking Wendy and I to stay put for a minute, the dean headed in alone.

"I'm so sorry this happened," Wendy said, turning to face me in the back seat as soon as it was just the two of us. "Don't worry about your physics homework for this week. I'll take care of it. And I'll give you an extension on the lab work that's supposed to be due Monday. In fact, I'll help you get it done. If you want."

Despite the physical agony I was in, I had to smile. Partly, I was touched by her concern, but I was also thoroughly amused that she thought I'd be worried about my homework right then. I'd just become the world's first time traveler. I'd been hit by a bus, caused a multiple-car accident, saved a little girl's life, and been gnawed on by Spuds Mackenzie's evil twin. And I hadn't even had lunch yet! Like I gave a crap about physics.

"That'd be great, Miss Octover" I said. "I'd appreciate the help." I tried to give her my best charming smile, but I think the pain kept me from quite achieving it.

She smiled back, blushed, and then hurried the conversation in a new direction, saying, "Please, call me Wendy. Your stitches couldn't come back with you. Only the things that were with you inside the ring could come back."

"And those things *had* to come back apparently, because my shirt wasn't even with me when my time ran out." I noticed the worry lines deepen in her forehead and guessed her next question before she could ask it. "I was alone. No one was watching when I . . . left."

"That's good," she said. "You understand how it could have affected someone if they'd seen that? I can't even imagine what most people would think. It's bad enough you interacted with people at all. What if you'd seen someone who'd just seen you somewhere else? What if you'd seen yourself? I know you were in the science building yesterday."

"No I wasn't," I corrected her. "My classes yesterday were all on the other side of campus, and then I spent the evening at the arena— the basketball game."

"You *were* in the science building at least for a while, Brody. Remember, you complimented me on last week's lecture. Then you took off running down the hallway."

And then she had it. I could see it on her face.

"You mean that wasn't the . . . *original* you? I remember talking with you yesterday afternoon. Are you telling me you remember that same conversation happening like . . . just a little over an hour ago?"

I nodded. Slowly. I was thinking hard again, and it was making my head hurt worse.

"You knew my name," I recalled, suddenly struck by the realization. "For you, that would have been the first time we'd ever spoken outside of class, but you already knew my name. And it's a big lecture. Do you know everybody's name in there?"

"What?" she said. "Oh . . . no. I guess not. I mean . . . I know some of them. A lot of them, actually. Not just yours."

She was blushing again, which took the edge off my pain, if just briefly.

"Why did you leave the lab anyway?" she continued, redirecting our conversation again. Her tone shifted, becoming accusatory. "Dr. Flannigan told you specifically to stay in there, that the room was locked and empty during that hour, and that you should keep out of sight the whole time."

My jaw literally dropped open. "Umm, no she didn't. I mean she did tell me about the lab being empty yesterday, but she didn't tell me to stay in there. She told me—we all agreed—that I'd try to save the girl, which I did. It didn't go according to plan, obviously, but she's safe. It worked. The dog ended up attacking me instead of her."

Wendy looked over her shoulder toward the rear entrance to the fitness center. Where was Dr. Flannigan? What was taking her so long?

"Wendy, you can't tell me you don't remember us talking about the little girl? The pit bull?"

"Listen to what you're saying, Brody. Of course I don't know what you're talking about, but that doesn't mean I don't believe you. You say some little girl was attacked by a dog yesterday, but you also say you stopped it from happening. How could I remember something that didn't happen? It happened for you, but not for me, or Dr. Flannigan, or anyone else. Understand?"

Oh, yeah. Sure. Who couldn't understand that?!

"So which is it," I asked, nearly flabbergasted, "the little girl *was* killed by the dog, or she *wasn't?*"

"Yes," Wendy answered. "Both. But only for you."

"Thanks for clearing that up."

Dr. Flannigan returned a moment later with a seriously unhappy looking man in a crisp beige shirt and a paisley tie. The man was carrying a Woodsmen football jersey, which he tossed into my lap as soon as the car door swung open.

"Put this on so we're not walking you in shirtless," the man said. "Maybe we'll get lucky and nobody'll notice us." Then turning to Dr. Flannigan, he added, "Or maybe somebody will."

"Relax, Alan," the dean whispered in a severe tone. "You'll sow him up, give him something for the pain, and we'll be out of your hair. It'll be fine."

The man, Alan, looked decidedly unconvinced.

"Are you a doctor?" I asked as he helped me into the football jersey, which fit me more like a muumuu.

"No," he answered curtly. "I am *not* a doctor." He faced me as he said this, but I got the impression he was speaking to Dr. Flannigan as much as to me.

"Mr. Rigby is trained and highly experienced in first aid medicine," the dean explained, her own voice shifting back to its usual coolness.

As we made our way toward the back of the building, Alan Rigby supported my injured arm with the same care you'd show a tray loaded with full Champaign glasses. Once we were inside, we slipped into the first door on our right, which turned out to be an examination room so small Wendy was forced to wait outside. Rigby went to work on me immediately. He may not have been a doctor, but he certainly did seem to know what he was doing, for which I was grateful. And he had a cabinet full of painkillers, for which I was doubly grateful.

"It was a pit bull," I offered.

I saw his jaw muscles tighten, and he said, "I don't need to know."

"I dislocated my right shoulder, too, and I think I might have a concussion. I hit my head really hard, and I've puked a couple times."

At this, Rigby stopped working and glared at Dr. Flannigan. "You hear that? He thinks he may have a concussion. I hope there's no nerve damage in this arm. I hope it doesn't need surgery in order to heal properly."

"If it needed surgery, then they wouldn't have sown it up already at the . . ." Dr. Flannigan's voice trailed off, and she looked away, staring at the wall.

"The doctor here doesn't want me asking questions about what happened to you," Rigby said, facing me again. "She says for my own sake it's better if I don't know any more than I need to, but I say I *need* to know quite a bit more than I do."

The tension in the tiny room was so heavy I could feel it weighing down against my shoulders. Or was that just my second round of pain dope kicking in? Hard to tell.

Dr. Flannigan invited Wendy to listen in while Rigby gave instructions on how my arm should be tended over the following days. He also took a moment to go over the appropriate dose and frequency for my pain meds, the dangers and symptoms of concussions, and the immorality of blackmail. Dr. Flannigan cut him off before he could finish that last part.

We walked back out to Wendy's car in silence, but as soon as we were in and the doors were shut, Dr. Flannigan said, "Alright, Mr. Wyoming, start talking. You woke up this morning, got out of bed, and then what?"

Wendy started up the car and headed us back toward the science building while I recapped my day, and also that extra hour of the day before. The two women never interrupted me with questions. They just listened.

"And then *poof,* I was back in the lab, and you two were there at your computers, right where you'd been when I left, with parts of your memories erased."

"Our memories were altered," Dr. Flannigan said when I was finished, "not erased. You changed past events, and history had to *correct* for those changes. You remember me sending you back to save a little girl, but I remember sending you back to spend one solitary hour in the lab, out of sight. Why? Because once the little girl was saved, she didn't need saving anymore. There was no longer a reason for me to risk sending you out from the lab. Your actions eliminated the motivation to do so."

"But you remember the watch test the same way I do. And the ice cube."

"That's because neither of those things caused any changes," Wendy jumped in. "They didn't interact with anyone or anything. The reason we sent them was still valid, even after they'd been sent."

I dropped my forehead into my right hand and squeezed back against the terrible pressure that was building there again. "I'm sorry, but I can't talk about this, think about this, anymore right now. I just want to lay down and . . . not think for a while. Okay?"

Dr. Flannigan sighed and said, "Yeah, that's okay. Actually, why don't you drop me off at the lab, Wendy, and then head right on over to your place. Mr. Wyoming will probably need to stay with you for at least a couple days."

I think Wendy looked more shocked then than when I showed up in the lab topless and *masticated.*

"Dr. Flannigan," she protested, "I don't think that's such a . . . great idea. He's a student in one of my classes. You can't expect me to—"

"I expect you to do what needs to be done in order to see this project through," the dean said matter-of-factly. "That was our agreement when you signed on for this. Right now what needs to be done is the care, observation, and evaluation of our first test subject. Would you prefer to go stay in his dorm room?"

Wendy looked stricken.

"I'm sure I'll be fine," I said. "My roommates can keep an eye on me."

Dr. Flannigan was already shaking her head before I'd finished speaking. "No they can't. It has to be Wendy or me. I am duly concerned about your arm and your head, Mr. Wyoming, but I'm also concerned about any unexpected side effects of the mulligan itself. We two are the only ones who know what really happened to you, and so only we are qualified to be your tenders. And we will remain the only ones who know. Is that clear?"

"Yes," I agreed automatically. "My lips are sealed. What did you say about a . . . *mulligan?*"

Dr. Flannigan hesitated and then explained, "That's sort of what I've nicknamed this whole project. In golf a mulligan is sort of a . . . do-over."

I couldn't help but smile at that. I was battered and bloodied and confused, but I understood what a mulligan was, and I understood that whether or not anybody else knew about it, little Sara's mulligan had been an amazing success. Granted, I got pretty beat up in the process, but I'd live. And so would she.

I had one last surprise waiting for me that night at Wendy's town house. I was sitting at her kitchen table, waiting for her to convert the futon into bed-mode, when I noticed the newspaper, which was opened out to the funny page. At first I didn't recognize the opportunity it presented, but then it dawned on me. I flipped back to the front page, where I found no articles about dog attacks. Nada. Nil. Zippo. It was as if I'd erased the letters right off the page, and someone had filled in the leftover space with something new. Unbelievable.

I suppose there might have been something in there a few pages deeper about a dog briefly latching onto some unidentified guy, but I'd lived, so it wasn't front page worthy. Whether it was in there or not, I wasn't interested in seeing it, so I didn't look. I was about to push the paper away when my gaze drifted to the top of the page, where the lead story's headline read, *Woodsmen Can't Make the Grady.*

Reading the article was murder behind my eyes, where the headache was still intense, but I couldn't wait to find out what it said. According to the article's author, the Woodsmen had fallen behind early in their big rivalry match-up, and only continued to lose more and more ground as the game went on. Most of the lackluster effort was attributed to the absence of Grady O'Hare, the team's star guard, who couldn't play after suffering a concussion from a car accident only hours before the game.

I already knew that last part, even before I read it. As soon as I saw *Grady* in the headline, it triggered the connection in my frazzled brain, and I knew. Grady O'Hare was the guy in the Firebird. It wasn't from a class that I recognized him, but from the basketball games. I'd caused the crash that kept him from playing, and in turn caused our team to lose the biggest game of the year, a game they should have won. A game they *had* won!

Not that the game was more important than Sara's life, not even close, but it was such a *big* thing involving so many people. That I could have changed it so dramatically without trying was . . . terrifying.

The Mulligan Man

Both Wendy and I had been so apprehensive about my having to move in with her for a few days, but it turned out to be no problem. In fact, when those few days were up we discovered that neither of us was in any hurry for me to move back out. She was tired of living by herself, and I was tired of living with a bunch of guys with hygiene deficiencies. So I traded in three stinky dudes for one foxy lady. Go me, right?

That's not to say things turned romantic between us right off the bat. At that point we were just realizing we made good roomies, and we were becoming friends.

We turned out to have a surprising number of things in common. We both loved running and movies and chess. We were both reading *Harry Potter* at the time of my move in, me for the second time and her for the *fifth!* Van Gogh was both our favorite artist, though his self-portraits, his best works in my opinion, creeped her out. And then the real kicker, the absolute, undeniable proof that we were destined to share a DVD player: of the five Star Trek TV series, I owned every episode of three, and she owned every episode of the *other* two. Fate, beyond doubt.

Even our differences seemed to make us more, rather than less, compatible. She loved to clean, but hated to cook, and I was just the opposite. I was good with cars, and the Le Sabre was a particularly needy one. Wendy was an ace not only with physics, but with organic chemistry, too, which was exactly the help I needed right then.

The new arrangement made us both happier than we'd been, so we stuck with it.

I healed quickly as the weeks went by, and when she thought I was healthy enough, Dr. F gave me the green light to take another mulligan. The first good candidate turned out to be the community center for the arts, which was housed within one of the oldest buildings in town, a former Catholic church that was constructed in the late 19th century. The building's caretaker, who was nearly as old, took an accidental nap with a lit cigarette dangling from his fingers and ended up burning the place to the ground. In an interview with a local reporter, the caretaker claimed not to have smoked in over three decades before that night, but when he found a half-full pack left lying on the sidewalk, he decided to try one again, just for a treat.

It was a bit of a risky mission, just because we couldn't be exactly sure about the timing of events, but it turned out to be easier than fishing in the Cabela's aquarium. I'd been leaving my bike chained up outside the science building all the time, just in case, and so it was right there waiting for me when I went back that evening. My arm still wasn't good for much, and I was forced to ride more or less one-handed, which required extra caution and slower speeds, but I still made it to the arts center in less than twenty minutes. I spotted the smokes from at least fifty yards off, lying right where the old man said he'd found them, and transporting them to a garbage can was a job of about ten seconds.

And that was it. Where there were no smokes, there was no fire.

Wendy and I had eaten dinner that night at a restaurant just two blocks away, so I used my extra time to pick a sprig of chicory, her favorite wildflower, from the roadside and leave it for her to find on the table where I knew we'd sit. The hostess assumed I was just being cutesy for my girlfriend, so she promised to make sure the flower stayed put until I returned. This was exactly the sort of thing Dr. F warned me not to do, but I loved the idea as soon as I thought of it and just couldn't help myself, especially because Wendy and I had spent the whole afternoon and evening together. She'd wonder when I'd managed to *plant* the *plant*. And when she asked, I'd tell her I hadn't, because I hadn't. Yet.

She knew by the time I *arrived* back in the lab, though. The smile on her face made that clear enough. Not to mention the fact that she silently mouthed the words *thank you* as I was stepping out of the ring. Oh yeah, that's me: Brody Wyoming, smooth operator.

I made three more successful trips after that. Successful, that is, in that I did a good thing each time and managed to do it without hurting myself or causing any traffic accidents or other major collateral damage.

I helped the head of the chemistry department down the stairs one day when the elevator was on the fritz, saving him from a misstep that would have broken his hip. Did it earn me any extra credit in organic? No.

I barely made it in time to stop an unsupervised third grader from drowning. I was driving Dr. F's car—she'd given me her spare key just in case—and should have had plenty of time, except that a passing train blocked my way, holding me up for several minutes, and I arrived at the riverside park just in time to see the swinging rope break and the boy disappear into the muddy current. I splashed in after him, dragged him out by one of his wildly thrashing arms, and swallowed about a gallon of the nastiest water on the face of the planet in the process. I also scared him to death apparently, because as soon as I let him go, he sprinted away and never looked back. Not even a thank you. And it's a wonder I didn't catch something.

Oh, and I stopped a bank robbery, too. The police were there before the robbers, and everybody ended up yelling *stick 'em up* at the exact same moment. The bad guys were in cuffs before anyone even had a chance to realize they were trying to hold the place up with black plastic water pistols. The worst heist ever attempted? Maybe.

That one only took a minute. I made the phone call right from the lab. I would have had plenty of time to go tinker with the future again, like I did with the flower, except for one thing: the lab wasn't empty when I got there. Dr. F was seated at one of the computer consoles, engrossed in work. Neither of us noticed the other until I picked up the phone, which was on the other side of the room, and started dialing. I startled her, but she seemed to realize almost immediately what was going on.

"Don't say anything," she told me. "Just do whatever you came back for." She eyed the phone in my hands curiously and then asked, "Is a phone call all there is to it? Is that all you have to do? Just answer yes or no, nothing more."

"Yes."

At that, she put her computer to sleep, stood, and crossed the room to the door. On her way out, she said, "Make your call, and then stay put."

I did. I sat in there for the next hour, so bored I actually ended up leafing through a physics text from one of the shelves. I needed to start leaving a magazine in there or something, just in case. That hour seemed like three while I waited to hear the chime that meant my time was almost up. Wendy had picked up a new watch for me, nothing too fancy, but not a dollar store cheapo either, so I could set its timer at the beginning of a mulligan and know when my return trip was imminent.

The next day's Campus Bugle printed my favorite article of all time. It was entitled, *Mysterious Tip-off Results in Bank Robbery Miss.* It was my favorite article ever because it was, finally, proof that I was really doing the things I said I was doing. Because Wendy didn't *know* about any of the things I'd done on my other mulligans. Neither did Dr. F. Neither did anyone else. Every time I poofed into the lab from the previous day, there were the two women, seated at their work stations, clueless about the real reason I'd gone back. They didn't know about any fire or broken hip or drowning, because for them none of those things had ever happened. I'd stopped them all. But a mysterious call from an anonymous tipper at the exact time I was gone—and Dr. F had seen me on the phone—that was proof.

Not that I thought they didn't believe me the other times, but now they didn't have to believe me. Now they *knew*.

It seemed like a vitally important distinction to me at the time, but only because I didn't know what lay ahead. If I'd known our experiment, just getting going really, was soon to come to a close, I'd have felt differently. I wouldn't have been worried about credit if I'd known our next effort to repair the past was going to be our last, and that one of our trio was about to step not forward nor backward along the road of time, but off it completely. Forever.

And it was my fault. She died because of me.

Tight on Time

I remember the day of the accident started like a dream, a crisp winter morning, quiet and white with fresh snowfall. It was a misleading entrance to a day that would end like a nightmare. It was a beautiful morning, but it was a hell of a day, tragic and terrible.

Twice.

It was Wednesday morning of finals week, and though neither Wendy nor I had to be on campus early, we were both up in time to watch the sunrise, which we did over two steaming cups of coffee beside the townhouse's only easterly facing window. It had started snowing sometime during the night, and by first light the flakes were as broad as nickels and falling so slowly they seemed to defy gravity. Wendy never said a word the whole time we sat there, and neither did I. And thank goodness. It was a perfect moment already, and any commentary could only have diminished it.

It was such a beautiful morning. Ironic.

Wendy headed out before me, to her daily news meeting with Dr. F. They watched the morning news every day on a TV in the dean's office, and then they leafed through the paper, checking for potential mulligan candidates. Just the two of them.

"Because three's a crowd for some jobs." That's what Dr. F told me when I asked her why I was never invited to the morning meetings.

I thought it was about the lamest excuse I'd ever heard, and I felt more than a little slighted, but a part of me was also relieved. Ever since that very first mulligan, when I'd inadvertently cost our team the basketball game, I'd been all too aware of the potential for collateral change every time I visited the past. It's not like I was still losing sleep over the outcome of one college sports event, but I had no illusions about the possibility of my going back and screwing up something that really mattered.

For instance, if Grady O'Hare's Firebird had been going another ten or fifteen miles per hour faster, he might have missed out on more than a basketball game. A little more speed could have meant the difference between a minor concussion and a fatal head injury. That's what I lost sleep over: not what had happened, but what *could* have happened. And what *could* happen the next time.

Taking the mulligan was my job, and my job alone. That's how it had to be. If the ladies were determined to keep the job of choosing the mulligan just between the two of them, then so be it. There was plenty of responsibility to go around, and I was happy to share.

So Wendy headed off to campus to administer a freshman physics exam, and I waded back into organic chemistry at our dining room table, which is where I'd spent most of the night. There was a smear in the middle of the first page of notes I opened up to, and it only took me a second to remember I'd drooled there a little after passing out from severe brain cramps. I really did hate that crap! *Carbon, carbon everywhere, and not an ounce of zinc.*

Thanks to the expert tutoring of my new roomie, I'd actually got a pretty good handle on my physics by then, so organic was my only major mountain to climb during finals week. I'd been hitting it hard for days, barely sleeping, and praying a lot. I wasn't going to be the top of the class, *obviously*, but I was going to pass. I was pretty sure. And then I was going to sleep for like a week straight.

I beat my head against it for another three hours, fueled up with another coffee and a scrumptious early lunch of Pop-Tarts and Ramen Noodles, and then headed off to my showdown with the molecules.

The only thing that could possibly thwart my victory was six inches of fresh snow and a gale force wind that made my eyes water the instant I stepped outside the door. It usually only took me about fifteen minutes to walk to campus from the townhouse, five to ride my bike if it was a nice enough day, but that day was way outside the norm. The bike was out of the question, so I pulled the collar of my coat up over my nose and trudged out into the storm. Wendy had suggested I ride along with her when she left, but I'd declined the offer, preferring to finish my studying where I knew I'd have quiet and solitude—not the greatest choice I ever made. It took me almost half an hour to walk to campus that day, and I reached the exam room just as the professor was closing the door, cutting it way too close for comfort.

The test was grueling, and by the end my brain cramps were severe again, but I felt like I'd done okay.

I was in a fog as I bundled back up and left the science building. I mean I was really in a blizzard, but I was *in a fog* at the same time. I was out of it. However, I did have just enough observational power left to notice a little commotion over on one of the intersecting sidewalks. One of the campus security officers was practically nose to nose with Mr. Fitz, the janitor. I couldn't tell what they were saying over the howling wind, but they were serious about it. In fact, by their body language I thought they might be close to coming to blows.

I paused to watch for a moment, morbidly amused. Whatever it was all about, I was sure the crotchety, old sucker had it coming. The next thing I knew the two men were playing tug-of-war with a camouflage backpack that must have been Fitz's.

Ah-ha. Now I thought I probably had it. The ex-hippie turned herbal entrepreneur was in the process of being busted with a bag full of *merchandise.*

"Go Fitz!" yelled another student bystander encouragingly. I couldn't tell if he was really pulling for him or just rooting for more entertainment. Maybe he was a client.

And then the show climaxed with what appeared to be an awkward judo throw by the guard. Whatever it was, it landed Fitz flat on his back. The officer rolled him over, burying his face in the fresh snow, put a knee between his shoulder blades, and pulled out his radio, presumably to call for some backup.

A few students clapped appreciatively, one booed, but then everybody moved on. It was too crappy outside to linger, even for such a bizarre spectacle.

"Adios, Fitz," I mumbled through my collar as I moved away with the crowd. One less problem for the mulligan team.

I turned and found Dr. F standing behind me. Apparently she'd been spectating as well.

"Never a dull moment around here, is there?" she said through a half-smile. She looked almost as tired as I felt. "Have you seen Wendy?"

"No. But I was sort of hoping to. I'd ride home with her today if I could."

"I'd take you myself, but I've got a pile of work three feet deep waiting for me and the rest of today to get it done. Sorry."

"No worries," I said, waving away her apology. "Blowing snow and biting cold are probably the only things that can keep me awake right now anyway."

"I hear you," she agreed, wincing away from a flake-filled gust of wind. "This is a long week for everybody. Go home and rest up, and I'll talk to you later." And with that she turned and headed inside.

I meant to go straight home, but couldn't quite bring myself to pass by Starbucks. I ordered my usual cappuccino, and on impulse, a London Fog for Dr. Flannigan, too. It was her favorite, I knew.

It only took a minute to walk it back to the science building, and the dean seemed genuinely touched I'd thought of her. She even went so far as to hug me, which was way out of character. At the risk of sounding sappy, I guess I was a little touched, too, by the gesture.

I headed out again feeling marginally rejuvenated, but I was still about as far behind on sleep as I'd ever been, and my brain was so overtaxed I almost started down the sidewalk in the wrong direction. On top of that, the weather reminded me of that scene in *Rudolph* where the little plastic trees blow right off the screen. The blankets were calling to me like never before, and I heeded their call.

It seemed like it took me an hour to walk back to the townhouse, but as soon as I got there I pitched my empty Starbucks cup somewhere in the general direction of the kitchen sink, left a trail of boots, gloves, and various other pieces of winter apparel from there to my bedroom door, and crawled directly into bed, still dressed. I didn't want to slip into my pajamas or close the shades or brush my teeth. I just wanted to sleep.

And sleep I did. In fact, though I didn't immediately realize it upon waking, I'd slept longer in one uninterrupted shift than I had in years.

I kept my eyes closed when I first came around, and the light that weakly penetrated my lids seemed to be of about equal intensity as when I'd crashed, leading me to mistake my slumber for a short one. I thought it was still early evening, and that only an hour or so had passed by. It wasn't until I clicked on the TV and found the wrong shows playing that I realized my estimation was off by half a day. I'd missed the tail end of Wednesday, the whole night, and the first chunk of Thursday morning, too. *The Price is Right* was already coming on.

I poked around for a second and decided I was alone. Wendy must have left already. I couldn't remember what her schedule was for the day, and I knew there was probably no point in trying to call her cell phone as she never, and I mean *never,* kept the thing on. She hated talking on the phone, and had told me more than once the only reason she had a cell at all was so she'd be ready to call the tow-truck when the Buick finally kicked the bucket. That was Wendy, always thinking ahead.

Still, stranger things had happened, and I was in the mood to celebrate. I had, I was pretty darn sure, passed my organic exam, and after that marathon sleep was feeling almost completely recuperated. I decided I'd love nothing more than to treat her for lunch, and not cafeteria fare or mystery nuggets with fries, but something served on a placemat with appropriately mellow satellite radio drifting down from overhead. Maybe I could even leave a flower for our table before we met up and let her wonder if I'd gone time-traveling again.

I reached for the house phone, but before I could lift it from the cradle it rang.

I barely got my *hello* out before Dr. F's voice cut in.

"Brody, I'm on my way to pick you up. Something's happened. Wendy's in the hospital."

"Is she okay? What—"

"Look, I'll be there in a minute, and I'll fill you in then. I'm halfway to the townhouse already, and I need to concentrate on my driving. The roads are still pretty bad, and we . . . well, we need to make sure we're ready to work this afternoon. Be ready to go."

The phone went dead. I slid it back into the cradle with some difficulty, missing its slot on the first couple tries with my trembling hand. My mind was racing, and I could already feel my quickened pulse pounding at my temples. My celebratory mood had turned to dread.

I still had on the clothes I'd worn the day before, having slept in them, and I didn't care about changing into fresh ones right then. All I cared about was getting to see my friend as soon as possible. I stepped into my boots, slipped into my coat, and headed out to the roadside, not bothering to lock up behind me. Honestly, I don't even know if I closed the door.

It was snowing again, but just barely, and somehow the sun was out at the same time. It would have been another beautiful morning had I been in the frame of mind to see it.

Traffic was light, but the cars passing by were crawling. It must have been pretty slick.

I started walking down the curb as soon as I saw Dr. F's car coming, which ended up forcing her to pull over at a bad spot, nearly getting her rear-ended by a pick-up. I should have just waited by the drive where she'd have had more room, but I couldn't wait—not another second.

"Is she okay?" I asked as I slid into the passenger's seat. "Tell me she's okay."

"It sounds like she's in rough shape right now, but she'll be fine. One way or another."

Dr. F told me what she knew. Wendy had been in a car accident, not that morning, but the previous afternoon. She'd been in the hospital all night, and I hadn't even realized she was missing. She'd lost control of the car a few miles outside of town, hit a tree, and slid out onto the frozen surface of Grassy Lake. The only witnesses, two fishermen, said the car stayed up for a minute or two, but then broke through the ice, plunging into the frigid water with Wendy still inside. The two men, regarded as heroes in the morning paper, managed to pull her out in time to save her, risking their own lives in the process. But now she was lying in intensive care, battered and unconscious.

"She didn't show up for our news meeting this morning," the dean continued, "which was when I first suspected something was up. You know she's never late for anything. I guess no one knew she was missing."

I saw her glance my way from the corner of her eye as she said this.

"I went to bed early yesterday and slept through the whole night," I explained. "I thought she must have come and gone when I woke up." I could barely even get the words out, and they left a sickening, sour taste in my mouth.

With a clenched jaw, Dr. F nodded her understanding. "I turned the TV on in my office, and the first picture they showed was of the lake and the hole in the ice where the car went through. They said the young woman who'd been driving hadn't had any identification on her person, and that due to unsafe conditions no one had been able to dive to the car yet. They gave a brief description, and I knew it had to be her. She's in critical care. She has major lacerations as well as internal injuries, and she was underwater for a while before the fishermen could get her out. The doctor's say even if they can keep her going, because of how long she was without oxygen, they just don't know . . ."

My stomach and chest were so tight as I listened I could barely pull in any breath. I was shaking. She had to be okay!

"Brody. Brody! She'll be fine, because you'll go back for her. Right? You'll go back and stop it all from ever happening. Right?"

"Right," I agreed after a moment. I'd been so upset by the news I'd completely overlooked the obvious, that we had a legitimate recourse for just such an incident. "I'll go back and find her before she leaves campus. I won't let her drive. I'll make her walk home with me. How soon can we . . ." And then I noticed we were *not* headed toward the hospital, which I'd assumed was our destination. We were headed back toward campus instead. As usual, Dr. F was way ahead of me.

"I know it's going to be hard for you, Brody," she said, her words slow and deliberate, "but you're going to have to be patient. I've always had Wendy at the second work station on our mulligans. I can do it myself, I'm sure I can, but I'll need to do some prep work first."

I wanted to object, but I had no idea how. I was ready and willing to take any risk for Wendy's sake, but I still knew next to nothing about the functioning of the machine and about what it took to make a mulligan *work*. If the dean said she needed time, then that was that. But patience was going to be difficult, if not impossible.

I spent the next three hours, the longest of my life, pacing back and forth through the lab in the bottom of the science building. I was just about driving myself crazy, but Dr. F didn't seem to notice me at all. She worked steadfastly at her computer the whole time, oblivious to my fretting, and though I desperately wanted to, I never said a word to break her concentration. I thought *hurry the hell up* at least a thousand times, but I kept it to myself. I had no idea what she was doing, but I was sure she was doing it as quickly as she could. She knew as well as I did what—no, make that *who*—was at stake.

According to the two men who'd pulled Wendy from the car, her accident had occurred at right around two-thirty in the afternoon, which would have given us plenty of time if we could have been *green light* as soon as we got to the school. As it was, almost all of that cushion of time had elapsed while Dr. F prepped the machine for single operator functioning. It was now one-thirty, and our window was closing fast.

At last the long cadence of the dean's keyboard fell silent.

"Are we ready?" I asked.

She sat frozen with her back still to me and didn't reply. I saw her head turn back and forth as she shifted her gaze from one monitor to the next. Then she lifted her hand and covered her eyes in a gesture I'd come to recognize as her deep-thinking reflex.

I swear she must have sat like that for two full minutes in perfect silence. I could hear the clock ticking behind me, and I was almost overcome with the urge to snatch it off the wall and smash it just to shut it up.

"I think so," she finally whispered.

I pulled my coat back on, stepped into the circle of spheres, took a deep breath, and readied my fingertip over the start button on my watch.

"Since we don't know where she was after her morning exam, you'll have to go straight to the scene of the accident," Dr. F said. We'd gone over this already, but I could see she was thinking it all out loud one more time, making sure she hadn't overlooked anything. "That's the only time and place we can be sure of. She was headed east, so you'll need to be west of the lake and far enough down the road to stop her in plenty of time. You have my car keys, and the car was in the lot yesterday afternoon. I wasn't down here then, so the room will be empty when you arrive."

"Actually, it'll be shortly before I saw you outside, remember?" she asked. "When Fitz got arrested. You should still have time to be out of here by then, avoid seeing yourself. The roads were bad, so be careful. You can't do her any good if you wreck yourself halfway there. But you won't have much spare time either. Sorry. Anything else you think of? Any questions?"

I shook my head. "Let's go."

She turned back to the computer consoles, stared at them in silence for several more grueling seconds, and then started tapping keys again. My heart was already hammering in my chest, harder than it had since the very first trip back.

"Here we go," I heard Dr. F whisper, and the machine started to hum.

With some difficulty I pulled a deep breath into my chest, held it in for a moment, and then blew it slowly out through puckered lips. The spheres became blurry as their humming voice gained a rhythm. I clenched my jaw and promised myself it would all work out fine. I'd get there in time. She'd be okay.

When the tempo of the machine's pulsing told me the mulligan was imminent, I hit the start button on my watch, setting the alarm for a fifty-nine minute countdown.

Then the silence and darkness came rushing in.

Wednesday afternoon—round two.

I didn't hesitate. I hopped over the ring of spheres and ran to the door, which I could have done with my eyes closed by then. The hallway outside was empty. Even Fitz was nowhere to be seen, which was a rarity. Though he seemed to be adhering to Dr. F's out-of-bounds order on the lab, he'd definitely been spending an inordinate amount of time lurking in the basement floor.

I bolted to the stairs, took them two at a time up to the ground level, and found it sparsely populated with other students who were sauntering along at their leisure, sharing casual conversations in twos and threes. Absently, I noticed most of their faces were familiar. It was the first of my organic classmates just finishing their exams. I was in there, I realized, just a few doors down, double checking my answers right then.

I had no time to ponder the weirdness of being in such close proximity to myself.

I flashed through the door, hit a patch of ice on the sidewalk and slid right into one of the campus security guards, catching him forehead to nose. That's my forehead and his nose. I actually heard a crunch, and as much as it hurt my head, it must have been killer on his honker.

"I'm sorry," I said breathlessly. The guy had both hands at his face, and there was blood everywhere. I realized it was the same officer I'd seen wrestling with Fitz. What a day he was having!

"My nose," he mumbled. "You broke my nose."

"It was the ice. I didn't mean . . ." And then I was off again, fleeing the scene of the accident. The shock of the collision had cost me my train of thought for a moment, but now I remembered what I was there, make that *then*, to do.

"Hey, wait!" the guard yelled from behind me, but I didn't turn back.

Sixty seconds later I was in Dr. F's car and headed away from campus.

On Thin Ice

The strange sense of déjà vu I'd felt on every other mulligan was somehow intensified that day, and I think it was mostly because of the weather. So many days are average, partly cloudy, partly sunny, maybe a little breeze from the west, but that day was extraordinary. The wind and the snow were ferocious in a way you only get a couple times a year in southern Michigan. As I struggled to peer through the blizzard, which became basically opaque at about fifty feet, I could have no doubt this was indeed the same crappy afternoon I'd trudged home through once already.

Despite my burning sense of urgency to get to the site of Wendy's accident as quickly as possible, I had no choice but to take my time. Dr. F's warning about not being able to help if I wrecked myself echoed in my ears, and the driving was treacherous to say the least. Outside of town, on the country roads, the plows obviously hadn't run in a while, and it took all my concentration just to make sure I was still on the road and not veering off into a bean field or something. Everything looked the same.

I wondered what in the world Wendy had been doing way out there anyway. I knew she sometimes eased her nerves with a drive and some classical music, but this was hardly the day for that. This was murder on the nerves.

I didn't see my last turn until I was going past it, and without thinking I stomped on the brakes, sending the car into a slide I had absolutely no control over. By blind luck I skidded straight down the road, coming to an eventual stop sideways across both lanes. I caught my breath, cursed myself for being so stupid, and started jockeying back and forth to get pointed back in the right direction.

I crept up to the corner this time, and as I eased the car around I spotted the lake. I was there. I'd driven down this road before, but not many times—not enough to remember it clearly. To my amazement, I saw there was only one big tree anywhere in sight, and from its drooping shape I could tell it was a willow. It stood alone in the strip of land that separated the road and the near shore of Grassy Lake. And it was huge. Its trunk must have been nearly as big around as the mulligan machine's ring of spheres. Immense. Immovable.

I stopped there and for one sickening moment my imagination betrayed me and I pictured what a tree that big might do to a speeding car. I shuddered at the thought.

I had another major panic moment then when I turned back to the road and spotted a set of headlights coming toward me. I glanced quickly to my watch, terrified that I was already too late, that I'd arrived in time to witness the accident, but wouldn't be able to do anything about it. But no, my watch said I should still have ten minutes of my hour left, which meant about five before the time of the accident. It had to be someone else. *If* those timetables were accurate, which I couldn't be sure of.

I flashed my brights because I couldn't think of anything else to do, but I could tell by then that whoever it was, they were slowing down anyway, pulling over to park just off the road where it was closest to the lake. As I started creeping forward again, I realized it wasn't actually a car at all, but a full sized truck.

I pulled up alongside the truck just as two men stepped out from either side, both dressed up like modern Eskimos. They were ice fishermen. And they were lunatics! I'd never been ice fishing, but it couldn't possibly be fun enough to warrant braving the elements on a day like that. Not to mention risking their lives on what I knew was dangerous ice. I did not have time to rescue anybody else.

"Hey you guys," I hollered after putting down the passenger's side window and letting in a shocking blast of frigid air, "I don't think you'd better go out there. Someone went through the ice yesterday." Which was nearly the truth.

"Hell with it," called the driver after a moment's hesitation. "It's nasty out here anyway, and nobody'd be around if one of us did go through."

He was right. There was no one else around. That's when it hit me. How it took me until then, I can't fathom. Stupid. Stupid, stupid, stupid!

"You guys, wait. Hold on." The truck's doors were already slamming closed as I said the words, and I knew they'd gone unheard. I jerked on the door handle, but found it wouldn't budge, and by the time I tracked down the button to unlock it they were pulling away. I stepped out into the snowy gale, thought about chasing after them, but froze instead. Metaphorically, that is. Well, literally, too. Both. What was I going to say to them anyway, *You guys mind hanging around for a few minutes in case there's a car accident on this deserted road?*

I glanced at my watch, which read seven minutes and thirty-one seconds. I didn't have time to kick myself for sending away the very men who had rescued my best friend. Or *would have.*

No matter. There wasn't going to be any accident anyway. That's why I was there.

My eyes were watering like crazy as I slid back into the car and slammed the door. It was so cold! I glanced once to the frozen lake as

I put the car in gear and tried to imagine what it would feel like to go through. I wondered if your heart might stop from the shock before you had time to drown.

Dr. F's directions rang in my ears. I needed to get farther west to make sure I could intercept Wendy well before she reached the lake. I sped up as much as I dared, barely able to see a thing through the dense flakes.

I hadn't gone a hundred yards before I reached a fork in the road and a life or death choice I had absolutely no intelligent way of making. The snow-covered pavement split to the left and right in front of me at small angles, and it didn't matter that one way had the right of way for approaching traffic. In those conditions Wendy could easily miss the stop sign and go sliding right through, and she'd still be pointed basically toward the big willow from either direction. I had no way of knowing which way she'd be coming from, and I was almost out of time.

Damn! I glanced back to my watch—five minutes and forty-eight seconds. The headlights of her car could appear at any moment. If I stayed there she might not see me in time for it to do any good, but if I continued up the road in the wrong direction then I couldn't hope to change anything. No, I'd already changed something, I reminded myself. I'd sent away the only other people who could help.

Short on time and options, I hit the gas and slid away to the right.

I knew almost immediately I'd made the wrong choice. The road curved sharply to follow the lakeshore, which I would have been able to see from the intersection if the day had been clear. There was no way Wendy could be coming from that way. Under those conditions, no one could make it around that curve doing more than fifteen or twenty miles an hour, and after losing it, Wendy had hit the tree hard enough to ricochet out onto the lake, which must have taken considerably more speed.

I hit the brakes, slid to a halt, and threw it into reverse. There were no driveways to turn around in, and judging from the looks of the roadside I could easily have ended up stuck if I'd tried to jockey around off the pavement, so I kept on going backward. I cranked my head around over my shoulder, but the back window was caked with snow. Panicking anew because I knew my time had to be nearly up, I put the window down, reached through, and wiped the side mirror clean. I still couldn't see crap, but I sped up anyway, doing my best to stay in the tracks I'd just made.

I was halfway back to the fork when I spotted the dim glow of headlights coming down the other road. My pulse hammered in my head so hard I could feel it behind my eyes. I couldn't breathe.

I stepped harder on the gas, desperate to get ahead of her. I was closer, but I could tell she was going much faster. Easy to do when you're going *forward*.

It came down to physics, over which my will held no sway. I simply couldn't accelerate through the snow fast enough. I was forced to watch her car sail through the view of my mirror, already spinning hopelessly out of control. I cranked my head around instinctively, but the back window was still blocked, which I suppose, in retrospect, was a blessing. Had I been able to watch the impact I so clearly could hear, even over the whistling wind, I'm sure it would have haunted me for the rest of my life.

I slammed the shifter into park even before the car had come to a complete stop, scrambled out the door, and sprinted down the road. Wendy's car sat pointing away from me out on the lake, maybe forty or so feet from the tree, which now bore a fresh scar on the bark of its trunk. I'd failed. Everything had happened just the same. Only now there was no one else to help her. If I couldn't get there in time . . .

Knowing I had precious little time before the car would break through the ice, I dashed out onto the frozen lake, and panicked as I was, I couldn't help but take note of the strange groaning sound that emanated from beneath my feet. I clenched my teeth as I approached the old Buick, trying to steady myself against what I was sure to see.

As I drew nearer I could see the front end of the car was trashed, as I knew it would be, the hood crumpled up like an accordion. The windshield was smashed out. The driver's side door appeared relatively unscathed, but when I tugged at its handle, it only opened about an inch. Something was catching. I could see Wendy inside, slumped forward so her hair was hanging down over her face. She wasn't moving.

I wiggled my fingers into the crack at the edge of the door, took a deep breath, planted my right foot against the side of the car, and heaved back with all my strength. I felt like I could rip the damn thing right off its hinges. There was a loud creak of warping metal, and the door flew open.

There sat Wendy, and right beside her sat a V-8. The damage to the car was incredible, and the fact that Wendy was sitting there all in one piece was beyond incredible. It was miraculous.

I cautiously reached into the ruined vehicle and slid back the hair that was draped across Wendy's face. Her left side seemed okay, just a few little cuts that were probably from the shattered windshield. Her serious injuries, I realized, must be on her right side, where the engine had come crashing in. I leaned across, barely daring to look. My face was inches from hers when her eyes flashed open.

"Brody?" she mumbled. "What happened? I have a headache." She reached to her forehead with her right hand, which also looked fine, and squeezed at her temples.

I was so shocked that for a second I couldn't respond. I couldn't even move. She seemed okay. When my momentary paralysis subsided I reached my hands up to cup her face. Then I ran my fingers through her hair and around her neck and down her sides and legs, searching for the injuries I knew had to be there—somewhere. And yet they weren't. Miraculous.

"Knock it off," she ordered, swatting my hands away. "Get your touchy-feely fingers off me."

And then I kissed her. I didn't mean to. I didn't think about it. I just did it, and when I pulled away she was smiling. Thank goodness!

"Was that you in the other car?" she asked suddenly, her smile falling away in a heartbeat. "Going backward? I hit the brakes when I saw you coming. I crashed because of you."

So I hadn't been too late after all. Reacting to me must have changed the timing of her slide just the tiniest bit, and that's all it had taken. She'd still hit the tree, but instead of sustaining life-threatening injuries she was left with just a few scrapes and scratches. Unbelievable.

Wendy's eyebrows pulled together like opposite magnets, and I knew she was thinking things through. "What were you doing out here anyway? And why do you have Dr. Flannigan's car? Why . . . oh. Ooooh." She got it.

She was about to say more when a horrid cracking sound grabbed both our attention.

"We need to go!" I exclaimed, remembering in a flash that we weren't yet out of danger. "Come on, help me!"

I grabbed for the seatbelt buckle at her hip, but it was jammed back into the crack of the seat by a protruding piece of the transplanted engine. I tried to slide my hand down to it from every angle, but it was no use. In desperation I grabbed the shoulder strap and yanked back against the pinned buckle, but all that did was cinch the lap strap down painfully over Wendy's stomach. It wouldn't budge.

"Hey. Ow!" she gasped. "Take it easy."

Another horrifying crack sounded from beneath us, shutting any further complaint from Wendy behind her suddenly clamped jaws. I froze, sure for an instant that we were going through right then.

"Where are we?" Wendy whispered.

"We need to get out of here right now," I repeated. That was all she really needed to know.

She tried to reach down to the buckle, but even with her smaller hands it was hopeless. I tugged against the belt at her hip and her waist and her shoulder, but it wouldn't budge. It was locked into place.

"Can you cut it with something?" she asked, her voice now laced with panic.

Of course! With some difficulty I jammed my quickly numbing hand down into the pocket of my jeans. My fist closed immediately over the familiar shape of my trusty pocket knife, right where it always was. I pulled it out, fumbled it once to the floor between Wendy's feet as I tried to open its stubby blade. The cold was really starting to take its toll on my fingers. My dexterity was crap.

I put the knife to the belt beside her left hip, kneeling down for better leverage. I gasped as I felt my knees sink through several inches of freezing water before hitting the ice. The feeling was already gone from my feet so much I hadn't even realized I was wading. The lake was surging up through the cracks in the ice, adding more and more weight atop the brittle sheet.

And then another chilling sound reached my ear, not a crack or creak, but a beep. My watch! I'd been so preoccupied with Wendy's wellbeing, I'd completely forgotten I was about to be pulled back to the lab, to the next day.

I doubled my efforts with the belt, sawing frantically, but it was tough stuff, and the knife was sadly dull. I couldn't go fast enough!

I glanced up to Wendy's face and found her expression inappropriately calm.

"It's okay, Brody," she whispered. "I know you're out of time. You did your best. Please don't blame yourself for this."

I wouldn't look at her while she spoke. I couldn't. I just kept sawing. I was halfway through, but the seconds were ticking by. The chime marked fifty-nine minutes after the start of my mulligan. Sixty minutes would mark its end. I couldn't have more than thirty seconds to go. The muscles in my arms and hands shook from strain and adrenalin. I was three-quarters of the way through, with maybe ten seconds left. And then I was out of time. The failing ice groaned beneath us.

I thought for a second about handing the knife to Wendy, telling her to keep working at it after I disappeared, but no, it would go back with me, whether I was holding it or not.

"I'm sorry, Wendy!" I cried. I raised the knife to eye level and slashed down like a wild man, incredibly slicing back into the belt and not my own fingers or Wendy's hip. "I'm sorry!"

And right then, in those final seconds before my hour was up, I understood perfectly what I'd done. I'd saved Wendy from being grievously injured only to sentence her to death. Instead of fighting for her life in a hospital bed, she'd be dragged down beneath the ice, helpless, to drown. She was doomed.

And it was my fault. She would die because of me.

Then something very strange happened. No, I take that back. Actually, it's that something didn't happen—that's what was strange. I didn't disappear. No poof.

"I don't understand," I mumbled, feeling disoriented. What had just *not* happened wasn't possible. It couldn't be. Was this all just some twisted nightmare, I wondered? I hoped.

"Whatever, just keep cutting!"

Wendy's frantic voice shook me free from my stupor. I renewed my attack against the seatbelt, and within seconds I was through.

"Come on," I urged, grabbing Wendy beneath the armpits and jerking her out of the car with all the gentleness I'd have shown a bale of hay. All that mattered was that we get away—fast! The water she stepped down into was ankle deep.

I pushed Wendy toward the shore with an equally not gentle two-handed shove, leaning back against the side of the Buick as I did so, and the car lurched as if in response. I'm sure it was just a coincidence in the timing, not that I had moved it, but that's what it felt like. A great popping sound accompanied the Le Sabre's shifting weight. I slid back with the car, unable to right myself. My arms flailed wildly, grasping for any purchase. What I found was Wendy's hand. Her fingers laced together with my own in an unfeeling grip, and she pulled me away just as the car sunk to its windows.

Still holding hands, we hurried away. Twice Wendy fell to her knees, and both times I hauled her back harshly to her feet, practically dragging her along. More cracks and pops erupted behind us, along with a gurgle of surging water, but we didn't look back.

"Slow down," she gasped as we neared the bank, but I wouldn't. I hauled us both onward with such urgency that I might have been trying to escape a burning building instead. Not until we had solid ground beneath our feet would I trust that we were safe.

We both collapsed to our hands and knees when we finally stepped off the ice. I gulped air hungrily down my throat, needing oxygen, but every breath of the frosty air burned inside my chest.

Wendy reached over and took my hand again, and though I couldn't feel it I could see the skin stretch over her knuckles as she squeezed.

"We made it." She was shivering so hard I could barely understand her words, but I'd have understood her fragile smile anyway. "We're okay."

I still wasn't entirely convinced we were okay, but we had made it, and that was a miracle. Another one.

Past Due

The drive back into town took even longer than it had on the way out. The weather was still brutal, only now the snow had piled up that much more and my hands and feet were numb. Even with the heat blasting out the vents full power I couldn't feel the wheel beneath my fingers until we were halfway to the hospital, and I never did feel the pedals under my feet. I could feel Wendy's hand on my shoulder, though. She kept it there the whole time, and that small contact was comforting beyond words. Already I knew we would be bonded now in a whole new way, as people sometimes are after standing together at the edge.

When she asked me what I thought had happened with the mulligan, I said that Dr. F must have found a way to extend the trip, at which point it occurred to me that I might still disappear at any moment. We were almost to the hospital by then anyway, so I kept going, hoping the car wouldn't become suddenly driverless.

When I asked Wendy what she'd been doing way out there anyway, and in such a hurry, she explained that she'd offered to drive home one of her students whose car wouldn't start, but then, delayed by the weather, ended up running late for a tutoring session.

"What Jen must think after I don't show up for our session or call or anything," Wendy said with a sigh. She was clearly upset by the thought. "And during finals week no less."

Seriously?! Was she really worried, right then, about missing a study appointment? The first one she'd ever missed, I was sure. Give me a break. I showed some restraint by not reminding her she'd just escaped death—barely—*twice!*

They rolled her into the emergency room in a wheelchair, just as a precaution, and I followed after parking the car in order to attend to the necessary paperwork. I was still expecting to be whisked away to the lab at any moment, but the moments kept slipping past one by one, and nothing happened.

The ER was a madhouse. There were moaning and groaning people everywhere, many of them the right age to be students at the University. Nurses darted back and forth through the melee wearing cheerfully bright scrubs that did not at all match their grim expressions.

I wondered at the size of the crowd. Sure, the roads were awful, but this was ridiculous. Did no one remember you need to slow down when driving on ice through a white-out blizzard? Was this everyone's first winter in Michigan? Morons.

Just as I turned away from the reception desk, scanning the congested room in the hopes of finding an unoccupied seat, a blast of cold air drew my attention to the entryway. And there she was.

"Clear the way!" yelled an EMT from just inside the automatic doors. The strain and authority in his voice parted the crowd instantly. The man hurried forward, pushing a gurney upon which laid Dr. F. Her reddish-gray hair, usually so neatly ordered, hung helter-skelter around her agonized face. The skin of her forehead and right cheek were blackened.

The shock of seeing her, and in such a state, froze me all over again. As the gurney wheeled past, I saw her eyes find me and flash from a look of indescribable pain to one of utter surprise. She shook visibly, and her thin lips, also half-charred, opened and closed in the rhythm of silent speech. Then she smiled. In fact, she beamed. Such an array of emotions in the span of a couple seconds! She reached out toward me as they sped her by, splaying wide the fingers of one ruined hand.

And then she was gone, just like that, swallowed up by one of the anonymous hospital corridors that branched away from the lobby like the legs of a great white spider. In the wake of her passing the crowd resumed its mad scurrying, dozens of people rushing around, bumping into each other like bees in an overcrowded hive, and right in the middle of them all, me, feeling very, very alone.

I couldn't know it then, but that was the last time I'd ever see Dr. F alive. To my understanding she died mere minutes later. In all likelihood, I was the very last person she spoke to, though her words were, and remain, a mystery to me. However, knowing what I know now about the fateful events that led up to that dreadful moment, and knowing what I know about the woman she was, I believe I can make a pretty good guess at their meaning.

I stayed there in the ER lobby for another hour, feeling painfully lonely amid all those people, and completely disoriented. I thought about calling someone, but who? There were only two people in the world who could possibly counsel me, and they were both right there in the hospital, and yet they were both out of reach.

I even considered going to the school, to the lab, where awaited the technology that could allow me to undo whatever grave misfortune had befallen Dr. F, but without her that technology was as useless to me as a laptop to a Neanderthal. Besides, I was still out of place, or out of *time* as it were, and who knew what would happen if I slid back again from what was, to me, already the past?

I had no idea what to do, so I did nothing.

Thankfully my wait was cut short when Wendy reappeared. Her injuries were as minor as they looked, and with hospital space at a sudden premium, she was released after having her several small abrasions cleaned and bandaged. She seemed surprised to see me still around. No doubt she'd also been wondering about when the second leg of my mulligan would finally arrive. Her concern about my continued presence there turned quickly to distress when I told her about Dr. F. We asked about seeing her, but were denied. No surprise.

We'd been waiting there together for another hour or so when Dr. F's family arrived. We were close enough to the receptionist to hear their inquiry at the desk, but we needn't have been. The red-haired beauty leading the group was obviously the dean's daughter. I didn't even know she had one, but the resemblance was unmistakable.

We headed back to the townhouse then, mainly because we didn't know where else to go. I asked Wendy to go in first and check on *me*. I told her I'd be sleeping soundly in my bed by then and that in accordance with Dr. F's wishes and warnings it would be safest if we kept quiet and let me sleep. Passing by the classroom where I sat taking a test was one thing, but the idea of actually looking myself in the eye was too strange and frightening to consider.

I held an arm supportively around her waist as I walked her to the door, and though she insisted she didn't need any help, she didn't seem to mind either. I waited while she tip-toed inside, but not for long. She returned a moment later wearing an unsettling expression—part confusion, part concern.

"He's not home," she said. "I mean, *you're* not home. I checked every room. The place is empty."

"Is it because I'm still here?" I asked, struggling to put my racing thoughts into words. "Maybe because I didn't go back to tomorrow, the me that belongs here's been, I don't know, cast into oblivion or erased from existence. Is something like that possible?"

Wendy stood there scrunching her eyebrows together and shaking her head, but she didn't say a thing. I waited, biting back the dozens of other questions that were piling up on the tip of my tongue. I knew better than to interrupt when her brain was revving like that.

I was relieved when she finally spoke, but my relief turned immediately to dread as her words sunk in.

"Somehow," she mumbled softly, "all this must be your fault. Oh, I'm sorry. I didn't mean it like that. I just meant . . . well, all of these things are going differently from how you say they were *supposed* to go. Somehow, your coming back must have caused all these changes."

"But I never even saw Dr. F after I came back," I argued, feeling frightened and defensive. "I hardly even spoke to anyone before you. I did send away these two ice fisherman from the lake, which was dumb because I'm sure now they were the guys who originally rescued you, but I don't even know who they were. I can't imagine they could have caused whatever happened to Dr. F, or that they're the reason I'm missing from my bed right now."

"The lab was empty when you arrived?" Wendy pressed.

"Yes."

"How many people saw you leaving the building? Was there anyone who knew you?"

"There were a bunch of people from my organic class just leaving from their exam, but I didn't speak with any of them. I suppose one of them could have noticed I was still working on my test as they left the room. Maybe. But even if they did, they'd probably just have wondered how I caught up with them so quickly. Unless someone was actually curious enough to go back in the room and check. They would have seen me still sitting in there right after watching me run out of the building. Could that have . . . could that be it?"

Wendy shrugged and asked, "And there was no one else, no one you bumped into on the way to the car?"

"Actually I did *bump into* one person, literally, but it wasn't anyone who knew me. I slipped on the ice right outside the science building and cracked heads with one of the campus security guys. I'm sure it hurt, and he was definitely ticked, but . . ."

And just like that, I knew—not every piece of the puzzle yet, but the biggest one, and the others were quickly falling into place.

"We need to go to the school," I said.

Wendy didn't argue, nor even ask for an immediate explanation. She nodded her understanding that I'd found a vital clue and held out her arm so I could walk her back out to the car.

We were still a mile from campus when I spotted unmistakable proof I'd come to the right conclusion. Even from that distance, and even through the blur of still-falling snow, the column of black smoke rising from the science building was clearly visible. Not that I could see from there which specific building was burning, but I knew. And I knew why.

I explained most of it to Wendy while we drove. The only thing I left out was the quickly shifting expression on Dr. Flannigan's face as she passed me by in the hospital. I suspected it was another important clue, but one I hadn't deciphered yet. Besides, I needed a little time to come to terms with the implications before I discussed them with anyone, even Wendy. She was probably already thinking along the same line as me anyway. After all, I should have been asleep in my bed right then.

It turned out we couldn't even reach the science building because the streets surrounding it were blocked by orange construction cones and yellow police tape.

"Do we need to try to get inside?" Wendy asked.

I shook my head. "No. I just needed to see, to be certain."

"Then let's go home," she suggested after a moment. "If the machine's destroyed, then we don't have any more choices to make. What's done is done, and we don't have a way to go back to undo it anymore. So let's go home."

It sounded almost like a plea the second time she said it, and her logic, as always, was impossible to argue against. What was done was done—this time for good.

Chronological Disorder

We fell asleep that night watching old movies on TCM from the couch. We leaned close and covered our legs with a cozy, old afghan to fight away the cold and the sadness of the day. I have no recollection of which black and white classics those were dancing before our eyes, and I doubt Wendy does either. It didn't matter.

I awoke the following morning, Thursday again, to find Wendy's face resting gently against the next sofa cushion over. The image was bitter sweet. Despite the numerous scrapes and scratches, she looked more lovely to me right then than she ever had. But those blemishes were proof that the jumbled memories in my head were genuine and not lingering echoes from the worst nightmare of my life. I managed to extricate myself from the couch and the afghan without waking her, but the gurgling sound, or perhaps even the smell, of freshly brewing coffee roused her minutes later.

"Good morning." The words came out sounding half-hearted, but I meant them. Despite the tragedies of the previous day, Wendy was there with me, alive and all in one piece, and that fact alone made it a good morning.

She smiled weakly in response and joined me by the coffee pot. She reached her hand to mine, and we laced our fingers together while we waited.

We were sipping our first cups by the east window, watching the horizon brighten, shifting from lavender to peach to a breathtaking amber-gold, as the sunrise approached. Arriving first by a small margin was the paper man, and at the sight of him I leapt up from the table and dashed outside, not bothering to retrieve my coat or hat despite the fact it was still snowing, though lightly.

I slowed when I reached the box and slid the paper out with needless caution, treating it like a bomb that might be triggered by the slightest mishandling. Even before I unfolded it I could see the big picture on the front page was the science building. The smoke at the time of the photo was tenfold what we'd seen, and open flames were visible through a window that had been either battered in or blown out on the first floor. Several firemen were battling the blaze with high-pressure hoses.

Oblivious to the cold wind biting at my exposed face, I walked the paper inside with deliberate steps and spread it across the table before Wendy so we could look at it together. The article that accompanied the picture of the burning hall didn't have the whole story, obviously, but it did fill in some of the details where my own understanding and conjecture were incomplete.

Actually, I should use a little more care with my choice of words. I don't think I'm willing to categorize my own death as a *detail*.

The explosion, it read, occurred in the lower level of Nimoy Hall, the university's main science building, at shortly before two o'clock, Wednesday afternoon. None of this, including the time, was new to me. It was about ten 'til two when I'd delivered Dr. Flannigan's London Fog to her in the lab.

Witnesses reported seeing Jim Fitz, the building's chief custodian, entering the building not long before then with a camouflage backpack, in which was hidden, presumably, the explosive device that destroyed one lab and started a fire that caused heavy damage to several other rooms before being extinguished. One faculty member,

Dr. Evelyn Flannigan, and one student, Brody Wyoming, died from injuries sustained from the initial detonation. Numerous other students suffered mild to moderate burns and smoke inhalation from the resulting fire. Fitz was placed under arrest after having his own injuries, which were minor, treated at the County Hospital. He was quoted as saying that he took what he deemed to be the necessary action against the "unnatural science" being conducted there.

"It was my fault," I whispered, turning away from the table. There was more to the article, but I'd read enough. I half-expected Wendy to argue the point with me, maybe try to convince me it was Fitz's fault alone, or even no one's at all. Instead she took my hands again in hers and gave them a good, hard, reassuring squeeze.

"So what was it?" she asked. Her voice was low, but stronger than mine. "What triggered all the changes?"

I took my time before beginning, strategizing, and eventually decided to start with the campus security guy, whose nose I'd broken outside the science building. I reminded her that was right after I'd taken the mulligan back. I explained that I'd also seen him ten or fifteen minutes *later,* after finishing my organic exam, when he was struggling with Fitz. I told her about the bomb bag, too, and how I'd initially assumed it was full of homegrown.

"Homegrown what?" she asked, interrupting for the first time.

Instead of answering, I just paused and fixed my *you've got to be kidding me* face on her until she got it.

"Oh," she said when the light bulb finally came on. "Ohhhh."

I laughed, as charmed as amazed at how naïve she was sometimes.

"Maybe the security guy caught a glimpse of what was really in the bag," I continued, "or maybe Fitz was already under suspicion and they were keeping an eye on him. I don't know. But the guard would have caught him, stopped him, except he wasn't where he was supposed to be—because of me. He was probably in the bathroom jamming toilet paper up his nose."

"And because he wasn't where he should have been," Wendy interjected, "Fitz was able to get into the building and set off the bomb that killed Dr. Flannigan and . . . *you*. But because of the mulligan there were actually two of you occupying the same time then, right? And because the machine was destroyed in the past, it no longer existed in the future to pull you back. You stayed here, a day before when you should be, and replaced yourself."

I nodded in agreement, thinking it all through again.

Wendy tilted her head to the side, smiled just a little and said, "You died, but you're still alive, Brody. That's . . . incredible. You should be grateful, I suppose. I suppose I am."

"I am, too," I agreed, "because the same chain of events that took Dr. F's life also saved yours. Remember, if the machine hadn't been destroyed, if I'd been pulled back when I was supposed to, then I wouldn't have had time to get you out of the car. You'd have still been trapped in the Buick when it went through the ice. You'd have drowned. Fitz's bomb saved your life."

"I wish Dr. Flannigan could have known that," Wendy whispered, squeezing my hands again. "If she'd held on a day or two, just long enough for us to talk to her again, then we could have explained everything. She could have died knowing something good came of all this."

With those words, she handed me the final piece of the puzzle. This last one was pure supposition. There wasn't, and never will be, any way to know for sure, but I'm confident it's right.

"She might not have known about your miraculous survival, but I think she knew about mine. When she saw me in the ER, she looked completely shocked at first, but then she smiled. She looked happy, just for a second there, and I think I know why."

"Because she realized you'd taken a mulligan," Wendy cut in, picking up my train of thought. "She must have known you were too close to the bomb when it went off. Maybe she even saw you . . . *dead*."

"She was shocked to see me alive," I said, "but she knew there was a way for me to be in two places at once. I doubt anybody else could have figured it out that quickly, but she could have. She must have. So . . . she did know some good came of it all."

It wasn't the greatest news ever, but it was some consolation, and it was enough to upgrade Wendy's smile from half to three-quarters, which was probably as good as I could hope for right then.

We spent most of the day on a series of joyless chores, starting with phone calls to all my family members to assure them I was alive and well despite whatever they may have heard to the contrary, and ending with returning Dr. F's car to the faculty parking lot outside the science building. Who knew whether anyone would notice that it had gone and returned, and quite frankly, who cared?

Likewise, I didn't really give a rip that they had a spare body at the city morgue that was now wearing a *John Doe* tag on its charred toe. I'd stopped into the police station to let them know someone must have screwed up and misidentified the body. Then I called the newspaper and asked them to print a retraction. It would make for a mystery, maybe even a scandal. I'd probably end up being questioned about it a hundred times, a thought I dreaded, but compared to the thought of being dead . . . not so bad.

Over the course of the following years, which Wendy and I have spent together, we've talked less and less frequently about the mulligan machine and the events it precipitated. It's too incredible to leave behind forever, but . . . well, life goes on.

We do, however, always drive back to SMU for the anniversary of that fateful day. We get fancy coffees from Starbucks and sip them as we walk around campus, swapping memories from our college days and feeling our age among the students. Then we ride out to the cemetery where Dr. F is buried to visit her grave. We don't stay long, but it's nice, just for those few minutes, to have the whole team together again, we two that survived and we two that died.

All three of us.

THE MAGIC MIRROR

Tragedy

"Harold, stop it. You're hurting me. Harold, please!"

Dr. Harold Olden ignored his wife's pleas. He didn't let her go, but tightened his grip instead, digging his fingers into her arm. Yes, he was hurting her. He knew that. He wanted that.

Not in a million years would he have thought himself capable of even thinking such a thing, but there he was, dragging Jessica through the house against her will, causing her pain, and feeling undeniably gratified by it. He'd become a different man, someone he never dreamed he'd become, never wanted to become, and it was all her fault. What she'd done, what he'd *seen* her do, was unthinkable, and unforgivable. It had unhinged him completely, and now, suddenly, he felt capable of . . . anything. He was a good man, but didn't good men do terrible things all the time? Of course they did, and now he knew how.

"Harold, talk to me, please. Where are we going?"

"I'm taking you back to the basement," Harold growled. Jessica recoiled from the venom in his voice, which pleased him further. She was afraid. Good.

"What do you mean *back?*" she asked, mumbling her words between sobs. "I'm telling you, I wasn't down there. Neither was Trent. He couldn't have been. He was never out of my sight. Why won't you believe me?"

Harold gnashed his teeth together so hard it made his jaw ache. How could she speak Trent's name to him with that innocent look on her face. Incredible. *Infuriating!*

"Go," he ordered when they reached the basement door. He threw the door open with his free hand and shoved her through. She stumbled, missing the first step, and teetered precariously on the second for a moment before finding the railing and righting herself. The sight made Harold's heart skip, an instinctual reaction that utterly betrayed his anger. The word *careful* had surged up over his tongue, but he'd snapped his teeth closed just in time to keep it from escaping. He forced that word back down his throat with a hard swallow and offered another in its place. "Move!"

The hum of idling electronics filled the air as they descended. Quite the opposite of most people's basements, Harold's was immaculately clean and so brightly lit it was almost blinding when first entered. Evenly spaced fluorescent bulbs formed three long lines of light that stretched from one end of the room to the other, and sheets of clear plastic covered almost every inch of wall space, a preventative measure against dust, which even in minute amounts could affect some of the doctor's most sensitive instruments.

Waiting for them at the bottom of the stairs was the device. Jessica walked right past without giving it so much as a glance, which struck Harold as nothing short of astonishing. He had to remind himself that it was probably the most innocuous *looking* piece of equipment in the lab, and that Jessica couldn't have any idea of what it was, of what it could do. If she had, then she would have been more careful. She would have entertained her houseguest somewhere else.

As Jessica begged for an explanation, still playing dumb about the whole thing, Harold went about powering up the device. He'd fire it up, adjust its view accordingly, and then she would see for herself the undeniable proof of her transgression. He'd make her stand there and watch right along with him, he'd make her own up to it, and then he'd . . . well, he honestly didn't know what he'd do then.

Five minutes later the room had been transformed, its condition shifted from practically sanitary to completely chaotic. A large section of the plastic that covered the walls had been torn down and lay in a heap on the floor. Harold's equipment was strewn about as well, much of it broken. Even one of the overhead fluorescent lights had failed to survive the confrontation. Brittle shards of the shattered bulb added to the debris, as did the device's ruined frame. A jumble of multicolored wires spilled out from its side, giving it the look of a dead animal, eviscerated by some vicious predator.

The glistening stripes of crimson that decorated the wall and the floor and even part of the ceiling, however, weren't oil, or grease, or any other mechanical fluid in disguise, but exactly what they appeared to be: blood. And it wasn't the smell of astringent cleaners and ozone, usually dominant in the lab, that now filled the air, but that of gun smoke. And death.

Drudgery

(Six Months Earlier)

Harold cringed as he turned the final corner, bringing his house into view. There was a strange car parked in the driveway, a late nineties Toyota sedan, the likes of which he'd never willingly park next to in his Mercedes. The rusting Corolla would have looked shabby parked at a dollar store in that part of southern California, and in his cobblestone driveway, in front of his brand new, two-story suburban home, it looked like roadkill, like something that had been caught briefly under someone's wheel and managed to crawl that far off the road before finally, mercifully, dying.

"I swear, I am not in the mood," Harold grumbled as he hit the button to raise the garage door. Annoyingly, the Toyota was parked centrally in the drive, preventing him from pulling into the vacant side of his two-car garage. He parked instead halfway into the yard, leaving, hopefully, plenty of room for his guest, whoever it was, to back out past him without clipping his side mirror, or worse. He'd know soon enough, because whoever it was, they'd be leaving promptly. He was not in the mood.

As he stepped out of the car, a jolt of pain raced up through his right hip and into his lower back, making him wince and swear under his breath. "Damn it." He'd been working hellacious shifts in the lab, and all those hours on his feet were taking their toll. He needed an adjustment from his chiropractor. He needed a new pair of shoes, too. He needed to be twenty years younger again. Back then he could work all day and half the night in the same sneakers he'd owned since college, catch up on his journal reading before bed, and then get up and run a couple miles the next morning before the sunrise. He couldn't even afford a dentist then, let alone a chiropractor, and he couldn't have cared less. Those were the days.

A quick glance at the sporty little BMW parked in the garage, his wife's car, reminded Harold that not everything had turned for the worse in his life over the past two decades. He'd been younger back then, sure, stronger and more energetic, too, but he'd also been suffering through Midwest winters and dating a soul-sucking manicurist who'd made belittling him and spending his money her two favorite pastimes. And he'd let her do it for years. That's what really made him shake his head in retrospect.

Of course back then he was yet to discover how much a good woman could elevate your life, shift your outlook and your priorities. Meeting and marrying Jessica had changed everything for him. She was the best thing that had ever happened to him, and the best thing, he was sure, that ever would. Compared to her, the house and the car and all his other *stuff* were negligible in worth, merely details. Because of her, his steadily receding health and hair were . . . tolerable. Or nearly so, at least.

Carrying his laptop in one hand and a thick binder of notes and printouts in the other, Harold pushed down the latch to the front screen door with the point of his elbow and backed his way inside. He kicked one foot back just in time to keep the door from slamming shut, a seemingly simple maneuver that nonetheless triggered another bolt of pain up through his hip and back. "Damn it."

"Hi, honey," Jessica's voice called from the next room. She sounded cheerful, as always, and despite the day he'd had, Harold couldn't help but feel a bit of relief. She was such a naturally positive person, had been ever since he'd know her, and every single time he saw her, day after day, every time he heard her voice, he was cured a bit more completely of the sad, lonely life he'd known before. She was the ultimate medicine for his innately dreary personality, and he was the perfect pillar of stability to keep the winds of her often whimsical tendencies from blowing her too far off course. She, the artist, and he, the scientist. Yin and Yang.

"Hey," he offered as he stepped into the living room, his eyes shifting quickly from Jessica, seated at her favorite end of the sofa, to the unfamiliar brunette beside her. The other woman was fit and pretty, though not beautiful like Jessica, and about her same age, thirtyish, nearly two decades younger than himself.

"This is Katie, Harold," Jessica said by way of introduction. The tone with which she spoke told Harold immediately that he was missing something. "Katie, this is my husband, Harold. He was glad to hear you'd be visiting. They're into some new project at the lab, and he's been working crazy hours—way too much, and I think he'll be glad to have you keep me entertained for a couple days, get me out of his hair."

"That's nonsense, and she knows it," Harold said with a smile, trying his best to be charming in case Katie turned out to be someone he needed to be charming for. For the life of him, he couldn't remember Jessica having said anything about expecting company, but then he wasn't always the best about keeping up in every casual conversation. Too often part of him was still working, even when he was sitting at his own kitchen table having dinner with the woman he loved. He had *heard* about Katie, he was sure, but he probably hadn't been *listening* when he'd heard. "Not only is Jess never in my hair, she's the only thing that keeps me sane. Like anyone could really get in my hair anymore. There's not much left."

Jessica offered a genuine laugh at his lame joke—it was another of her special gifts, another bit of proof that she was meant for him. Katie, on the other hand, barely managed an obviously forced giggle. She was giving him the strangest look. What was she thinking?

"Have we met before, Katie?" As soon as the words were out, Harold wished he could take them back, suddenly sure this was one of Jessica's friends he'd met at their wedding, or maybe at the class reunion she'd dragged him along to. Neither event was so distant as to adequately justify his lapse in memory.

"No, we haven't," Katie answered, her expression quickly morphing to one of generic friendliness. "We should have met at your wedding, but I'd just started my new job then, and I really couldn't take any time yet, even for that."

"Well, we certainly understood," Jessica assured her, patting her on the knee. "I'm just so glad you could make it out here now. It's so good to see you. And we're going to have a great couple days. I've got it all planned out. And no, Harold, I'm not going to let you starve while we girls are out gallivanting around. There's a bunch of stuff in the fridge I cooked ahead. All you have to do is heat it up in the microwave and eat it."

"Thank you," Harold said automatically. He was having trouble taking his eyes off Katie, still wondering about the odd look she'd given him. "Well, I don't want to interrupt your catching up, and I've got some work yet to do this evening down in the lab, so . . . have fun, and let me know if you need me for anything, or . . . whatever."

"He's got a lab of his own down in the basement," Jessica explained, responding to the question on Katie's face. "That way he can work all the time instead of just most of the time like regular obsessed people."

Harold smiled and nodded, acknowledging the undeniable truth of her observation. "It was nice to meet you, Katie. And thanks for the stockpiled fridge, Jess. I appreciate it."

With that he turned and strode out of the room, passing through the kitchen on his way to the basement door. He pulled the door open when he reached it, swinging it wide with a familiar groan of its hinges, which were still practically new. Ten minutes work and a little grease would probably cure that simple mechanical complaint, he knew, but even ten minutes represented a precious chunk of what was, to him, the world's most precious commodity: time.

Just before stepping through the door and starting down the stairs, Harold hesitated, pausing to think back to when he'd eaten his lunch. He discovered that he barely remembered eating it at all, but he knew he had, and that it had been a long time past. Though he wasn't particularly hungry, he knew he was overdue for food—brain work required fuel just as much as muscle work. The four or five steps back to the fridge, from which he retrieved an apple and a can of soda, were just enough to bring him into earshot of the conversation from the next room.

"It just caught me off guard for a second," Katie was saying. "When you showed me that picture, I assumed your husband was the other guy, the younger one. It didn't even occur to me it could be him. I mean Harold seems great. I like him. He's just not what I was expecting. It just caught me off guard . . . for a second."

Her words seemed to float through the house and come to rest squarely upon Harold's shoulders, weighing down on him so heavily he felt his knees quake under the pressure. Perhaps because he'd already used up his entire reserve of annoyance for the day, what he felt instead in response to Katie's admittance was simply . . . *old*. Of course Jessica's friend expected her to have married someone younger and fitter and better looking, because she was young and fit and good looking herself. He, on the other hand, was old and bald and pudgy. And his back hurt all the time. That was the truth of it, and at that moment it was a very heavy truth to hold.

"So who else from the old group do you stay in touch with?" Jessica was asking as Harold slunk back across the kitchen. She was changing the subject, steering the conversation away from what was obviously an embarrassing topic for her: him.

With all possible finesse, Harold pulled the door closed behind him as he started down the stairs, turning it on its hinges as slowly and steadily as he could, which was, he knew, the only way to silence its usual groan. Unlike the door, the stairs were as solid as stone and offered not even the slightest whisper of sound to announce his passage over them.

With a groan of his own, Harold sat himself down onto the bottom step when he reached it, dragging the edge of his hand down across the wall and over the light switch as he did. What the garish fluorescent light revealed was a lab of modern electronic equipment that would have roused jealousy in many a university professor. Here, among his machines, his experiments and investigations, was where he felt most at ease.

The lab at work, the government facility where he'd been employed for the past twelve years, was superior to his own basement shop, but it wasn't *his*. There, he was bound by the mandates of his sanctioned projects and the parameters of their endless official policies. He wasn't free there to follow every flash of inspiration to wherever it led. And then there was the ceaseless barrage of distractions when he was at work; meetings with what they called parallel project personnel, briefings with the higher ups, and most hindering of all, most annoying of all, Trent—the other guy in the picture, the one Katie had supposed to be Jessica's husband.

Trent Penner was all of those things Harold was not—good looking, fit, charming, and *young*. He was, in fact, the youngest person in history ever to be awarded the Presidential Award for Scientific Advancement, an honor that had been bestowed upon Harold and him two years earlier for their joint work with deep space radio scanning technology. They'd done the work together, accepted the award together, and then Trent alone had appeared on the front page of Scientific American and been interviewed by the people from National Geographic, the Discovery Channel, and, believe it or not, The Late Show.

The picture Katie must have seen was of the two of them and Jess on the night they'd received the award. Harold couldn't remember how, couldn't imagine how, but Trent had ended up in the middle when the photograph was taken, separating husband and wife. It had been a great, happy night, but Harold hated that picture.

That evening, instead of throwing himself into his work like he usually did, like he should have, Harold sat for a long time on that step. Unengaged, his mind was free to wander, and it did, far back and forward through time, from the distant days of his youth to his rapidly approaching *golden* years. More like rusty years! By the time he went back upstairs, all was dark and quiet. A sandwich and a note awaited him on the kitchen counter, right next to the microwave—the usual spot. *Eat, and then get some sleep,* it read. *Goodnight. I love you.*

Not only was Jessica young and vigorous and all those other more obvious things, she was also the kindest, most thoughtful person Harold had ever met. How had he ever convinced her to marry him?

He didn't remember. He couldn't imagine. How could he hope to keep her happy? How could he hope to keep her at all?

Harold shook his head, trying to chase those parasitical thoughts away, but they persisted, gnawing their way deeper and deeper into his psyche. He climbed into bed without touching the sandwich, and after finding himself unable to drift off, spent most of the night continuing to wander through the gray haze of exhaustion and despair.

Epiphany

When morning finally arrived, announced by the first dim rays of easterly sun, which snuck into the bedroom through the slender crack between the drapes, Harold sat up and swung his legs out from beneath the covers. For the sake of his still slumbering wife, he stifled the groan that pushed up into his throat in response to the sudden movement. His back was killing him, but that was no reason for Jessica to have to join him up at that ridiculously early hour. He knew where the aspirin was, and all she could offer him beyond that was sympathy, which would do nothing to alleviate his discomfort. If anything, it might actually make it worse. Hearing her say how sorry she was that he was old and speeding toward infirmity was the last thing he needed—not good medicine.

Spotting an unfamiliar purse hanging from one of the dining room chairs, Harold was reminded of their houseguest, who was, presumably, still sleeping as well in the spare bedroom. The idea of having to try to be personable to her if she awoke before he was gone was enough to convince him to forego his normal breakfast routine. He opted instead on an earlier than usual departure and a mystery meat and muffin value meal. Not a lot of medicinal qualities there either, but it was cheap and fast and it would keep his motor chugging along until lunch.

A little time to himself in the lab would be nice anyway, he mused as he approached the Mercedes, still parked out of place behind

Katie's Corolla. Maybe Trent would be late, *again,* and he'd have a couple good hours to work in peace and quiet, without the constant barrage of chit chat and the grating screeches of what apparently passed for rock and roll music these days.

"You'd probably have liked this if you'd heard it on the radio," Trent had suggested the previous day about a particularly offensive song. "You're convincing yourself you don't like it because you know I do, and you're determined to prove we have absolutely nothing in common. But you're wrong. We might not like the same music, but I *know* we have the same taste in women, and if you get hit by a bus on the way home tonight, I'll prove it. Jessica will be mine within a month."

This was followed by the little half-smile chuckle Trent always used to let everyone know when he was *just kidding.* Kidding or not, his words had been the catalyst for the spiral Harold had spent the rest of the day and that whole night sliding down.

"But not today," Harold vowed as he threw the Mercedes into reverse and hit the gas. He would not let that . . . *twerp* get to him again, no matter what.

The strength of his conviction hardly even wavered when he saw the ugly brown stripe he'd made in the yard with his manly peel out.

Thirty minutes later, Harold sat idling at the guardhouse station positioned outside the government buildings that housed his lab. It was the first of three separate lines of security he had to pass through before getting to work. Every. Single. Day. And of the three, this one was by far the biggest pain in the butt.

"Doctor O. What's up?" the guard in the station asked once Harold had the window down.

"Oh, same old, Kevin. How're you?"

Kevin was the real problem with this particular part of the daily security routine. Taking sixty seconds to have his card swiped and smiling into the *first* camera wouldn't have seemed like much hassle at all if he could have done it without the annoying banter. Kevin represented the lowest ranks of all government employees as far as Harold could tell, and was, he imagined, a dropout cop that hadn't quite made it as a real badge man. Before that, Harold supposed he'd been a high school star athlete in one sport per season, and probably prom king to boot. But now, in the real world, none of that meant crap. In the real world, it was the brainy kids who didn't even go to prom, namely him, who made the big bucks and drove around in a Mercedes and got married to the prom queen.

So why could Kevin still make him feel like the same insecure geek teenager he'd been all those years, *decades,* ago? He did it so easily, and in all likelihood without meaning to, which only made it all the more frustrating.

"You catch the Lakers game last night, Doc? It was epic. Kobe put up thirty-six. He's unstoppable."

"I missed it," Harold answered simply. He'd actually gotten into the habit of checking the results of the games on his phone some mornings, just so he could have something to say when Kevin's invariable queries came. That he did this, that he went out of his way just to try to fit in, for that's clearly what it was, with the least paid man on the staff, the lowest rung on the ladder, was absolutely maddening. And yet he did it anyway.

"At least tell me you missed it for some quality time with that hot wife of yours. Don't tell me you were working at home all night on the same boring crap you work on all day here. But you were. I can see it on your face. You gotta live, Doc. You can't work all the time."

"I hear you," Harold answered, struggling to keep his frustration out of his voice. "But hey, you gotta work, right? Gotta pay the bills."

In response to this, Kevin only sneered, probably annoyed himself at hearing the guy in the brand new Mercedes complain about money. He handed Harold's card back in silence and turned back to his video monitor, which was currently displaying SportCenter instead of the regularly shifting views of the property that should have appeared there in perpetuity.

"Have a good day," Harold offered weakly as he pulled away, but no reply followed.

How he could always, *always,* be the one who ended up feeling like a schmuck after the morning check-in, seemingly regardless of the line of conversation, was a mystery. It was a nuisance he shouldn't have had to deal with, and he was, as he was with so many things at the lab, fed up with it. He couldn't keep on with things the way they were forever, he knew. Something, at some point, had to change.

As Harold swiped his keycard one final time at the entrance to the lab, the third and final security checkpoint, he glanced at the sign on the door, a stamped sheet of some silvery metal, which read, *No Unauthorized Personnel Beyond this Point—RVW Project Team Members Only.*

It was a pretty fancy sign, Harold thought, considering when they'd first hung it no one had known whether the project was going to last two weeks or two years. They could have taped up a sheet of typing paper with the same words scribbled across it in black marker, which is exactly what they'd have done back at the University, and it would have served the same purpose. Mostly. The only thing a sheet of paper couldn't do nearly as well was remind everyone who saw it that this was a government facility, and money was not an issue.

When the light beside the door's handle switched from red to green, Harold twisted the knob and slipped inside. As he paused to wait for the sound of the door's lock reengaging once it swung closed behind him, as was his habit, he glanced ever so briefly up at the video camera mounted at the corner of the ceiling, just above his head. This was another habit, one he'd tried, and failed, to shake. It was disconcerting to know someone was always watching, that he never had any true privacy in which to work, even when he was alone in the lab.

A step inside the door, Harold slipped into his white lab coat, left hanging neatly on the hook as usual, and then headed for the CD player on the nearest countertop. He popped out the disc Trent had been playing last, something called, strangely enough, *Wolfmother,* and swapped it for Vivaldi. Who knew how late his young colleague would be that day? Or, heaven forbid, he might even be on time for once. Regardless, Harold knew his window of opportunity for "grown ups only" time was limited, and he had to take full advantage while it lasted.

With the sounds of *Autumn* drifting through the room, he went about powering up several laptops which sat networked at his main workstation, the electronic brain that carried out the incredibly complex simulations that were the heart of their work with RVW.

Then, on a whim, Harold turned and crossed to the far side of the room, where a piece of machinery was covered by a translucent sheet of milky white plastic. Another ceiling mounted camera was positioned nearby, its tiny lens fixed permanently on the concealed equipment, and a hand-held digital recorder sat atop a tripod before it as well, its electronic eye fixed on the same spot like a tireless sentinel, waiting patiently to see something worth recording.

With the utmost care, Harold pulled the tarp away, starting at one side and folding it over itself, one arm-length segment at a time, until it finally dropped to the floor in a neat pile, like a crinkly bedroll. To anyone else, the apparatus that had been hidden underneath wouldn't have looked like much, just a thick, aluminum picture frame with a tangle of cables hanging from its side, and no picture within, but Harold saw something else entirely. What he saw was the potential to advance modern science in one of the most significant steps forward since the splitting of the atom.

With the thoughtless ease of an act performed in repetitions beyond count, Harold typed in a long series of commands, and with the last press of the enter key, a steady humming sound came to life within the machine as power began feeding through the wires and shunts of its electron streaming circulatory system.

Normally, the device would have remained inert until later in the day, if they got around to powering it up at all. More simulations needed to be run, more equations tweaked and machinery recalibrated, before there was any point in trying again, but for some reason that day, while Harold had a few moments of relative privacy, he just wanted to turn it on and listen to it, to hear the whirring voice of the energy cycling through it, and to think.

RVW, or *Remote Viewing Window,* was by far the most exciting project Harold had ever been a part of. At the time, the work he and Trent had done with the deep space scanners seemed like a probable pinnacle for his career as a scientist, but now, in retrospect, it seemed almost trivial in comparison to what they were trying to do with RVW.

It was ironic in a sense that the aims of the two projects ran nearly in parallel, while the means to accomplishing those aims couldn't have stood further apart. In both cases, the goal was to find new ways to see into hidden places. With the ultra-sensitive radio scanners, it was into deep space that they peered, scrutinizing for the first time some of the most distant mysteries of our vast, mostly unknown, universe. With RVW, the goal was much smaller, and yet infinitely more profound. All they wanted to accomplish with the Window was to see across the room, but to do so via a shortcut—through space.

It was a notion that had first come to Harold while they were still working with the radio scanners, a wild idea that had, initially, only tickled his curiosity, but not settled immediately into place for any serious scrutiny. But it wouldn't go away. The possibility that trying so hard to see across space might be unnecessary, that there might be a way to see *through* space instead, via a shortcut, a hole, took root in his mind and slowly, bit by bit, grew into the theoretical framework behind RVW. So it was that even as he was striving to perfect the deep space scanners, he was already thinking about how to make them obsolete.

"A hole in space." Harold whispered the words so quietly the sound barely reached his own ears. It had become his litany during the past months, a way to stay focused, to keep himself from forgetting, even for a second, the core purpose of the project. Sometimes, if he wasn't careful, he could get too caught up in the math, in the numbers, and lose sight of the ultimate goal of the work, and that was dangerous. The math always posed mysterious paths of its own, interesting lines of conjecture that often led to nowhere. He had to stay focused. "A hole in space."

The previous day, after completing the most recent series of simulations and recalibrating the device for what must have been the hundredth time, Harold and Trent had tested the machine, and in similar fashion to every other test, it had failed. They had failed.

Again. But as Harold stood there, staring at the unrealized potential of his theory, the unripened fruits of his labor, he simply couldn't imagine what it was that kept going wrong. He hadn't expected the Window to be working perfectly at this point, but he'd been wholly confident it would be working . . . somehow. Maybe just a murky glimpse of an off-target view, but . . . something. Anything! And yet what they saw instead, over and over again, was nothing.

With no real intention of following through to the completion of the process, Harold began moving deliberately from one preliminary step to the next, scrutinizing each one in the hopes of discovering some potential oversight that might explain their ongoing failures. He reconsidered the strength and consistency of their power source, reexamined the integrity of each and every plug, port, and connection. He even hushed Vivaldi so he could have a few moments of complete silence during which he could focus on the humming voice of the machine, listen for any pitch or volume fluctuations that might offer a clue.

That's pointless, spoke Trent's voice in Harold's imagination. *And ridiculous.*

"Shut up, Trent," Harold said aloud. They were words he thought often in the lab, but rarely voiced, and only, ironically, when he was alone.

All the equipment looked perfect. It sounded perfect. It should've worked.

Glancing at the clock, Harold estimated Trent was already late by fifteen minutes. He couldn't hope for much more than that. With a sigh of defeat, he turned away from the still-humming machine. His first coffee of the day was already wearing off, and he was feeling the hollow void inside him that opened whenever he neglected his caffeine addiction.

The fifty dollar microwave sitting next to the nine thousand dollar centrifuge wasn't exactly standard issue for the facility, but it was a simple, practical way to keep the go-juice flowing all day without pulling Harold away from his work. Without giving it any conscious thought, he pulled open a drawer and withdrew a tea bag. He plucked his mug from the autoclave, gave it a quick rinse in the sink, and filled it with cold tap water. He was still on autopilot when he reached down and pushed the button to spring the microwave door, which is why he didn't notice the empty beaker sitting in front of it. When the door popped open, it brushed the fragile glassware over the side of the counter and sent it crashing down to the floor. It shattered at his feet.

"Damn it!" Harold hissed, startled by the breaking of the glass and of the relative silence. "Trent. Moron."

Harold was already halfway done cleaning up the broken glass when it occurred to him he shouldn't be cleaning it up at all. What he should have done was leave it for his lab partner to deal with, since it was surely Trent who'd left it there instead of putting it away. But then another idea presented itself, one Harold liked even better. He finished with the mess, retrieved his tea water from the microwave, and then put another beaker, just like the one he'd broken, right back where the first one had been, if not a bit closer to the edge. He reset the trap.

"It'll never work," Harold grumbled. He wasn't that lucky, he knew, but then again, nothing else was working, and *something* had to go right eventually. Maybe this would be it.

The door swung open just then, and in walked Trent, late as usual.

"You've got it powered up already? How early did you come in? You did go home last night, didn't you?"

Harold moved quickly away from the microwave and the beaker he'd planted in front of it. He felt his cheeks flush and was immediately annoyed by it. For goodness sakes, it wasn't like he'd committed some criminal act!

"I was just going over the preliminary steps, seeing if I could track down any glitches in the hardware," Harold said, avoiding eye contact. "And I just got here at the regular time. *On time.*"

"Yeah, right!" Trent shot back, his voice full of disbelief. "That's total garbage. What you were doing was running a test without me here because you think it's my fault it keeps failing. I don't know why you think that."

"No, Trent, that's not it. I wasn't even going to run it. I was just going through the power up steps. I didn't find anything suspicious, so now I'm going to power it down and go back to simulations."

"Whatever, man," Trent grumbled as he smoothed down the sleeves of his lab coat, which he'd already been wearing when he'd arrived. As far as Harold could tell, he wore it all the time, everywhere he went. He said it got him more attention from *the ladies* than the fanciest suit and tie ever could.

"Do you mind?" Harold said when Trent then stepped to the CD player, plucked out the Vivaldi disc, and dropped it haphazardly on the countertop, less than a foot from its case.

Trent turned to him, rolled his eyes, and then with deliberateness worthy of a tea ceremony master, returned the CD to its case. "There. You can breathe easy now. It's safe and sound."

"That's not even what I meant, Trent, and you don't need to be such a . . . wise guy about it."

"Ooooh, a *wise guy,* huh? Such a foul mouth today, Doctor."

Harold felt his annoyance shift, felt it grow and approach the point where it would become outright anger instead. It was a feeling he'd become familiar with lately. He and Trent had never been bosom buddies, but they'd made good partners in the lab, two keen minds positioned at different angles, so to speak: good compliments for problem solving. Lately, however, the tension between them had become almost palpable. The source of the increased volatility was no mystery, at least not to Harold. It was Jessica. Ever since Trent had started in with his little pokes about her and her *old man*, about their mysterious marriage, and about her obviously bizarre taste in men, Harold's ire had been growing. He tried to convince himself it was just harmless, albeit tasteless, kidding around, but that argument was wearing thin.

"Look, all I want is to leave the CD player off for a while, okay?" Harold said, struggling to keep his voice even.

Trent rolled his eyes again and said, "You still think you'll be able to hear the problem somehow with your magic ear, huh? Fine. Let's fire the sucker up and see if you can."

"That's not what I meant either," Harold shot back as Trent stepped to the keyboard beside the Window and began typing in commands in rapid succession. "I told you I wasn't running a full test. I just wanted to go over the preliminary steps."

"And you did, right? And you obviously didn't find anything, right? Well, it's already powered up. It's ready to go. Let's go."

Harold started to argue further, but stopped himself. There really was no reason not to proceed, except that it was what Trent wanted, and he couldn't let that become his driving motivation, not in the lab. In there, the science had to come first, always. And the truth was, he really did want to run it once without any background noise. Although Trent insisted it was a futile gesture, Harold wasn't so sure. Sometimes the tiniest hints, like a little unidentified click or buzz, or a barely noticeable revving or slowing in one of the cooling fans, could be the clue that eventually cracked the case.

"Alright then, go ahead," Harold said with a nod. "You run the test, and I'll just stand here and listen, learn what I can with my magic ear."

"You got it, Doc."

As Trent continued pecking away at the keyboard, Harold drew a thick curtain that had been mounted on the ceiling. It was only six feet across, just wide enough to block the view between the Window and the painting hanging on the opposite wall, one of Jessica's. It was an oil of the weeping willow that grew behind their new house. She'd only finished it a couple weeks earlier, and grudgingly allowed Harold to hang it in the lab. She'd intended it to decorate their dining room, but now it had the chance of becoming something much more than mere decoration. When the Window finally worked, Jessica's art would not only become *known,* it would become an item of genuine historical significance. It would become the first image ever seen by human eyes through a hole in space.

Harold stepped back and positioned himself behind the Window. Through its empty frame he saw only the plain, opaque surface of the curtain. He pictured the painting in his head, saw it in his mind's eye hanging there mere feet beyond his view. He imagined seeing it coalesce in the Window, making him the very first human being to experience true sight beyond sight. He wouldn't be seeing a data transfer after all, not an image passed along to be reformed on a visual monitor, but an actual unobscured view. And if it worked here, across the span of a single room, then there was no reason with further refinement it couldn't work across the span of a continent as well, or the universe.

"We're almost there," Trent called over from his workstation, raising his voice to be heard over the climbing voice of the machine. Its hum had become a buzz, and was rapidly spiking both in pitch and volume. Instead of shying away from the abrasive noise, Harold leaned in closer, straining to hear any softer sounds or unsteadiness to the rhythm he might have missed before, and all the while he kept his eyes focused through the Window.

"Come on, come on," Harold whispered softly to himself. "Work!"

When Harold suddenly found himself struggling to focus clearly on the curtain through the Window, he knew the moment had arrived. The fabric of the cloth barrier suddenly looked fuzzy and indistinct, like he was looking at it through a pane of dingy glass. Then the actual space within the frame became visible. A thin swirling film seemed to stretch across it. It was hard to focus on, barely there, but it grew rapidly denser, quickly blocking his view of the curtain completely.

"Come on, come on."

The machine was oppressively loud now, practically screeching, but it sounded like it always did, and beneath its voice Harold couldn't hear anything out of the ordinary, no new clues. As he had so many times before, he stared hard at the shadowy smears of black and gray that had filled the Window, searching for some discernible shape among the mishmash, but there was nothing.

Long seconds ticked by, and Harold knew this fresh opportunity had nearly passed. The machine could only remain active for a brief period of time, and then it shut down automatically.

Risking a quick glance away, Harold shifted his eyes to Trent, who also looked up just then from his computer screen and shook his head in dismay. His unspoken message was clear. Another failure.

And that's when it happened. Harold's gaze was still directed away from the Window, but his ear was wide open to it. As Trent gave a thumb down, Harold heard a very faint but sharp sound beneath the din, like breaking glass. He swung his head quickly back to the Window, but it was already too late. The frame stood empty once again. Silence had refilled the room.

"Well, that sucks," Trent said, but his words fell on deaf ears.

Rush hour traffic had descended on the highway of Harold's mind, every speeding car another new question or possibility. Could he have been mistaken? No. No way. He'd definitely heard something, and it really had sounded like . . .

Then it hit him. Yes, he had heard something, and breaking glass is exactly what it was. Of course it was!

"Maybe we're still off on our targeting," Trent was saying. "Maybe it's working, but we're trying to look into the middle of the wall instead of at the painting. Or . . . I don't know. I don't know why it won't work. Maybe we should try . . ."

He kept talking, but Harold didn't hear a word of it. Moving very slowly, he made his way back toward the entrance of the lab.

"I'm not feeling good, Trent," he said as he replaced his lab coat on the hook beside the door. "I'm going home."

"What?" Trent asked. "Are you serious? You're taking a sick day? I didn't think you knew about sick days."

Harold didn't reply. He disappeared through the door without another word, made his way back through the building in a daze, and then didn't even wave at Kevin as he sped past the gatehouse in the Mercedes. His mind raced as he drove home, consumed with the incredible opportunities suddenly presented to him, and the terrible responsibilities to which he was now yoked. A hole in space was one thing, but a hole in time? That was another matter entirely.

Necessity

By the time Harold arrived back at the house that morning, the most important of the decisions now facing him were made. First and foremost, he'd decided not to let anyone else know about his discovery. No one. He could justify helping to further his nation's spying capabilities, perhaps even enabling them to peer into the most secure facilities of their rivals across the globe, but handing over actual space-time technology, the first ever to exist outside the realm of science fiction, was something he couldn't do. At least not until he'd had time to explore the full potential and limitations of the Window on his own, until he understood what it could really do.

Looking into the past could offer the ultimate means of correcting the mistakes in every history book, of ferreting out the truth behind every government's propaganda and every media outlet's sensationalism. It could mean the end of wrong convictions and acquittals, but it could also mean the end of privacy, and though the scientist in him balked at the idea, the man in him knew certain secrets were better left buried. And what if the technology eventually led to something more than hindsight? What if it ultimately led to the ability to manipulate the past, to actually interact with the timeline? It didn't seem possible, but he couldn't be certain of anything anymore, not without further experimentation. And until he was sure, he had to keep it to himself.

Yes, the idea of being able to claim sole ownership of the greatest discovery in modern science also entered into Harold's mind, but only briefly. That was a peripheral matter, an afterthought, really. But it was there, and it was impossible to ignore completely.

Jessica and Katie were already gone when Harold arrived back at the house, probably sipping lattes somewhere and planning out their day, spending a little of his money and preparing to spend a lot. Good. Great! The arrival of Jessica's company couldn't have come at a better time, Harold realized, as the two of them would undoubtedly be out and on the go together for most of the next several days, which would allow him the perfect window of opportunity to work alone at the house. He'd encourage it. He'd tell them to live it up, to shop with abandon. After all, no matter how carried away they got flexing his credit card at the mall, it wasn't going to amount to a tiny fraction of the currency he was about to move.

The lab in Harold's basement had been redesigned in his mind during the car ride home, rearranged and modified to a degree of detail only someone with his extraordinary intellect was capable of. There would barely be enough space down there for everything he was going to need, but he could squeeze it in. A few of the new pieces of equipment would be difficult to maneuver down the stairs as well, but he thought he could manage. He might have to find a way to supplement the power he pulled from the local grid, too, but again, it was doable. The biggest hurdle he faced was money.

Harold had done well for himself over the years, particularly since joining the ranks of the federally employed. He'd made a lot of money, and he'd invested it carefully, taking full advantage of the swelling market. There'd be a hefty government pension waiting for him at retirement as well. He'd also refrained from the extravagant spending habits that had become the norm for Americans of all economic strata. True, he had a nice house and a nice car, but he didn't have a time share down south and a cabin up north and a pole barn full of power toys he made payments on and hardly ever used. He didn't take off jet-setting for Europe or the Caribbean three times a year, hurrying to spend his money as quickly as he could make it. Or quicker.

Harold had thought himself sitting pretty where money was concerned, but now he realized what he had wasn't going to be enough—not by a long shot. The lab where he worked housed a set of cutting edge equipment that could make top university researchers green with envy. Recreating that lab on his own, purchasing all those same technologies himself, would take a fortune he didn't have. Yet.

Harold set to work immediately at the house, shifting around the equipment he would still need and carrying the pieces he wouldn't up to the garage to get them out of the way, making room for the machines he had, as of that moment, no means of acquiring. Not for a single second, however, did he consider the possibility that he wouldn't be able to . . . somehow. What he would accomplish with those machines was far too important to be obstructed, or even delayed, by something as petty and erroneous as money.

Money was only important because people chose to see it as representative of the goods and services it could buy, but scientific advancement, growth in human understanding, was intrinsically valuable. Knowledge, Harold knew, was the ultimate measure of wealth, and truly monumental leaps forward in knowledge were worth more than all the money in the world. This would be one of those rare leaps.

Despite his confidence, Harold quickly came to realize there were going to be a very limited number of options available to him for getting his hands on so much money, and quickly. And some of them wouldn't be *technically* legal. Law might be more fundamental than money, but even law ranked below understanding, and thus it could not be allowed to be a limiting factor either. The importance of his work was adequate justification for whatever rule bending might be required. He would do what needed to be done. There was really no other choice.

Besides, when he eventually announced his findings, the world would only care about what he'd done, not how he'd done it. Of that Harold was absolutely certain. The great accomplishers were always forgiven.

Ironically, it was Jessica's shopping habits that started Harold down the line of thought that led to his plan of action. He was rummaging through the garage, trying to make space, when he accidentally tipped over one of his wife's recently collected junk items. At least that's what it was to him. It was a rusting old gumball machine that probably hadn't worked in half a century. Two weeks earlier it had been someone's trash, but now it was Jessica's treasure. She referred to it, and all its fellow refuse collectibles, as *nostalgia art*. Harold didn't get it, but he didn't mind it all that much either. If it made her happy, got her artist's juices flowing or whatever, then fine.

Thankfully, the thing somehow snagged up in his long ignored golf clubs on its way down, sparing the glass globe from reaching the concrete floor, where it would certainly have shattered. There was a clunk as the thing's base collided with one of the golf clubs, the wedge, Harold thought, and off popped a small metal cap with a key hole at its center. A stream of pennies, as vintage as the machine by the look of them, came pouring out from behind the cap, tumbling down in a steady stream and piling up on the floor. The sight of them, and the sound of them, sent Harold's thoughts racing . . . to the east.

What Harold needed was money, a lot of it, and he didn't have the time or the means to acquire it by any conventional strategy, but it so happened that just four short hours from his southern California home lay a place where big money changed hands more freely and frequently than perhaps anywhere else in the world.

The plan was coming together as Harold made his way back into the house, headed for the fridge to investigate the pre-fab meals Jessica had left him, and by the time he popped the top off a Tupperware container of meatloaf, mashed potatoes, and peas, he had it more or less worked out. Some of it would have to be ad-libbed when he got there, but he'd make it work. Whatever it took.

He didn't wait for Jessica to return, but chose instead to leave her a note. In it he explained that he'd left the lab early and was driving out to Las Vegas that afternoon, all of which was true. He went on to say that a guest speaker at UNLV was the reason for his road trip, which had been the real reason for his making that same drive once before. Somehow this made it feel like less of a lie. It had been the truth in the past, after all, and so it was only a matter of time, and maybe time wasn't such an absolute distinction anyway. That, of course, was the real reason behind the trip, to find out whether it was or not.

Still, Jessica and he had always maintained a very honest relationship, and even this little fib, quickly scribbled across the back of a discarded envelope from the previous day's mail, gave him pause. But what could he do? Explaining that he was headed to Vegas in the hopes of getting his hands on enough money to rebuy their house—twice, was hardly an option. He hated having to be dishonest with her, even in this small way, but it was necessary, and he was committed. There was no turning back. Whatever it took.

Harold arrived in Vegas at five o'clock. He noted a digital sign outside a bank as he passed the city limits that read one-hundred and three degrees. It was hardly the appropriate weather to break out the only nice suit he owned, had ever owned, but the clothes made the man, he knew, and that night he needed to be another man, one who might do things he would never do.

Following the directions from his GPS, Harold drove straight to one of the largest and most famous casinos on the strip. It was a place he'd visited once before, a little detour he'd made during his trip to UNLV. He'd enjoyed the buffet, enjoyed watching the incredible array of people, some radiating exuberance and others seemingly on the verge of catatonia, but he'd only been able to force himself to gamble away about ten dollars of his own money before losing interest in the machines. He understood the odds well enough, and was not in any way thrilled by the remote possibility of beating those odds—not then, and not still. His cause was one of much too great importance to be left to chance. He couldn't count on winning the money, and he didn't intend to. He'd intended to borrow it.

While driving, Harold had wondered about the timing of his arrival in Vegas, unsure if it would be reasonable to try to play the part of the drowning gambler at the supper hour, but his first glimpse of the machine floor quelled that doubt. The place was a circus, loud and bright and crowded full of people who'd clearly lost all track of the hour, and perhaps even the day. The casino was a time machine itself, a place where the pace of the passing seconds surged and dragged with the luck of the deal and the draw.

Not more than fifty feet inside the door, Harold paused to watch a man about his age who was trying, and failing, to depart from a slot machine depicting a vicious tiger with electric red eyes that flashed like four-way stop lights. Maybe, Harold thought, they worked the same way, too. Three times in the span of as many minutes, the man rose from his seat, shaking his head and massaging his temples with quivering fingers. He'd start away each time, but never make it more than a few steps before turning back and hurrying to reclaim his spot. He'd fallen deep, deep down the rabbit's hole.

Harold studied the man, noted the way he blinked his eyes at something like twice the normal rate and constantly tilted his head from side to side, perhaps trying to loosen a stiff neck, or perhaps just trying to keep himself awake. The man made a sad sight, but he was just who Harold needed to see, just who he needed, for a short while, to become.

"You can do this," he said to the men's room mirror a few minutes later. He rumpled his clothes and washed his face repeatedly in cold water until his cheeks glowed red, hopefully giving the impression of spiking blood pressure or intoxication. Either one would do. It wasn't going to take any great acting from him to look desperate—that's exactly what he was.

Before he lost his nerve, Harold barged out of the restroom and headed back across the casino floor. He was so anxious he could hear his own ragged breathing, and his shirt was becoming rapidly soaked in perspiration. The suit was hot, but not *that* hot. He was sweating like a cold can of beer beside a hot barbecue.

When he was near what he took to be the middle of the room, he spotted a youngish man wearing the clothes of a dealer walking his way. He'd planned on picking out a security officer, but he didn't really think it would matter. He could start with a waitress, and the result would be the same. No one from the casino could get him the money he needed anyway. That wasn't the plan.

"Excuse me," Harold said with a shaky voice, catching the man's attention. The guy looked immediately on guard, no doubt in response to Harold's panicky expression.

"Yes? Are you alright, sir? Do you need help?"

Harold froze for a second, so nervous and so far out of his element that he suddenly couldn't remember the lines he'd rehearsed over and over in the car.

"This is ridiculous!" he finally managed, forcing out his words at the top of his voice, shifting his tone from quiet to crazy. "I've never been so insulted in my life!"

The young dealer stepped back, startled by Harold's sudden vehemence. His mouth fell open, but he remained silent, perhaps too surprised to respond. Around the room, heads turned in their direction.

Knowing full well no one could make a scene long in a place like that, where security was everywhere, Harold forged ahead, shouting, "I'm worth thirty-eight million dollars, and this place can't run me credit for a couple hundred grand? Ridiculous!"

"Sir, I'm not sure what your situation is," said the casino man, "but I'm sure we can attend to whatever problem you've run into. Why don't you come with me, and we'll find someone—"

"I'm probably the richest guy in here," Harold yelled, cutting the man off and forcing him back another step. "All I'm asking for is a little advance, and you're telling me this place can't handle it? Ridiculous!"

As the man continued to do his best to placate Harold, the crowd around them swelled, vacationers mostly, eager for some variety in their entertainment. And then came security. Not one or two, but *five* well dressed gentlemen, who ushered Harold roughly out the door. It took about ten seconds. They were very efficient.

"I'm worth . . . thirty-eight million dollars," Harold yelled again as he was dragged along, stuttering as he struggled to remember the specifics of his lies. "And you can't loan me a couple hundred grand? Ridiculous!"

Despite himself, Harold felt thrilled as he was sent stumbling back out onto the street. Whether his ruse led to the desired result or not, he'd forced himself to do something way, *way* outside his comfort zone, and the adrenaline rush that had come with it was something he'd not experienced in a long time.

As he struggled to catch his breath, Harold spent several minutes standing outside the casino doors, frozen in the evening's lingering heat.

"Hey, you okay, man?" asked a passerby, a man walking with his elbow linked to a much younger woman. "You look like you're about ready to pass out. You'd better peel that suit, or else get inside, find some AC."

The comment was enough to break Harold free from his momentary reverie, and besides that, it was good advice as well. He was roasting, and although that probably only helped him look more the part he needed to continue to play, it was also robbing him of the energy and focus he needed to proceed. Before the street's heat could sap his strength further, he pushed his way out into the crowd, which was starting to swell outside now that the sun was dipping, and followed the sidewalk to the very next casino down the row. He took a few deep breaths at the door and then headed inside and repeated his performance, practically word for word, this time to a middle-aged woman who was so surprised by the exuberance of his tirade she could hardly utter a single word in response. Nevertheless, security was once again quick to respond and efficient with his ejection.

So he did it again, at the next casino, and then again at the next one after that, and that's when he finally found who he was looking for. Or rather, they found him.

Harold was standing halfway down a long, grandiose staircase that connected the street to the entryway of his fourth casino, from which he'd just been expelled, when the man approached him. By then the streets and sidewalks were packed, which was part of the reason Harold didn't notice him right away. The man also looked nothing like who Harold had expected him to be. He was as much kid as man really, not more than twenty years old, with a face so clean Harold wondered how long he'd been shaving, and a dress shirt so crisply pressed he might have been preparing to deliver a sunny Ivy League dissertation rather than a shadowy backstreets proposition.

"Excuse me, sir," the young man said once he'd maneuvered his way beside Harold, stepping down to the same stair so as to meet him eye to eye. "I couldn't help overhearing your . . . conversation inside, and I just wanted to say I'm appalled at the way you were treated. Establishments like this ought to know better how to treat their . . . preferred clientele, especially in this town."

Harold, caught momentarily off guard by the young man's appearance, took a few seconds to respond. "Yes, well, considering the fortune I've spent here in the past, I think they'll regret offending me this way. I'm a busy man, and it's not often I find the time to spend a few days here in Vegas to gamble and relax. That the time I've allotted here for amusement might be cut short by this casino's apparent inability to run me a little credit is maddening. It's not as if they don't know full well I'm good for it. And then some. And then *plenty*."

Now it was the young man's turn to hesitate, deliberately pausing in consideration. Harold had rehearsed his lines over and over in his mind during the car ride east, but now, hearing them aloud for the first time, he was suddenly terrified they sounded scripted and unnatural, and that he had, in all likelihood, blown his shot at making the plan work.

"I work with someone who runs a sort of . . . savings and loan here in Vegas," the young man said finally. "As you'd expect, lots of people here need to borrow a bit from time to time. He's a good business man. He's fair. He might be able to help you out, float you a loan so you don't have to cut your fun short just because the casino's being stingy. Would you like to meet him?"

"Absolutely," Harold answered too quickly. "Is he nearby? Within walking distance?"

"No, we can't walk, but it's just a short drive across town. What do you say we take your car?"

Harold pretended to consider this for a moment before acquiescing, but it was, to his reckoning, a great idea. The Mercedes was by far the most extravagant purchase he'd ever made, and it would suggest he really was the man he was pretending to be much better than his best entitlement act or his fieriest casino floor temper tantrum. The car, as well as anything, would help to give the wrong impression.

The young man, who introduced himself as Alvin Clemens, shed much of his easy demeanor after sliding into the passenger's seat of Harold's car. As they pulled out onto the busy avenue, he slid an iPad free from a neoprene case he'd been carrying, and within seconds it was powered up and displaying Harold's likeness on its screen.

"Whoa, is this you?" Alvin asked, angling the iPad toward Harold so he could see a familiar clip from the New York Times, which was titled *Seeing Across the Cosmos*. Inserted halfway down through the text was a picture of Harold and Trent. Harold was holding an old fashioned telescope, of the sort you might see in a pirate movie, while Trent was holding, or appeared to be holding, a graphic they'd inserted of a tiny spiral universe. Somehow it had never occurred to Harold until that very moment, driving across Vegas those years later, that the Times had really screwed him over there. They'd given him something old, and they'd given Trent something amazing. It was just one more annoying thing on that front.

"Yeah, that's me," Harold confirmed. He quickly swallowed down the twinge of irritation he felt in response to the photo, a reaction that would not serve his current purpose. "And that younger guy's Trent Penner, my research partner. That article was about a deep space radio scanner we designed. It was one of our biggest tech developments. We've had a few. Some big patents, too."

Harold made purposeful eye contact as he spoke that last bit, smiling suggestively. People generally assumed his work somehow paralleled that of Bill gates or Steve Jobs, that all those "tech guys" were big bucks rich. That wasn't the case at all, not even close, but if young Mr. Alvin Clemens might be encouraged to make the same faulty presumption, then great. And honestly, it wasn't even so much a matter of truth as it was a matter of time, because with his next breakthrough he really would join the ranks of those super-rich moguls. In fact, he'd probably surpass them. He wasn't merely going to advance an existing technology, after all, but introduce a whole new scientific field. His work with the Window was going to become historical, and it was going to make him beyond famous. How could it not?

And with fame came fortune—the more of one, the more of the other. Accumulating monetary wealth wasn't Harold's purpose, of course, but it was going to be a peripheral consequence. A few months from then, six at the most, and he'd never have to bother himself with money concerns again. Which was, of course, why he could borrow whatever he wanted without having to worry about being able to pay it back.

Alvin nodded in response to Harold's suggestion of his own personal wealth, but failed to return his smile. Instead, he continued to work diligently on his iPad, typing and swiping with practiced efficiency, and looking up only periodically to relay further driving instructions.

Harold continued to prattle on about his research, trying to maintain a careful edge with his exaggerations. A little embellishing could work to his advantage, but he sensed that if he let himself get carried away for a second, the young businessman beside him, for that's clearly what he was, would be all over it. Despite his youth, Harold had no doubt Alvin was razor sharp, and no stranger to that sort of situation. Quite the opposite, he'd probably gone through this little interview process repeatedly, whereas Harold was feeling his way through it for the first time. He was, in essence, trying to bluff a more practiced gambler in a very high stakes game. With his eyes locked on the prize, the possible consequences of losing that game never entered into his field of vision.

But they should have.

Civility

On the far side of town, after about a half-hour's drive, Alvin directed Harold into the parking lot of a custom cabinetry shop. It seemed an unlikely place to stop until Harold saw the office in the back of the building, and the man sitting behind the desk within. Here was the character Harold had envisioned meeting when he'd first devised his plan.

"Smokey" Joe Simms, as Alvin introduced him, fit almost exactly into Harold's preconceived idea of a Vegas loan shark. He was big, broad-shouldered, and though he wore a crisp dress shirt like Alvin, dark, ugly tattoos snuck just beyond its collar and cuffs. It was hard to make out exactly what they were, but the tear drops inked onto his cheeks were plain enough, and strangely menacing. His smile, a bit too broad, revealed a shiny gold tooth that sat awkwardly out of place right in the center of his mouth. His handshake was a crusher, less a greeting than a demonstration of power.

"Wow, that's quite a grip," Harold said, trying to keep his voice steady through the pain. If Smokey Joe was going for intimidation, he was succeeding. "It probably takes strong hands to build cabinetry. Unless . . . maybe that's not really your business. I mean, maybe somebody else does that part . . . up there, and you do . . . other stuff . . . back here."

Joe's smile spread wider yet. The gold tooth was like a bull's eye in the middle of his face, and Harold had trouble looking away from it.

"You seem nervous, Harold," Joe observed. "It's okay if I call you Harold, right?"

"Sure, yeah. Harold's fine. Anything. Whatever."

"Harold, you seem nervous. Are you?"

Harold discovered his throat had gone quite dry, and he had to take several hard swallows before he was finally able to answer, saying, "Yeah, I guess I am . . . a little bit. I guess I'm just feeling a little . . . out of place."

"Ah, I see what you mean. Why don't we get right down to business, and then we'll get you on your way again as quick as we can? Sound good?"

Harold just nodded. Something was still wrong with his voice.

"Let's see here," Joe continued, glancing over a sheet of notes Alvin had scratched down in the car. The younger man now stood idly some ten feet away, leaning back into the corner of the room, keeping quiet, but observing the conversation intently. "This says you are Harold Olden, make that *Doctor* Harold Olden, and that you are quite the renowned scientist. You spent some years as a university man, but now you're in the employ of the government of these glorious United States of America. How's Uncle Sam for a boss? You gettin' rich off him, fattenin' up your accounts with taxpayers' dollars just like all them greedy politicians?"

"I'm . . . fine," Harold stuttered. "It's good. I'm . . . doing good."

"Well good," Joe said with another toothy grin. "Glad to hear it. What else we got here? It says at the bottom of my little cheat sheet from Alvin that you're tryin' to front like you're loaded way past what you really got. What's up with that? You might be out of place, Harold, but anybody, especially a smart guy like you, must realize that frontin' for a loan in a town like this, for a *fat* loan, is risky business. Right? You get that, yeah?"

"Sure, yeah," Harold agreed automatically. A drip of sweat ran down between his eyes, stalling just at the tip of his nose. He wiped it away with his sleeve. The suit coat felt like it had caught fire.

"So, what's the deal? What kind of trouble you into that you need money so bad?"

Harold glanced back over his shoulder and found that Alvin was no longer leaning into the wall, but standing erect on the balls of his feet. His hands were open at his sides, and his shoulders were visibly tensed. He looked poised, like Wyatt Earp standing at the gates of the O. K. Corral, ready to draw down on the outlaw cowboys.

"I'm not in trouble," Harold managed. "I'm just . . . taking a few days away from work, doing a little gambling. I got a little behind, but I don't want to have to quit yet, and I don't . . . want to have to shift around my own money . . . because I don't want my wife to see how much I've lost."

"That would be Jessica, right?" Joe interrupted him.

This time Harold couldn't bring himself to respond. He couldn't even breathe.

"At least it says Jessica here on my cheat sheet—that's what Alvin says her name is, and he's good at this kind of stuff, information gatherin' and whatnot. He can practically run my whole business through that little electronic pad of his. But anyway, what kind of trouble are you in? Now this is the second time I've asked, and if I don't get the real answer this time, I'm gonna be insulted, so don't tell me again about your casino binge and your personal fortune that's all tied up in the market or whatever. Because it also says here in my notes that Alvin doesn't think you're a gambler."

To that, Harold had nothing to say. He'd moved beyond being nervous to being wholly terrified. Suddenly this whole plan seemed foolish to the point of absurdity. Hearing that man, that *thug,* speak Jessica's name was like hearing a wolf howl in the middle of the night.

"Come on, Harold, you can do it," Joe said in mock encouragement. "Spit it out. Tell the truth."

And that's exactly what Harold did. He'd been called on his bluff, and he didn't dare try another. More than that, he knew somehow he'd moved past the point where he could simply change his mind about the whole thing and walk back out the door. It wasn't going to be that simple.

"I've made a discovery at the lab where I work, a big one. I mean it's the kind of thing that'll make front page news everywhere in the whole world when it comes out."

Harold wasn't done. He was ready to spill out the whole story from beginning to end, but a soft chuckle interrupted him. He turned back to see Alvin, now standing just one short step behind him, smiling and shaking his head, obviously amused.

"I have to admit this isn't what I expected," he confessed. "This is way better. I thought this was going to be about you digging out of a money hole, but it's not, is it? This is about you climbing the slopes of a money mountain. You're onto something big in your research, you're smelling the cash on down the path, and you're looking for a way to make sure it ends up being *yours* instead of *theirs.* Am I right? I know I am. I can see it in your face."

"Yes, that's it, but no," Harold stammered. "I mean you're right about the what, but not the why. I am onto something big, like I said, something huge, but I'm not trying to hoard it for myself, for the money—not mostly, anyway. Mostly I just need to explore it on my own before anyone else knows about it, make sure it's safe, make sure it can't be exploited for terrible purposes. But I need money to do that, so I can reproduce the apparatus setup from my work lab at my house, so I can continue the work on my own, in private. That's the truth."

From behind his desk, Joe smiled and held his hand up in the *whoa boy* gesture. "Alright, alright. Take a breath before you pass out. I believe you. Most of it. Maybe even all of it other than the part about the money. I don't care if you're a scientist or a day trader or a freakin' ballerina, it's all about money, always. That's how the world works these days. That's how it is for everybody. That's how it is for me, that's how it is for Alvin, and that's how it is for you, too, Doc, even if you don't realize it."

"You have to believe—" Harold began, only to be hushed by another wave of Joe's stop sign hands.

"There's no need to argue here, Doc, no need to defend yourself. In fact, I'm just now, for the first time, thinkin' maybe I'll really loan you the money, not because I'm convinced you're into some sort of noble cause, but because I'm suddenly thinkin' this could all turn out to be a nice payday for me. If you really have made some big discovery, and I believe you have, then big money is probably headed your way. But you can't get there without a start up loan. That's why you're here, right?"

Joe paused briefly, but when Harold failed to reply, he continued on, saying, "So here's how this would go: I would loan you the money you need to set up your private lab, which you would use to complete your work. Then, when you go public with it, when the patents and the interviews start feedin' your accounts, then you pay me back what you borrowed plus . . . an extra fifty percent again of the original loan. Now that's a high interest rate, but it's a big loan, a big risk for me, and you have full confidence your work's gonna pan out, right? You're sure this thing'll make you just as rich as you were pretendin' to be? If so, then payin' me back shouldn't be a problem. Right?"

Harold tried to say yes. He wanted desperately to say anything that might keep him safe for another five minutes, anything that might serve to hasten his escape from this dangerous predator's lair into which he'd been lured. No, into which he'd entered voluntarily. He'd sought the place out! Now, however, he wanted nothing more than to flee, and yet that simple affirming word that might allow him to stuck stubbornly in his throat.

"Doc, you look like you're gettin' close to a pass out again. Breathe, man, breathe. I ain't callin' the paramedics if you—"

"Yes!" When Harold finally found his voice, it came bursting out with such sudden energy that it caused Alvin to jump beside him and nearly fumble his iPad. Smokey Joe, entertained both by the outburst and his assistant's jittery reaction to it, threw back his head and laughed.

"Yes, what?" he asked "I can't even remember now what I asked you. You're sayin' yes, you're gonna make lots of money? Or you're sayin' yes, you agree to the terms of the loan?"

"Yes." Harold had found his voice, but his vocabulary had apparently been reduced to that single syllable.

Joe laughed harder yet. From a desk drawer he retrieved a fat, brown cigar, expertly trimmed and lit it, and between puffs, mumbled, "Okey-doke. Alvin, go draw up the necessary paperwork so we can send the good doctor on his way while he's still conscious? And before he scares you anymore."

"The contract's done," Alvin said, his voice laced with irritation. "I've been getting it ready on the pad. All I need to do is print it out, get a couple signatures, and then we can make arrangements for the transfer of funds."

"Oh, so . . . a contract," Harold said, still struggling for words. "I guess that'll make it . . . legit. Right?"

This elicited another bout of wheezing laughter from Joe, but this time it quickly morphed into a coughing fit that swirled the blue-gray cigar smoke gathering above his head like a pet rain cloud.

"Yeah, sure, Doc. It's all totally legit. It's just like goin' to the bank. Only difference is we got better office hours."

Joe laughed so hard then that his eyes filled with tears. One trickled down over his cheek, pausing ever so briefly over a black ink rendering of a drop very much like itself. It was life imitating art in the most sinister fashion.

"Yeah, we even work holidays," Alvin added. His momentary embarrassment had passed apparently, and now he was also laughing. "But other than that, just like the bank."

Harold tried to join in, to laugh along with them—he thought he should, but he just couldn't.

"Damn, you're a funny guy, Doc," Joe offered in a tone that was almost affectionate. "I wouldn't have pegged you for the type, either. Hey, I wish I had more time to be entertained here, but I'm a busy man. Bank inspector's coming this week, so I gotta make sure all the books are in order and such."

Though Harold wouldn't have thought it possible, Joe's laughter raised yet another notch in spirit. He wiped his face with the sleeve of his shirt, clearing the tears from his cheeks. The real ones.

"Wasn't that guy we buried in the desert last week a bank inspector?" Alvin asked.

"Well, if he was a bank inspector, then he deserved it, right?" Harold chimed in, finally finding enough courage to play along.

But just as Harold started to laugh, Joe finally stopped. A look of deep contemplation came over his face before he said, "No, he was a . . . an auditor. Right? Yeah, a tax auditor. That's what he was. But you shouldn't laugh about that, Doc. It was an ugly bit of business I deeply regret. There was nothin' funny about it, nothin' funny at all."

"Except he was an auditor that couldn't manage his own accounts," Alvin pointed out. "That's a little funny, you have to admit."

But Harold agreed with Smokey Joe. It was anything but funny.

One might have expected that Harold would have driven away from Las Vegas at thirty over the speed limit, which the Mercedes was more than capable of, but he did just the opposite. He merged onto the highway doing fifty-five, and kept it about there, clinging to the right lane and jamming up traffic behind him.

He was experiencing the biggest adrenaline dump of his life, falling quickly from a state of acute excitement to one of overwhelming fatigue. His overstressed brain had slowed to a crawl, so much so that keeping his eyes on the road and keeping the car between the stripes was about as much as he could manage. He wasn't thinking about Smokey Joe anymore, or the money, which had already multiplied his saving account by a factor of ten, or that poor tax auditor, lying somewhere out there in the desert in an unmarked, and presumably shallow, grave. He wasn't thinking about the lab, either, or the Window and its monumental secret. He wasn't even thinking about Jessica. His only thinking, his only cognitive functioning, was of driving, of making slow, steady progress, mile by mile, closer to home.

Ingenuity

When Harold awoke the next morning, safe and sound, and alone, he found he could only vaguely remember having gone to bed, and he couldn't recall a single detail about his drive back from Las Vegas. He could, however, think back to every second of every minute he'd spent in the company of Smokey Joe Simms. He could recite each word that had passed between them, and would still be able to, he knew, when a week, or even an entire year, had passed by. He could smell the faint scent of cigar smoke lingering on the clothes he'd worn, now lying in a haphazard pile on the floor next to the bed. There was a dull ache in his hand.

He sat there for a long time with his legs thrown over the side of the bed, taking slow, deep breaths and waiting for the stiff muscles of his mind to limber up. His tired gaze shifted aimlessly around the room, already fully lit by the midmorning sun, until it settled on the oak nightstand beside him. Scattered across its surface was, among other things, a dollar or so in loose change. Money.

Money!

He'd done it. He had the money. He knew it was true, and yet the enormity of his success in securing such massive funds within hours of discovering his need for them was . . . incredible. It was hard to believe. A few minutes and a quick glance at his online banking, however, eliminated any shadow of doubt. It was a done deal. It wasn't the most important step in his plans, but it might well have been the most difficult, his biggest obstacle, and he'd overcome it in less than a day.

Now it was on to the real job, the science. It was sure to be difficult work, perhaps even the most challenging of his career, but his motivation would be unprecedented as well. He'd always been an exceptionally dedicated worker, as well as a gifted scientist, but now he was ready to give himself over to the dictates of his research like never before. He'd do whatever he had to do, whatever it took.

On the kitchen counter, Harold found another note from Jessica. It said she'd assumed he was taking the day off from work after returning home so late from his conference, and so had chosen not to wake him. She and Katie were out for the day again, and wouldn't be back until late that afternoon or evening. There was plenty to eat in the fridge.

It was the first part of the note that threw him, but only for a second. *The day off from work?* What day was it? Thursday? A work day. So why wasn't he at work? Hadn't his alarm gone off? Would Jessica have turned it off if it failed to rouse him? Could he have turned it off, gone back to sleep, and completely forgotten? He had no idea.

A flicker of panic swam through him, but it came and went in moments. Before that week, he probably hadn't skipped a day of work since high school. It might have seemed like something to fret about if not for the events of the previous day, compared to which his imperfect attendance was beyond trivial.

Nevertheless, he was still a long way from the finish line, and he couldn't just quit his job and go to work in his basement 24-7, especially since that project and his job were, by and large, one in the same. Now that he had the money he needed, he'd be able to retrofit his home workspace into an adequate facility for the research that lay ahead, but the government lab was already there, already set up with everything that had led to his discovery. It was also where he had direct access to any and every piece of relevant hardware and software for such research, not just the pieces he'd be ordering for himself. He had room for the necessities he foresaw, but who knew where things would lead, what else might be required? He couldn't wait to have new items delivered to him every time the need arose. No, when he ran into roadblocks, which he inevitably would, he'd need access to the government lab and its bountiful arsenal of equipment.

There was one other thing he might need from the lab at some point, another qualified mind to consider his ideas. There were very few such minds in the world, and though it pained him to admit it, he knew who one of them was. He'd have to be careful not to divulge too much, but sometimes a fresh perspective was required to get past a snag.

Already thinking of his lab partner, Harold picked up his cell and dialed his number.

"Hey, old man, you okay?" Trent asked instead of saying hello.

"Yeah, I'm okay," Harold answered. "Don't call me that. I'm not old. You're just . . . *young*. I'm middle aged."

"Whatever. You're sure you're alright, though? You had me worried when you bolted out of here yesterday, and then when you weren't here this morning, I started really getting nervous. I was afraid your new pimp ride might have got you in trouble, drove you right off the road somewhere or something."

"It's not a *pimp ride,* Trent," Harold argued, unable to resist being drawn in. "It's a . . . never mind. I'm fine. Just got a little . . . cold, or something. Anyway, I'm not coming in today—"

"Obviously."

"And I probably won't be in tomorrow either, so I'll see you Monday. Don't screw anything up in the mean time."

Trent laughed at the insinuation, and said, "Oh, yeah, because I'm so helpless when you're not around, being the junior partner here and all."

"That's not what I was saying, Trent, and you know it. I just . . . I'm just . . . not feeling very good . . . so I'm taking a couple days off. That's it. That's all I'm saying."

"Hey, fine, old man. You didn't even need to say that. You don't have to convince me you have a good reason to play hooky. I know you do. If Jessica was my wife, I'd have trouble ever making it to—"

And that's when Harold hung up.

With the house to himself and the next three days empty of any other responsibilities, Harold eagerly flew into motion. He gobbled down a bowl of cereal, made a pot of coffee, and carried his first cup down to the basement, setting it beside his laptop while he slipped into the lab coat he kept hanging beside the base of the stairs.

While the computer booted up, Harold thought back over his brief phone conversation with Trent. What was happening there? Not that the two of them had ever been buddies exactly, but things certainly hadn't been so antagonistic between them before. Anymore, the way that phone call had gone had become the norm for them, the way it went almost every time they talked. Trent had always been the way he was, cocky, an instigator, but Harold hadn't used to let it get to him, at least not so quickly and so regularly. So what had changed? Harold had. It was obvious, even to himself. And why? The answer to that was just as easy to track down. In fact, it was sitting right there on his desk, within arm's reach.

"Are we okay?" he asked the picture of Jessica. Harold had taken the photograph himself, on their honeymoon in Paris. They'd spent that afternoon at the Louvre, a check off her bucket list, and then walked the streets for the rest of the day, sipping coffee and wine and seeing the sights. The sun was sinking in the picture, revealing the late hour of the day, and in the background, shrunken with distance, was the Eiffel Tower, glowing, though not quite so brightly as Jessica. She was beaming, smiling with such obvious and unrestrained joy that even in that one still glimpse there could be no denying the perfection of the moment. Harold would never get tired of looking at that picture, or of remembering that day.

"Could we ever have a day like that again?" he whispered.

He couldn't see any specific reason why not, but still he had his doubts. Things just didn't feel the same as they had then. He'd been older than her when they'd married, but he hadn't been *old*. Now . . . he was getting there. Whereas Jessica was every bit as beautiful as she'd been, Harold had gained an extra twenty pounds, lost half his hair, and developed a bad back. While she remained in the prime years of her life, he'd clearly moved beyond his own.

Then again, there was more than one way to determine a man's best years, wasn't there? Of course there was. There had to be. Beethoven, for instance, was already well over fifty when he'd written his ninth symphony, his greatest in Harold's opinion. He was deaf by then, obviously past his physical prime, but clearly at the peak of his skill as a composer. And that's how it was going to be for Harold as well. No one would give a crap about his waistline or his hairline when he became the most famous scientist in history. No one would wonder how he'd managed to land a catch like Jessica when his name was plastered across the front page of every newspaper on the planet.

In the ways that mattered most, Harold realized, he was just entering his prime. As long as he could make the Window work, and he had every confidence that he could, then it would make the coming years the most celebrated of his life. It would be an achievement that would make him truly worthy of the woman he so dearly loved. It would be his masterpiece.

By the time Jessica and Katie returned later that evening, Harold had been working steadily in his basement for what, to most people, would have been a full day's work, but he was nowhere near ready to wrap things up. The hours had slipped away without his noticing, so engrossed was he with a series of minor revelations that unfolded as he repeatedly updated his equations. Now that he knew the true potential of the Window, he saw everything, every aspect of the machine's functioning and design, in a whole new light. He still didn't understand how it happened, how the Window was able to breach the laws of linear time, but knowing that was the mystery that needed solving allowed him to see new clues everywhere he looked. Little discrepancies in the machine's power usage, conundrums in the math, suddenly, for the first time, started to make sense.

The thrill of discovery Harold felt that night surpassed anything he'd felt before in his career as a scientist. It was exactly what every researcher dreamed of, forging ahead into completely unknown territory, exploring a land of knowledge where no other human mind had ever tread.

By the end of the day, Harold comprehended how the world worked more completely than anyone else did or ever had, more than Albert Einstein, more than Stephen Hawking, and most importantly, more than Trent Penner. Way more than Trent.

Irritability

"Any hungry scientists down there?" Jessica called from the top of the basement stairs. It was a few minutes to nine o'clock p.m.

Harold was so engrossed in his work he barely heard her. It took a few moments for him to refocus his attention enough to consider her words.

"No, it's just me, Jess," he finally responded. "I mean, yes, actually. I mean . . . I am hungry. I should be. What time is it?"

"It's almost nine," she answered, moving down two steps, just far enough so she could see Harold sitting at his laptop. That was as far down as she ever ventured, as close as she ever got to the delicate equipment in her husband's workspace. "Have you been down there all day? When was the last time you ate?"

Harold pushed back his chair from the tabletop and rose to his feet . . . slowly. With every centimeter he straightened his back, the vehemence of its protestations increased. It was agony. He'd been hunched over in the same position for way too long, since . . . when? He found he couldn't remember. He couldn't remember the last time he'd eaten either.

"I really got caught up in some work," he said from the base of the stairs. It wasn't exactly an answer to her question, but it was the best he could do. As he spoke, he slipped out of his lab coat, hanging it back on its hook.

"There's a shocker," she said sarcastically. "Well, get up here and get something to eat before you starve to death. My mother'd be ashamed of me if I let my husband die of malnutrition."

"You know the last thing I ever want to do is upset your mother," Harold said, trying to force a smile as he started up the stairs. Every step sent another jolt of pain up the length of his spine.

"That's the last thing Dad ever wanted to do, too," she pointed out, "but it's easier said than done. Obviously."

Her parents, who'd been separated in age by almost as many years as Harold and Jessica, had divorced not quite ten months earlier. It was the last thing Harold wanted to think about.

Jessica met him at the top of the stairs with a kiss, and then went about heating some lasagna she'd cooked ahead. It was delicious, especially since Harold discovered he really was starving. As he gobbled it down, she recounted the highlights of her day with Katie. Harold tried to pay attention as she did, but it was a struggle. His mind constantly wanted to sneak back down to the basement ahead of him, to keep working, keep exploring.

"Harold, are you listening to me at all?" she asked as he hoisted a forkful of pasta.

"Yes," he answered too quickly. "I'm trying to. I just started on something new, and I'm really excited about it. I think it could be . . . big. I think it could be huge, Jess."

She nodded her understanding, but couldn't quite manage a smile as she said, "That's great. It really is. I'm glad you love your job, but there's more to life than work, even for you. Like . . . you're married, for one thing. You remember that, right?"

Harold let the fork fall back to his plate. Despite himself, he felt a little prickle of annoyance. In a world full of deadbeat husbands who could barely hold down minimum wage jobs, here he was, pushing himself past the point of exhaustion on the most challenging work of his life, something that could, that *would,* radically improve their lives. And she was complaining about it?

"Of course I do," he answered, careful to keep his tone neutral. "I know I've been hitting it hard, but isn't it a perfect time for me to put in some extra hours, I mean with Katie here? I think it's worked out great. And I'm glad you two have been having fun. I hope tomorrow goes just as well."

"Tomorrow? I just told you she's gone. Had to leave early? Her boyfriend got in an accident? Any of that sound familiar at all?"

Harold didn't say anything. What could he say?

"I'm going to read for a while, and then I'm going to bed," Jessica said after a long, painful silence. "Are you?"

"Am I what?"

"Going to bed!" she shot back. "Are you going to bed or not?"

"No," Harold answered flatly. "Not for a while."

"Fine." Then, without another word, she turned and walked out of the room.

Harold slid his plate and the rest of his half-eaten dinner into the sink, and then he headed back down to the basement. He wasn't hungry anymore.

That scene, and that chilly conversation, became a template for many evenings over the following months. As the days went by, Harold spent more and more time in the basement and ever less time with Jessica. They still sat down together for dinner most evenings, but there was a constant tension between them that hadn't been there before. Harold's work was the only thing he could focus on and the one thing he couldn't talk about, which made for conversation that was disjointed at best, but more often simply one directional.

The situation at the lab deteriorated as well. After spending years stockpiling personal days, Harold suddenly began spending them with abandon, a shift that seemed primarily entertaining to Trent at first, but not for long. The jokes he made about it initially, mostly relating to Jessica as usual, soon changed to complaints as he was forced to shoulder more and more of the workload by himself and do his best to deflect the heat that started coming down from the higher ups. It was a role reversal he did not find entertaining in the least.

When Harold did make it to the lab, he was severely limited as to the work he could actually do. Because of the progress he was making on his own time, his understanding of the project had leapt ahead of Trent's, a fact he had to keep carefully concealed. It was frustrating enough having to take so much time away from his work at the house, but then it was made doubly so by having to spend much of that time pretending to help Trent with equations he'd already moved beyond and simulations he now saw as irrelevant.

"Are you even trying to figure this out?" Trent asked one afternoon, his tone making it clear Harold wasn't the only one feeling frustrated. "I mean for real, what is your deal lately? You don't even bother coming in half the time, and even when you are here, you're . . . lame. I mean you've always been lame, but now it's like you're lame with no motivation, which is . . . super lame."

"You're so articulate, Trent."

"Yeah, whatever, man. Say what you want, but you know exactly what I'm talking about. And I'm not the only one who's noticed either. The suits were down here yesterday grilling me, wanting to know what's up with RVW, and what's up with you."

"What'd you tell them?" Harold asked, suddenly worried. The last thing he needed was the bosses breathing down his neck. Or looking over his shoulder.

"Don't sweat it. I covered for you," Trent assured him. "Again. But I've been doing that way too much lately. You need to get it together, man. At least clue me in on what's going on. If you and Jess are having problems or something—"

"Jess and I are fine," Harold snapped. "We're great. And if we weren't, it wouldn't be any of your business, Trent. You're the last person I'd tell. And you don't call her Jess, either. I'm the only one who calls her that. You call her . . . nothing. I mean, don't call her anything. Don't even talk about her. I mean it. I'm sick of it."

Trent was visibly stunned by the outburst. He took a reflexive step back, opened his mouth to speak, but then closed it again, remaining silent instead. He turned away after a moment and returned to his laptop, where he began pecking away at the keyboard, maybe busying himself with work or maybe just giving the impression of being busy. It didn't really matter which.

Harold remained frozen in place for a few seconds more, and then he slipped out of his lab coat, hung it on the rack, and headed out the door.

"What did I ever do to you, anyway?" asked Trent without turning away from his computer. The question froze Harold halfway out the door. "I mean, to make you resent me so much? Is it just my music and my stupid jokes and crap like that? Because none of that matters. None of it means anything. If that's all it is, then . . . then you're the one with the problem, not me. I'm tired of taking heat from you for nothing. I'm sick of—"

Before Trent could finish speaking, Harold finished listening. He stepped through the door and slammed it shut behind him. He hurried away down the hall, but soon slowed, and was practically dragging his feet by the time he reached the Mercedes. He never achieved the speed limit all the way home.

Though he hadn't felt rested for months, he'd not, through that whole span of time, felt as utterly depleted as he did right then. Trent's harsh words had sapped the last of his reserves, leaving him so exhausted by the time he got home that he told Jessica he wasn't well, which was certainly true, and went to bed. It was three o'clock in the afternoon.

After spending several hours slipping fitfully in and out of consciousness, Harold became convinced any more quality rest was sure to remain stubbornly beyond his reach, so he headed back down to the basement to work. He was still there when the sun came up the following morning.

When another week had slipped by, the situation at the lab had not improved. Harold's attendance continued to be irregular, and because he had to drag his feet when he was there, Trent remained thoroughly frustrated with him. At home, it was the same. Although he was spending more time at the house than ever, Harold ascended to the ground level only infrequently, and since Jessica strictly avoided the basement, the forty or so feet that separated them most of the time might as well have been a hundred miles. For every five minutes he spent at the dinner table, or every hour in his bed, he spent half a day in his subterranean laboratory.

"If you could just help me understand what all this is about," Jessica pleaded on more than one occasion.

Strung out from too much work and too little sleep, Harold responded to the comment with less delicacy each time he heard it repeated.

"I can't tell you," he barked across the dinner table one night as he pushed away his half-finished supper. "How many times do I have to say it? Why can't you trust me? I'm your husband. If you can't trust me—"

"Are you kidding me?" she shouted, rising so quickly from her chair that it tipped over behind her. "You're the one acting like a crazy person, skipping work, hiding out in the basement all hours of the day, barely sleeping. You're the one keeping secrets—from *me*. You obviously don't trust *me*. And now you have the nerve to say I don't trust *you*? I can't keep doing this, Harold. I don't know what it is, what you're working on all this time, but you need to decide if it's more important than our marriage."

She practically ran from the table then, retreating to the bedroom and leaving Harold to consider her words in solitude. In all the time he'd known her, he'd never seen her so upset, and it genuinely frightened him. It was a slap in the face he shouldn't have needed.

He rose and followed her after a bit, but found the bedroom door closed. He laid his hand over the knob, but then hesitated, reluctant to push his way inside when he knew there was probably nothing he could say to makes things better. He could apologize, but he'd done that plenty of times already. Another *I'm sorry* wouldn't count for anything without some answers to go with it. Unfortunately, her answers were his secrets, and he still wasn't ready to share.

If only he could make her understand it was for her own good he was keeping things from her, to protect her. And that thought led, yet again, to the same conclusion at which he'd arrived so many times before: she *would* understand. Maybe there was no way for him to smooth things over between them right then, but when it was done, when Jessica, along with everyone else, found out what he'd accomplished, then she would understand. Then she would forgive him. How could she not?

Still stinging from their confrontation, but remaining confident things would eventually work out for the best, Harold released the doorknob and tiptoed back down the hallway. He took a minute to clean up the remnants of their supper so Jessica wouldn't have to, and then he descended once again to the basement. Instead of reconsidering his dedication to the project, he felt more motivated than ever. The sooner he finished, he reasoned, the sooner he could put his wife at ease, and his marriage back in order.

Frailty

It was just after ten o'clock that night when the phone began to ring upstairs. Both Harold and Jessica relied almost exclusively on their cells, so much so that it had become rare for calls to come in through their home line.

"Come on, Jess, answer the phone," Harold grumbled, glancing briefly upward. But it continued to ring.

The answering machine picked up eventually, but then beeped so quickly Harold knew no message had been left. Then, almost immediately, it started ringing again.

Annoyed at the disturbance, and at Jessica's reluctance to answer, Harold slid out of his seat and hurried to the base of the staircase. He'd been sitting for too long again, and his back had tightened up, making the climb agony. He finally reached the phone just in time for the machine to pick up again, and again no message came through.

Glancing down the hallway, Harold saw a thin bar of light stretching across the bottom edge of the bedroom door, which remained closed. She probably wasn't even asleep yet, he supposed. She was probably in there reading a romance novel with some long haired muscle man on the cover while he was grinding his gears at work, but she couldn't be bothered for the thirty seconds it would have taken to answer the stupid phone? Lazy!

As soon as the thought formed in Harold's mine, he hated it. He hated himself for thinking it. He remembered how upset she'd been when she'd retreated to the bedroom, how upset he'd made her, and he cringed at the memory. For all he knew, she might have been in there right at that moment, crying her eyes out. Trent had been right—he was the one with the problem.

When a few minutes had passed and the phone remained silent, Harold decided whoever it was must have given up. Just in case, he slipped the cordless receiver into his pants pocket before heading back to the basement. He was halfway down the stairs when it rang again.

Anxious to keep the machine from picking up, Harold hurried the phone back out of his pocket, slid his thumb to the talk button, but then froze when his eyes found the name spelled out across the little digital screen: *A. Clemens.*

Harold didn't make the connection immediately. The name ignited a spark in his brain, but one that failed to trigger a flame on the first try. Still, it was enough to make him hesitate. It was like catching the faintest whiff of a familiar scent, enough to realize you should know what it is, but not quite enough to recognize it.

"A. Clemens?" Saying it aloud did the trick, touched off a second spark, and this time it found adequate fuel to burn. "A for Alvin. Alvin Clemens."

Considering it had been one of, if not *the* most memorable encounters of his life, it seemed incredible Harold had hardly spared a single thought for young Mr. Alvin Clemens and his burly boss, the custom cabinetry man/loan shark/auditor dispatcher, but that was exactly the case. He'd made it home from Vegas, dove headlong into his work, and up the blinders had gone. His tunnel vision had allowed him a clear view of his future fame and fortune, but effectively obstructed his peripheral view as well as his hindsight. Unfortunately, that partial blindness had kept him from seeing not only the woman he loved, but also the man of whom he should have been very much afraid.

All the terror of that day in Vegas came flooding back through Harold. His heart pounded in his chest. He stared at the phone until it fell silent in his hand. The machine had picked up again, and this time a familiar voice spoke through its tiny, tinny speaker.

"Doctor Olden, this is Alvin Clemens. I'm sorry to call so late, but I've been trying to catch you with the phone for a while now. I wasn't having any luck with your cell, so I decided to try your home phone instead. I just had a quick question about the recent transaction you made at our office, so when you hear this, whenever you hear this, day or night, you need to get back with me. Okay, have a good night, and I'll talk to you soon. The sooner, the better."

Harold hurried back up the stairs, and was relieved to see the bedroom door still closed. He prayed Jessica really was fast asleep in there already, or else so engrossed in whatever book she was reading that she wouldn't have paid the message any attention, even if she'd heard it. The last thing he wanted was for her curiosity to be roused, although Alvin's carefully chosen words hadn't offered much in the way of incriminating suggestion. At least not on the surface, not for anyone else to recognize. For him, however, the veiled threat had been perfectly plain. *The sooner, the better. Day or night.* Despite how placid a voice had spoken them, they were words of urgency.

Harold erased the message without listening to it again, and then hurried back down the stairs. If Jessica had stepped out and confronted him right then, he'd have had no idea what to say, and if he'd tried to make something up on the fly, she'd have know immediately. He was a terrible liar, and she knew how to read him better than anyone else.

"Where is it?" he asked himself as he lurched off the bottom step onto the basement floor. He scanned around the room, searching

145

for his cell phone, and spotted it lying beside his voltmeter. It was powered off, as it had been for . . . how long? He tried to think when he'd had it on last, but couldn't remember. He'd been keeping it off so as not to be disturbed, neglecting it just as he'd been everything else, other than his work.

It seemed to take a long time for the tiny machine to come to life, and when it finally did, the message it relayed made Harold's heart sink right down into his shoes. He'd missed twenty-three calls, all from the same number, one which he wouldn't have recognized five minutes earlier. It was the same number he'd seen come up on his home phone, the one for *A. Clemens*. There were also messages, but he didn't bother listening to them. He had no doubt as to what they'd say, so what was the point?

He set his cell down and pulled the cordless back out of his pocket, bringing up the recent calls list. It also contained a lengthy record of Alvin's failed attempts to contact him. He clicked the down button, counting the repetitions of the number: one, two, three, four, five, six—

"Who's that?" Harold thought aloud.

Seven spots down from the top of the list, the long string of Alvin's number was broken by another, one that struck Harold as familiar, though he couldn't immediately place it. Switching back to his cell, he opened his contacts list. It only took a second to track the number down, and when he saw it, his breath caught in his throat. The entry read, *Trent cell.*

In all the time he'd worked with him, Trent had only ever called Harold's cell a few times, and he'd never, not once, called the house. Why would he?

"Because he wasn't calling for me," Harold answered his own question.

Staggering like a man afflicted by some grievous wound, he fell into the chair at his workstation, slumping over onto the desk before him, head in hands. The remainder of the night, he never moved from that position, and though he never slept, his mind was plagued by nightmares.

It was the worst night of Harold's life. Back and forth, over and over again, his mind shifted, swinging like the pendulum of a grandfather clock, and at the apex of each swing it touched upon one great fear and then the other in turn. It was difficult to judge which image hurt him more acutely, that of the criminal's hands, or that of his colleague's lips, both at his wife's throat. The combined power of the two, flashing in their relentless cycle, was enough to drive him to the brink of madness by the time the morning finally arrived, an event of which he'd have had no awareness if not for Jessica's voice calling down from the top of the stairs.

"Harold, can you hear me? Are you down there? Harold?"

Although true sleep had not found him all night, Harold's senses had fallen numb as the hours dragged by, making him oblivious to his surroundings, and even to the passage of time. With no windows, his underground asylum always felt and looked the same, whether it was midnight or noon, January or July.

"Harold, answer me!" Jessica's voice had risen in volume and urgency. "I'm coming down there."

"No!" Harold had the strange sensation of hearing himself speak the word, and being genuinely surprised by it. It was like the muscles of his throat and mouth had been briefly hijacked somehow, and that intruder, that spy, had spoken *through* him.

"You are down there. Are you okay? I called your name like ten times. You must have been out like a light."

"No, I wasn't sleeping," Harold's voice responded again without his ordering it to do so. Shaking his head to clear away part of the cobwebs, he added, of his own volition, "I mean, I wasn't quite asleep. I was . . . just . . . coming up. Don't come down. I'll come up. I'm coming up."

That was easier said than done. Straightening himself in the chair was enough to trigger a small explosion of pain in his back, and when he forced himself to stand, it went supernova. He let out a sharp cry, almost falling, but barely managing to catch himself with his hands on his knees.

"Are you okay?" Jessica called down again. Harold glanced up in time to see her feet appear as she moved down the first several steps. "I'm coming down."

"No!" Harold shouted the word like a curse, putting more intensity into it than he'd meant to as his pain forced its way out through his voice. "I'm coming up."

Determined not to show the full extent of his suffering, Harold clenched his teeth and willed himself to hold steady for what he knew was coming. With a monumental effort, he wriggled out of his lab coat and then took his first step up the stairs. The pain that small movement caused him was enormous, but he thought he managed to keep most of it from his face. It was the same for the second step, and the third, and the fourth. He kept it together until he was just a few steps from the top, almost as far up as Jessica had come down, and then, as he threw himself into the motion again, one more surge of pain proved one too many. His legs gave out, and he collapsed to his hands and knees.

Jessica rushed to him, terrified he was going to fall down the stairs.

"Oh, God. Are you okay? Don't move. Don't try to get up."

But that's exactly what Harold did, without any hesitation. Although his pain had multiplied again, he didn't think he'd hurt anything seriously: probably just a couple bruised up knees, maybe a jammed wrist. And however hurt he was, whatever damage had been inflicted, it couldn't equal his embarrassment and frustration. It couldn't possibly. He didn't care if he'd broken his leg in eight places, his priority right then was to get up, to stop feeling like a pitiful old man who lacked the strength to climb a single flight of stairs.

"Damn it, Harold," Jessica whispered as she stepped around him, supporting him from behind as he painstakingly negotiated the last couple stairs. "This is crazy. You're going to work yourself to death."

Harold said nothing to that, because he sensed anything he might say would only make things worse. He didn't want her helping him, he didn't want her seeing him in the state he was in, and he didn't want to hear her accusations of how *all of this* was his fault. He didn't want to look down at her delicate hands, wrapped around his waist, and wonder whether Trent had ever felt their soft touch.

Despite Jessica's repeated insistence that they should be headed to the ER, Harold stubbornly refused. He did, however, allow himself to be led to his own bed, where he laid down with the intention of resting for a bit, and ended up falling into a deep, dreamless sleep that lasted most of the day.

Vulnerability

When he awoke almost ten hours later, Harold found himself stiff and sore, but feeling as clear headed as he had in weeks. How badly he had needed to sleep, and how much better he felt now that he finally had!

The first thing he thought of was, of course, the Mirror. *The Magic Mirror.* Harold tried, and failed, to remember when he'd started calling it that. It was at some point over the past week or so, he thought, though he couldn't recall exactly when. It was overly dramatic for him, but a little theatricality fit with the images of triumph he so regularly envisioned. *The Window* lacked the flare needed for a great headline. Besides, now that he knew what the device really did, he understood that it didn't function like a window anyway. A window let you see through something, like a wall, whereas a mirror let you see *back,* back at yourself, or in this case, back in time.

Harold eased himself up into a sitting position, leaning his back gently against the bed's oak headboard. He looked over at the empty half of the bed and saw it as a blatant metaphor for his life, a significant portion of which had become similarly empty. The Mirror, as staggering an achievement as it would be, was still just a thing after all, and what good were all the things in the world without Jessica? Worthless. Did he work to live, or did he live to work? Once and for all, he needed to decide.

"Because the Mirror is just work," he whispered to his wife's pillow. "Jessica is your life."

He picked the pillow up and pressed it into his face, drinking in the scent of her shampoo which lingered there. He pictured her smile and struggled to remember the last time he'd seen it. It had been a while. He'd made her miserable. And then he'd been foolish enough to imagine her being disloyal, and with Trent of all people. His refreshed mind saw how preposterous an idea it really was, and he chastised himself again for falling so deep into that dark pit of paranoia.

Then, turning toward the dark rectangle of the bedroom door, he began to rehearse an apology, saying, "Jess, I'm so sorry. I've neglected you. I've taken you for granted. I've let myself get so caught up in—"

The sound of muted conversation elsewhere in the house caught his attention, truncating his monologue. He strained to make out any specific words, but was unable to do so. He could, however, tell one of the voices was Jessica's, and the other was a man's. Trent's? As he slid his legs over the side of the bed, he made a desperate wish it would turn out to be anyone else, any other man in the whole world other than Trent.

It was a foolish wish to make.

As Harold stepped out through the door, he stole his first glance down the hallway, into the kitchen, and there he saw Jessica leaning back against the countertop. She looked nervous, which made Harold all the more nervous himself. Was she nervous about the possibility of him waking up, finding her entertaining a guest that would be, to him, most unwelcome?

That's what he was wondering when she looked his way, but the shift in her expression the instant she saw him was enough to completely assuage his fears. She didn't look guilty, but relieved. She was glad to see he was up, happy to have him entering the scene.

As he walked slowly down the hallway, Harold wondered at his insecurity. When, in all the years they'd been together, had Jessica given him even the slightest cause to doubt her faithfulness? Just thinking the question was almost enough to make him laugh. He was so certain of the answer it might as well have been flashing in hot pink neon letters before his eyes. It wouldn't have been any more obvious to him if it had been. Never. Never ever, and she never would. She was the most honest and trustworthy person he knew. It was a big part of why he'd fallen in love with her, why he'd married her. He could trust her implicitly.

Could he trust Trent? The answer to that was equally clear. Who cared? Yes? No? Maybe? Whatever! He could trust Jessica, and therefore it didn't matter if he could trust Trent or not. Why should Harold concern himself with what his young coworker was doing in his free time, and who he was doing it with? It had nothing to do with him, or with his life. Or with his wife!

"Morning, Jess," Harold said as he stepped into the kitchen. He tried to fill the words with all the warmth and affection he could muster. His apology would have to wait until they were alone, but he wanted to get a head start, get off on a better foot for the new day.

"Mornin', Doc," responded their guest before Jessica could.

The sound of the man's voice struck Harold with so much force he nearly fainted from the blow. The sight of *him* standing there in Harold's home, mere steps from Jessica, was beyond terrifying.

"Sorry if I got you outta bed," the man continued. "Must be it's your day to sleep in. Well, you're up now, so what do you say we go have a look at that project of ours?"

"Joe Simms." Harold meant to say more, but that's all that came out, just the man's name.

Smokey Joe chuckled at Harold's awkwardness and said, "Hey, what a relief—you do remember me. Me and Alvin was startin' to worry you'd forgot all about us. You don't keep in touch, never answer our calls. What are we s'posed to think?"

"I'm sorry," Harold apologized quickly as he crossed the room, positioning himself protectively between the man and his wife. "I've been busy . . . been working . . . a lot."

"Well, that's good, Doc. That's good to hear. Now I know you just got up and all, but I got a busy day ahead of me, so let's get to it. Let's see how things are comin' with our project."

From the corner of his eye, Harold glanced at Jessica and found her wearing a quizzical expression.

"You're getting new cabinets for the basement?" she asked.

Her question confused Harold briefly, but then he noticed Joe tapping suggestively at the breast pocket of his shirt, where the words *Simms Custom Cabinetry* were embroidered.

"Yeah, I . . . I've let things get so cluttered down there, and I thought some new . . . cabinets . . . might help."

"*You* let things get *cluttered?*" she asked. "Oookay."

Harold didn't think she was convinced, but he thought she was going to let it pass without pursuing it.

"It's down here," Harold said, leading the way to the basement door.

Smokey Joe, grinning broadly, followed him down, closing the door behind them.

Softly playing classical piano greeted the two men as they descended. Harold kept the music playing in the lab all the time, even when he wasn't there.

"Alright, Doc, let's see it," Joe said when they reached the bottom of the stairs.

"What, um . . . what exactly do you want to see?" Harold asked. He felt dizzy from all the nervous energy coursing through him.

Joe smiled humorlessly and replied, "What do you think I wanna see? I wanna see *it*. I wanna see the thing. I wanna see it work. I wanna see something that'll convince me you're gonna be able to make good on your loan."

"Oh, of course, yes. Of course you do. It takes a minute to power up, and then it'll take another minute for me to calculate a set of coordinates for an opening."

"What do you mean by coordinates?" Joe asked, scrutinizing Harold as he moved quickly from a set of dials to a switchboard to his laptop. "And what's gonna open? The thing's gonna open?"

Harold paused briefly, his fingertips poised over his keyboard. After a moment of word searching, he said, "They're not coordinates in the traditional sense, like coordinates on a map, because of course it's the timescape that's being traversed, not geography, and it turns out the timescape isn't as simple as we thought, not just a line going back and forth, with us riding along at the present moment. There are branches everywhere, branches that keep splitting over and over in every direction, backward and forward—"

"Okay, Doc. It's fine," Joe interrupted.

"And as far as it *opening*," Harold continued, undeterred, "it's not like it makes a hole through something, like a window does through a wall. In fact, it turns out there's not really even a barrier there, separating times, to make a hole through. What the Mirror does is gather information from all the matter around it, the air, the floor, the aluminum in its own frame, even you and me if we're standing close enough, and it sorts through all these tiny bits of data it's collected, in numbers beyond our ability to reason, and it reconstitutes them—"

"Doc, stop. *Stop!* Good God, you're gonna give me an aneurism. Never mind the explanation. Forget I even asked. Just make it work."

Harold proceeded to do just that, but not quite to the extent his guest was hoping for. It took a few more minutes to get everything ready, and then, before activating the device, Harold stepped past Joe and killed the radio. In lieu of Mozart, the soft humming of the electronics and the buzz of the fluorescent lights became apparent.

"Sheesh, it sounds like there's a swarm of killer bees in the walls," Joe observed. "How much juice you got runnin' through all this stuff, Doc? I bet your energy bill this month's gonna be—"

"Ssshhh!" So intent was Harold on the equipment by then that he didn't even consider the wisdom of so harshly silencing the murderer beside him. "We're almost there. Listen."

The voice of the device was growing, filling the room, drowning out the other, dimmer sounds. It caught Joe's attention and forced him back an involuntary step.

"Doc, you're sure this is safe, right? You've done this before and—"
"Ssshhh! Listen!"

As the pitch of the sound coming from the Mirror continued to crescendo up, approaching a level of shrillness that was nearly painful, a faint melody became just audible behind it. A broad grin spread across Harold's face, and he pointed excitedly at the machine, making sure Joe knew where the music was coming from.

A moment later, Harold typed a quick sequence into his laptop, and the Mirror powered down, its voice dipping rapidly and then dying altogether. When it was silent again, he turned the radio back on, and then turned expectantly to Joe, who'd just become the second man in history to witness actual time manipulation. Harold assumed he would be thunderstruck.

Joe rubbed his chin thoughtfully, and said, "Well, that was . . . What was that?"

"What do you mean?" Harold asked, sounding incredulous. "That was it. *The music.* You heard it, right? It wasn't playing on the radio anymore. What you heard was the music that *had been* playing. What you heard was an actual echo of the past. You heard through time."

Still, Joe failed to react with anything resembling what Harold would have considered appropriate enthusiasm.

"You're sure? How far back were we hearin'?"

"I don't know *exactly,*" Harold answered as he reached for the radio, turning it back on. "I've had a little trouble directing it to precise coordinates. That's why I keep the music playing all the time, so there'll be something to hear, however far back I listen."

"I see," Joe said, leaning over the Mirror for a closer look. "I thought you were s'posed to be able to see through it, to see back in time. I'm sure that's what you told me when I agreed to loan you all that money. Right?"

Harold nodded eagerly and wiped his sweating palms on his pant legs. "I did, yeah. And you can. I mean, you will . . . be able to. It's been a little more complicated than I anticipated, but . . . I'm getting there. I'm making progress. I think I just need to . . ."

Harold's voice caught in his throat as Smokey Joe rose back to his full height and stepped purposefully into the doctor's personal space, practically on his toes.

"I don't care, Doc. I don't care about all that. All I care about, the only thing, is gettin' my money. On time. And that time's comin' up. You got a month, so if I was you, I'd get crackin'. One month and I'm gonna be back, and I'm gonna collect."

"But what if . . ." Harold started to ask, but then bit back the rest of the question.

"There's more than one way to collect, Doc. You know that, right? The money, that's plan A. That's the way I always want it to go, but sometimes, when people don't make good on their promises, it has to end up bein' plan B instead. You remember Alvin talkin' about the auditor we left in the desert? That wasn't just talk. That wasn't just us tryin' to work your nerves. That guy failed to make good on his promise to me, so I collected the only other way I could. That desert's full of bones, Doc, and I don't wanna add yours to the collection. Or *hers*." He didn't bother saying her name. He didn't even glance up toward the first floor. He didn't need to.

Joe turned then and started back toward the staircase. "I'll show myself out, Doc. I know the way. I got lots to do today, and I know you do, too. Alvin'll be callin' again soon, I'm sure, and when he does, you better—"

"I will," Harold blurted out. "I'll answer. And . . . I'll get it done. And then I'll get the money."

Pausing at the first step, Joe turned back and said, "Yeah, I think you will. I hope so. Have a good day, Doc."

A few seconds later, Smokey Joe Simms was gone, and Harold was left standing alone in what had been his sanctuary. Suddenly, it didn't feel like that anymore, though. It wasn't the safe place he'd thought it to be. Nowhere was. He glanced at the Mirror and saw it in a whole new light, not merely as his big chance at fame and fortune, but as his only means to safeguard his own life and that of the woman he loved. He had to make it work.

Fidelity

Following Joe's surprise visit, Harold's work on the Mirror shifted from obsessive to feverish. He drank copious amounts of coffee, slept sparingly and ran full tests with the device several times most days instead of once or twice a week, as had been more the norm beforehand. He made steady progress, but as to whether or not he could reach his goal in time, he remained uncertain. He sensed he was making his way down the right path, heading toward his ultimate destination, but it was a journey through uncharted territory, and the obstacles he encountered along the way were impossible to anticipate and exceedingly difficult to overcome.

Harold's superiors at the government lab rejected his request for a leave of absence, but he took one anyway. Given the thin ice he was on already, it might end up being an early retirement instead of a leave, he knew, but what choice did he have? He had to make the Mirror work, and he had very little time left to do it. He'd always been, he had to admit, a man who lived to work, not the other way around, but seeing Smokey Joe standing there next to Jessica, sensing the imminent danger she was in, made him realize his priorities had been wrong. She should have been first in his life, not work. He could live without the lab; he could not live without her. But for her sake, he would have to work now like never before.

The one thing that could pull Harold's nose away from the grindstone was the telephone, which he never ignored. As Joe had predicted, Alvin called regularly, around every third day or so, for a progress report, and he always called the land line, never the cell. It was, Harold suspected, a way to continuously reinvade his home, to keep him feeling vulnerable. If so, it worked.

When things weren't going well, Harold anticipated their next conversation with dread, but he didn't dare let the machine pick up for him. He didn't dare let Alvin wonder, even for a second, if another house call from the boss might be in order.

Less frequently, but still regularly, another familiar number would pop up on the caller ID, but when Trent called, Harold would just stare at the phone, listen to it ringing in his hand, and grind his teeth. He never answered. In a strange way, those calls were almost as frightening to him as the ones from Vegas. The logical part of Harold's mind told him it made all the sense in the world for Trent to be calling—for *him*. The two of them had been partners at work for years, and now Harold had, with no good explanation, vacated his post. Naturally, Trent would wonder what was up and look for answers from the source. That was logical. That was likely. That it wasn't actually Harold he was calling for was so unlikely a possibility it bordered on the absurd.

And yet he couldn't help but wonder.

There were, of course, other parts to Harold's mind as well, other voices, not just logic. There was also the low, growling voice of his jealousy. He'd subdued it briefly, but the longer and harder he worked, and the more exhausted he became, the louder it grew again. Every time the phone rang and Trent's number reappeared, it gained strength. It demanded to know why Jessica wasn't answering his calls either. If there was nothing there, nothing to hide, then why wouldn't she pick up?

They were questions Harold couldn't answer, and shouldn't have been spending time or energy thinking about. He didn't want to think about them. But he couldn't help it.

One month to the day after Smokey Joe's visit to the house, Dr. Harold Olden became the first man to see through time. Even in his state of extreme exhaustion, he did not completely miss out on the irony that such an event should take place just as he was, quite literally, running *out of time*. His days were no longer numbered—he was past that point, down to hours and minutes. Joe was returning that day, and the money he wanted, the money Harold owed him, wasn't there. But it was close. It was so close!

Harold had to believe the man would be willing to push the deadline back if doing so would mean more money for him. He was a businessman, after all, and to him it was all about the money. He'd said so. He'd grant Harold an extension if he could see the machine work and so be assured big bucks were just around the corner. Harold would offer him a larger cut of that money and hope they could work out a new deal. It was the only hope he had left.

The big moment, when it arrived, wasn't much more than that: a moment. But in that moment, Harold was offered a glimpse of an image that was, though fleeting, unmistakable. He could have no doubt it had worked.

His breakthrough came in the middle of the night. He awoke from an accidental nap, slumped over in his chair, fingers still tickling the edge of his laptop keyboard, and discovered to his surprise that at some point during his slumber, insight had arrived.

He practically leapt from his chair, letting out a grunt as fresh pain flared in his back, and hurried to his trusty white board. He cleaned the board with the sleeve of his lab coat, not giving a second thought to what he was erasing. The thoughts in his head were complex, and his hold on them felt tenuous. Before they could slip away, he scribbled them out with all possible haste, the marker squeaking madly as it flew across the smooth surface, sounding like a bath toy in the hands of an overexcited infant.

It took the rest of the night and most of the morning to integrate those ideas into his equations and then apply them to a fresh set of time coordinates. When his calculations were finished at last, Harold skipped past the simulations that usually preceded a test and fired up the Mirror. As the device came to life, he rolled the whiteboard, still covered with his scribbled thoughts, behind the empty frame, blocking his view of the wall beyond.

Despite the alterations he'd implemented, the machine powered up seemingly as it always had, emitting the same rising crescendo of sound, and peaking in the same time frame. The empty space at its center became first blurry and translucent, and then an opaque curtain of swirling gray, but then it continued to shift, growing lighter and brighter once again, and for one glorious moment it revealed a clear glimpse, not of the whiteboard, but of the plastic covered wall behind it. And it wasn't that he was seeing through the board, he knew, but that he was seeing through the empty space that had been there . . . *before*. He was seeing through time.

Harold didn't hesitate a second. As soon as the machine fell back into silence, he rushed to the cordless phone, still resting on his desk. He had to call Alvin, tell him the news, so that Alvin, in turn, could tell Smokey Joe.

It took three tries for Harold to hit the talk button with his quavering fingertip, and when he finally did, he was surprised to hear not dial tone from it, but a voice—the voice he knew better than any other.

"I'll see you soon, then?" Jessica asked softly.

"Count on it."

Harold heard the sound of Jessica clicking off the other cordless receiver. Instead of doing the same with his, he instead turned and threw it across the room with all his might. It tore through the plastic that covered the far wall and smashed into pieces.

Trent!

A screen of red dropped down over Harold's eyes. His heart pounded inside his chest and he struggled to breathe. It felt like he was cooking from the inside out, like all his blood had been flash heated to just short of boiling. It burned as it coursed through his veins. The basement walls pushed in at him from every side, making him feel trapped and claustrophobic. The weight of the earth outside those walls suddenly seemed like an imminent threat, barely held back and poised to crush him where he stood at any moment.

Panic and rage erupted inside his skull, flooding his brain, forcing out every other thought, including those of the Mirror, and of Smokey Joe.

If he could have run up the stairs, he would have, but his back wouldn't allow it. Instead, he shuffled up with all the haste he could manage and hurried out the door, ignoring Jessica's voice calling behind him.

In his rush to flee, Harold didn't wait long enough for the garage door to lift behind him and scraped the roof of the Mercedes across its bottom edge as he backed out. The screech it made was so grating, so visceral, it sounded like the car actually screamed out in pain, but Harold hardly noticed. Not so many weeks before, he'd have been livid about the Mercedes receiving even the slightest injury, but now he couldn't have cared less.

At the end of the driveway, Harold turned in the direction of his work commute. He had no intention of heading to the lab, or *to* anywhere else for that matter, but simply *away*. He was in no state of mind to make any sort of conscious decisions, so he simply followed the path of least resistance. After so many repetitions, his hands and feet could maneuver the car through the twists and turns and traffic between his house and the lab without involving his brain at all, and that's just what they started to do. Halfway there, however, he realized where he was headed, and that it was not somewhere he wanted to be. Thankfully, an alternative destination presented itself.

Danny's Four Leaf Tavern was a regular after work hangout for many of Harold's coworkers, but he had never been inside. Trent had extended repeated invitations for him to join them, but had quit trying at some point, much to Harold's relief.

The manager, a sharp-eyed man about Harold's age, met him at the door, unlocking it ahead of him. He was their first customer of the day.

"Sit anywhere," the man said. "One of the girls will be right with you."

Harold shuffled in and practically collapsed into the nearest booth. He was so tired he could barely keep his eyes open, but if he let them close his imagination immediately filled the void with images of Jessica and Trent. He heard their voices replaying in a continuous loop in his mind.

"Want a coffee?" asked the waitress when she arrived, sliding a glass of water across the tabletop. "You look like you could use a cup."

"Yes, please," he answered automatically. "No, actually what I want is a . . . gin and tonic. A double. Bring the coffee, too. I want both."

"Okey-doke," the girl said. "One of those mornings, huh?"

Harold didn't answer, and eventually the girl left to retrieve his drinks. She returned with them a few minutes later, and as she set them down, she said, "It seems weird to drink caffeine and alcohol at the same time, but we make these things with vodka and orange juice and one of those energy drinks, and people love them. I've never tried one, but—"

"Maybe I'll have one of those next," Harold said, cutting her off, "but this is all I want right now. Thanks."

With his waitress dismissed, and probably offended, Harold fought off a deep yawn, rubbed his eyes and took a tentative sip of his steaming coffee. Then he slammed the gin and tonic, not coming up for air once until the ice cubes slid into his nose. The alcohol hit him like hurricane wind blowing over a field of sunflowers. It flattened him.

Harold stared down into his tumbler, his eyes focusing on the ice, and then through the ice, and then somewhere in between. Suddenly he was falling forward, tumbling down through the air as if he'd stepped off the edge of a high cliff. He threw out his arms like wings, backhanding his coffee as he did so, sending it crashing to the floor.

As Harold leaned out of his booth and stared down at the broken glass and spilt coffee, he experienced a strange sensation of disconnect. Despite what he knew to have happened, it didn't *feel* like he'd made that mess. He examined his hand and discovered it was not only wet, but quite red as well. He was burned, and yet he felt nothing. He told his fingers to move, and they moved, but still they didn't *feel* like they were under his control.

His waitress was there in no time, sweeping up the shards of the mug and then wiping up the coffee with a wad of paper towels trapped beneath the sole of her shoe.

"No big deal," she was saying. "Happens all the time. Give me a sec to track down a wet floor sign and then I'll grab you another coffee . . . *Doctor?*"

"What?" Harold asked, confused momentarily until he realized he was still wearing his lab coat. In his rush to leave the house, he hadn't thought to take if off. "No, I'm a . . . I mean I am a doctor, but not the kind you're thinking of. I'm a . . . scientist . . . doctor. And . . . no more coffee. Another tin and . . . tonic. And gin. Please."

The waitress hesitated, perhaps wondering about the wisdom of granting his request, but then she smiled and walked away. She took his empty tumbler with her, removing it from harm's way.

Harold pressed his shoulders against the back of the seat, closed his eyes, and tried to slow his breathing.

"Here you go."

Harold was so startled by the waitress's return he let out a little yelp at the sound of her voice, which in turn startled her. She took a quick step backward and knocked over the wet floor sign, which landed flat against the floor with a bang that startled them both again.

As the two apologized over one another, Harold noticed the manager had reappeared and was leaning against the bar, eyeing him intently.

"Do you need anything?" the waitress asked.

"No," Harold answered, reaching for his drink. "This is fine. Nothing else."

"I don't mean, you know, just something to eat or drink. I mean do you need . . . *anything*. You seem like maybe you're not feeling so good. You okay?"

Harold forced himself to focus on the girl, really looking at her for the first time. Her expression revealed genuine concern. Her words reminded him of Jessica. It was the kind of thing she might have said under similar circumstances, to a stranger in need.

"Jessica," he whispered.

"I'm sorry, what was that?" the waitress asked, but Harold had already turned away from her, facing out the window in order to hide the tear streaking down his cheek. Although his mind was miles away, his eyes were still open, and the canary yellow Mustang that drove by just then, heading in the direction from which Harold had come, captured their gaze immediately. Harold would have recognized the car anyway, even if he hadn't glimpsed the driver, still clad in his usual white lab coat.

I'll see you soon, then?

Jessica's words echoed in Harold's mind, taunting him and torturing him. He hadn't dreamed she'd meant *that* soon, but where else could Trent be headed in that direction?

Harold rose awkwardly from his seat, knocking the wet floor sign over again. He bent over to right it, but felt immediately dizzy and abandoned the idea. He staggered to the door and didn't even hear the manager call after him as he passed through it.

"Hey! You forget something, buddy? Like your bill?"

Harold was just sliding into the Mercedes when the man finally caught his attention. He thought about starting the car up and making a break for it, but he hesitated, never having done something like that before, and that was all the time it took. The manager was there in moments, throwing his arm over the car door to keep it open.

"The easy way or the hard way, buddy? What'll it be?"

Harold opted for what the manager was referring to as the easy way, though there was nothing easy about it for him. Every second he delayed, his mind churned more raucously with images of Trent, perhaps already arrived at his home, with his wife.

It only took a few minutes for Harold to step back into the restaurant, swipe his credit card, and sign the slip, but it felt like hours. It was far too long a delay. Anything could have happened in that span of time.

Likewise, the drive home seemed to take forever, though Harold had certainly never traversed the same stretch of road in nearly so little time before. He pushed the Mercedes well beyond what would have been safe on any day, let alone that day, when he was in no condition to drive at all. He sped around cars with abandon and barely even slowed each time he should have stopped. He did slow, however, when he passed a yellow Mustang headed in the opposite direction.

"Trent!" Harold heard himself yell as he spun his head around to watch the Mustang recede down the road behind him. The blare of a car horn forced him to face forward again, and what he saw when he did was the grill of a moving van headed straight toward him. He swerved back across the center line, missing the van by inches, hit the curb after overcorrecting, and then finally settled back into his own lane.

If not for the near miss, he might have tried to whip the car around and chase after Trent, but with his heart lodged firmly in his throat, and the image of the van's headlights still staring him in the eyes, it was all he could do to creep along the last three blocks to get home. He pulled slowly into the garage, stopping when he hit the garbage can. He didn't get out right away, because he still didn't know what he was going to do when he went inside. But he had to get out eventually. He had to go inside. He had to do something.

Sanity

The door was already ajar, but Harold failed to realize it, so when he reached for the knob, expecting it to push back, it instead fell away effortlessly from his touch. Rather than stepping into the house like a man on a mission, he fell in like an overtired old guy with a buzz. It was not the entrance he was hoping to make, on his hands and knees.

"Oh, Harold! Are you okay?" Jessica was at his side immediately, steadying him as he scrambled back up to his feet. "I've been worried sick about you."

Harold quickly clamped his teeth together, biting back his first impulse, which was to say that he was fine. Reassuring her was not what he wanted to do. In fact, he wanted just the opposite.

Gripping her above the elbows, Harold pushed his wife back to arm's length. He held her there, needing the space and, regrettably, the support. Silently, he cursed himself for the gin and tonic. It was the last thing he'd needed.

After a deep, steadying breath, he was ready to begin. His first accusation was poised at the tip of his tongue, loaded and ready to fire, but before he could pull the trigger a single slow tear trickled down Jessica's cheek, giving him pause. Just what had prompted that tear, he wondered? Was it a tear of fear? Was she afraid of having been found out, afraid of what vengeance her jealous husband might now wish to exact for her discretion? Was she afraid of him? Or was she afraid *for* him? He hated the idea, but knew, on some level at least, that it might well be the truth.

The two of them stood there for a long moment, frozen in that position, arms locked in a way that was halfway between holding each other and holding each other apart, until the phone freed them at last from their impasse. It rang and rang, but neither moved to answer it, nor even broke eye contact to look its way. When the machine picked up, however, and the raspy voice of Smokey Joe Simms announced that he was on his way, it was more than enough to prompt Harold to action.

"Oh my God," He murmured as he released his grip on Jessica's arms. "He's on his . . . I have to . . . Oh my God!"

"Harold, what is it?" Jessica asked, sounding frantic. "Who was that? Why won't you talk to me?"

But her husband was already gone, disappeared like so many times before over the past months, down the stairs into his secret chamber. He slammed the door behind him, a clear enough sign that he did not wish to be followed.

Fortunately, Harold hadn't taken the time to power everything down when he'd rushed out of his lab, so the preparations for running another test of the Mirror were minimal. It was fortunate, because if he'd had to start with the initial sequences, he probably wouldn't have had time to duplicate his success with the machine even once before Joe arrived, and that would have been an awful risk to take. He knew perfectly well what the stakes were. It was life or death.

So how could he have forgotten? How could he have lost track of that imminent crisis point, even for a second, let alone an hour? As he typed in a new set of time coordinates, ones that should allow him to look back a mere fifteen minutes, he considered the answer. It was twofold. Firstly, there was his mental state. He was tired beyond anything he'd ever experienced before and stressed in a way he'd never dreamed of.

The other half of it, of course, was Jessica. At that moment, he didn't know if he still thought she and Trent had been fooling around behind his back or not, but he knew even the idea of it was enough to make him crazy. And crazy people weren't rational. He'd just proven that by going to the bar for a drink when time was almost up on the the first actual *dead*line of his career. Only a crazy person would have done that.

The machine was already winding up, its electronic voice rising, when Harold remembered the white board was still standing between the Mirror and the wall, and had been for the past hour. Unless he moved it out of the way, the view in the Mirror from fifteen minutes earlier would look exactly the same as the current view. He hurried across the room, almost tripping over a bundle of cables that snaked across the floor, and just managed to slide the white board out of the way before the machine climaxed.

Instead of rushing back toward it straightaway, Harold hesitated, confused by what sounded like voices coming from the Mirror. But how could that be, he wondered? He was sure he'd set the time coordinates right, and fifteen minutes earlier he still hadn't arrived home yet. The basement would have been empty.

Unless it wasn't.

Harold shuddered as he realized that fifteen minutes earlier, someone else could have been there. In fact, someone must have been. Jessica hadn't been alone. He'd passed Trent on the road, heading away from the house, and now here was the proof that's where he'd been. But why would they have been in the basement? Could Trent have found out about Harold's work with the Mirror? Might he be trying to steal that as well, along with his wife?

By the time he made it back to the Mirror, its cycle was almost complete. Harold only had time to catch the briefest glimpse before it shut down, and what he saw was exactly what he expected, exactly what he feared. In that single moment before the image disappeared, Harold saw Jessica embracing a man in a white lab coat—just like the one Trent wore all the time. He also heard a single phrase, barely audible over the whine of the machine, but clearly spoken in Jessica's voice. "I love you."

The man had been standing with his back to the Mirror, but that hardly mattered. Harold had no doubt about who it was. The coat was right. The timing was right. The motivation was obvious. The proof was incontrovertible.

A little over an hour earlier, when Harold had overheard the suspicious snippet of phone conversation, it had been enough to make him crazy, but now, with the image of that embrace fresh in his mind and that poisonous *I love you* reverberating back and forth between his ears, he became something worse.

With his powers of observation so severely hampered by stress and fatigue, it was no wonder Harold failed to notice the white board was missing from the scene he'd glimpsed in the Mirror. It was no wonder, but it was a shame.

Harold didn't rush back up the stairs. He moved up them deliberately, focusing on one step at a time, carefully guiding his feet, which were shaking like the rest of him. It appeared to him that the steps themselves were shaking as well, vibrating beneath him as if in the midst of an earthquake.

He found Jessica in the kitchen, cutting up an apple. On the counter beside her was the jar of crunchy peanut butter. It was Harold's favorite snack.

"Oh, Harold!" she said when she saw him. She hadn't heard him come up the stairs, and he'd startled her, enough to make her drop the knife on the floor. She made no move to retrieve it, but leaned back against the counter with one hand pressed against her chest as if trying to keep her heart from pounding its way right through her ribcage. Her eyes were red and puffy, and her face was flushed. Her chin was quivering slightly. "I . . . I was getting you . . . something to eat. I thought you might need something, that it might . . . make you feel better. I can't remember the last time I saw you eat."

"Trent was here?" Harold said it like a question, but he needn't have. He already knew the answer.

Jessica hesitated, swallowed hard, and said, "Yes. He was here. I asked him to come over. I was hoping he could talk to you. You wouldn't talk to me, so—"

"You were in the basement with him?"

"No. I never go down there. You know that."

"But you did today," Harold insisted. His voice didn't sound like his own, even to himself. He was practically growling out his words. "I *know* you did. With *him!*"

"Harold, Trent was only here for a minute." As Jessica said this, she slid back along the counter a step, away from her husband and the barely contained anger she felt emanating from him. "You were already gone by then, and I . . . I had no idea where you'd gone. I asked him to come back later. He barely even made it in the front door. He wasn't anywhere near the basement. And I . . . I never go down there. You know I don't. I never—"

Harold had heard enough. He couldn't bear to listen to one more desperate lie come spilling out of her. He lunged forward and grabbed her by the wrists, but she twisted away, retreating back several more steps into the corner of the room, where she buried her head in her hands and began to sob.

As she spun out of his grip, Harold lost his balance and stumbled down to the floor. He heard the sound of his knee impacting the hardwood, but it didn't hurt. He didn't even feel it. As he braced his hands to push himself back up to his feet, something hard pressed into his palm—the knife. He picked it up as he rose and slipped it into the pocket of his lab coat, not with any intention of doing anything with it, but thoughtlessly.

"Come on," Harold barked as he took hold of Jessica and pulled her out of the corner. This time she didn't resist.

"Harold, stop it. You're hurting me. Harold, please!"

Dr. Harold Olden ignored his wife's pleas. He didn't let her go, but tightened his grip instead, digging his fingers into her arm. Yes, he was hurting her. He knew that. He wanted that.

Not in a million years would he have thought himself capable of even thinking such a thing, but there he was, dragging Jessica through the house against her will, causing her pain, and feeling undeniably gratified by it. He'd become a different man, someone he never dreamed he'd become, never wanted to become, and it was all her fault. What she'd done, what he'd *seen* her do, was unspeakable! It had unhinged him completely, and now, suddenly, he felt capable of . . . anything. He was a good man, but didn't good men do terrible things all the time? Of course they did, and now he knew how.

"Harold, talk to me, please. Where are we going?"

"I'm taking you back to the basement," he growled. She recoiled from the venom in his voice, which pleased him further. She was afraid. Good!

"What do you mean *back?*" she asked, mumbling her words between sobs. "I'm telling you, I wasn't down there. And neither was Trent. He couldn't have been. He was never out of my sight. Why won't you believe me?"

Harold gnashed his teeth together so hard it made his jaw ache. How could she speak Trent's name to him with that innocent look on her face. Incredible. *Infuriating!*

"Go," he ordered when they reached the basement door. He threw the door open with his free hand and shoved her through. She stumbled, missing the first step, and teetered precariously on the second for a moment before finding the railing and righting herself. The sight made Harold's heart skip, an instinctual reaction that utterly betrayed his anger. The word *careful* had surged up over his tongue, but he'd snapped his teeth back closed just in time to keep it from escaping. He forced that word back down his throat with a hard swallow, and offered another in its place. "Move!"

Waiting for them at the bottom of the stairs was the Mirror. Jessica walked right past without giving it so much as a glance, which struck Harold as nothing short of astonishing. He had to remind himself that it was probably the most innocuous *looking* piece of equipment in the lab, and that Jessica couldn't have any idea of what it was, of what it could do. If she had, then she would have been more careful. She would have entertained her houseguest somewhere else.

As Jessica begged for an explanation, still playing dumb about the whole thing, Harold went about powering up the Mirror. He'd fire it up, adjust its view accordingly, and then she would see for herself the undeniable proof of her transgression. He'd make her stand there and watch right along with him, he'd make her own up to it, and then he'd . . . well, he honestly didn't know what he'd do then.

Clarity

Harold had trouble resetting the time coordinates for the machine, mostly because his trembling fingers kept mistyping the data into his laptop. It was also going to be difficult, he realized, to relocate that exact span of seconds again now that time had moved on. He tried to make some quick mental calculations and adjust the coordinates accordingly, but it was almost impossible to think. His mind was teetering, one wrong thought away from what would be a catastrophic fall.

Jessica was done pleading apparently, as she allowed Harold to reposition her in front of the Mirror without uttering another word. Tears still streamed down her face, but she was no longer sobbing. She looked like she could barely keep herself upright, like she might be on the verge of fainting.

Harold started up the machine, pointed one badly shaking finger at it as he turned back to his wife and said, *"Watch."*

She did. She stared into the Mirror with wide, alert eyes, awakened from her stupor by the inexplicable film that suddenly stretched across the span of what had been, only a moment before, an empty metal frame. The film swirled and darkened, and the machine's voice climbed in pitch and volume until it was shrill and oppressive.

Harold did not watch the Mirror as it powered up. Instead, he kept his eyes trained on Jessica, scrutinizing her expression, anticipating her reaction when the scene of her betrayal appeared. That moment was only seconds away, he knew. By the sound of the machine alone, he could tell it was almost there.

When it happened, Harold was disappointed. Jessica's reaction was all wrong, not even close to what it should have been. She didn't look ashamed. She didn't look terrified. She just looked . . . confused.

"What . . .?" she mumbled under her breath as she leaned in for a closer look. "When did we . . .? I don't . . ."

Harold's mind raced, searching frantically for an explanation to her behavior. Could it be an act? Could she still be playing dumb to try and protect herself? No. No, her reaction was genuine, he was sure. He knew her well enough to judge that. But how could that be? She'd been caught red handed, and now she knew it. She should have been at his feet, sobbing her apologies into the laces of his shoes, not standing there with that perplexed look on her face. Unless he'd miscalculated. Yes, that had to be it. He hadn't adjusted the coordinates precisely enough before starting up the machine again, and he'd missed his mark. Jessica was probably just seeing—

"Go. Go now!" Harold's own voice called through the Mirror, interrupting his thought. Then, in a pleading tone, "Please, it's working. I can get the money. I can get more, all you want. *Please.*"

Jessica's expression changed, the terror Harold had expected finally showing. She gasped. Her eyes bulged. "No. Oh, no!"

And just like that . . . he got it.

Harold didn't know exactly what he would see when he looked into the Mirror, but he knew *who* he would see. More importantly, he knew *when* he would see. His mind raced, searching frantically for answers to the multitude of questions which presented themselves in rapid succession. He found most of those answers quickly. They were obvious now that he realized what the Mirror really did. All that time he thought he'd been hearing, and then finally seeing, into the past! It had been the mistake of a lifetime.

He thought back to that morning in the lab, when he'd heard the faint sound of breaking glass through the Mirror. He'd assumed it was the beaker he'd broken, but there'd been another. There was also the beaker he'd replaced that first one with, the one he'd left as a booby trap for Trent. He hadn't thought it likely that the trap would work, but obviously it had. Trent must have broken that beaker after Harold left, and that had been the crash he'd heard through the machine, not from the past, but from the future. It was that one faulty assumption, Harold now saw, that had set him on the wrong path.

He recalled the image of what he'd thought to be Jessica and Trent embracing, but that wasn't what he'd actually seen. That hadn't been Trent in the lab coat, but Harold himself. He'd never embraced his wife down there before, but he was going to, and soon. And probably for the last time.

Jessica's whispered *I love you* had been for him! Or rather, *would be.*

As Harold stepped to Jessica's side, he reached down and took her trembling hand in his own. She didn't resist. She didn't even look away from the Mirror. She was transfixed by what she saw there, and mortified.

"Sorry, Doc," Smokey Joe Simm's voice spoke through the device, "but it's too late for that. I'm here to collect."

The sound of struggling followed. Finally turning his gaze to the Mirror, Harold saw two men go crashing through its view, their arms locked together like wrestlers, each searching for an advantage in leverage over the other.

Back and forth they surged, slamming one another into the wall and the countertops, sending lab equipment crashing to the floor. They shifted in and out of view repeatedly until Harold came flying through the space alone, thrown harshly down by his younger, stronger assailant. He was back up immediately, though, and in his hand, a familiar object had appeared.

Without looking away from the Mirror, Harold reached his free hand to his lab coat pocket and felt the shape of the knife there. He barely remembered having picked it up.

"Please, you have to stop," Harold's voice called back from the future. "I'll kill you!"

The two men came together again, each capturing one of the other's wrists in their grip so that Harold's knife, as well as the dull black gun that had appeared in Joe's hand, were held temporarily at bay.

The gun went off, shattering one of the overhead fluorescent bulbs, showering both men with slivers of broken glass.

Jessica shuddered. She leaned into Harold, grabbed a handful of the sleeve of his lab coat and squeezed it as if hanging on for her life. She kept her eyes on the Mirror.

The gun went off again, and again, and the sounds of the shots were shockingly loud, even over the shrill wail of the machine. But by the angle of the gun, Harold knew the bullets had gone high like the first, burying themselves somewhere in the ceiling above.

With a heave, Joe threw Harold away again, but failed to topple him, and as soon as Harold regained his balance, he lunged forward once more, slashing a steep arc down through the air with the knife. The gun fired again, and this time the bullet found its mark. Harold collapsed limply to the floor, a brilliant bloom of crimson staining the front of his snowy jacket. Joe spent a moment examining the knife handle protruding from his chest, and then followed him down.

The image disappeared as the machine powered down, and in the renewed quiet, Harold could just hear the creak of a floorboard above him. Smokey Joe was already inside the house.

Glory

Harold stared through the empty frame of the Mirror, replaying the whole scene over again in his mind, and he found it almost impossible to believe. Yet he could find no way to deny it either, to explain it away as being anything other than the next, and the final, minutes of his life.

Harold couldn't imagine lasting a second in a hand-to-hand struggle against Joe Simms, let alone proving his equal in a fight to the death, especially in his current state of diminished health, but that's exactly what he was going to do. It seemed incredible, and yet the evidence proved it was not only possible, but inevitable. He'd watched it happen with his own eyes!

I'll kill you!

They were words Harold had never spoken to anyone. He'd never have believed he would. He wasn't the threatening type, but then he wasn't really making a threat when he said it. He wasn't warning Smokey Joe of his intentions, but informing him of the eventual outcome of their confrontation, because he *knew* how it was going to end. He'd seen the final score before the opening kickoff.

As Harold wrestled with the conundrums of remembering things that hadn't happened yet, Jessica wandered across the room to the scene of her husband's imminent, violent death. She bent down, examining the floor, perhaps looking for blood or debris, and then she looked up to the fluorescent bulb above her, which remained undamaged.

Harold wished he could explain things to her, make her understand what had happened, and what was going to happen, but he decided there wasn't time. It was the last decision he'd ever have to make. From that point forward, he already knew exactly what he was going to do.

Besieged by a potent wave of déjà vu, Harold walked to Jessica's side and wrapped his arms around her. As they embraced for the last time, she whispered, "I love you."

Right on cue.

Harold scanned around the room. There was nowhere to get Jessica out of sight except behind the whiteboard, which wasn't much of a hiding place. Then again, it didn't need to be. "Go. Go now!" he said, directing her there.

A few seconds later, Smokey Joe was making his way down the stairs.

"Please, it's working," Harold said when he saw the man. "I can get the money. I can get more, all you want. *Please.*"

The words were bizarrely familiar to Harold, and he wondered at himself for saying them. What was the point? He already knew it was a futile gesture, that there would be no bargaining. That time had passed.

Before the two men came together, Harold had just enough time to consider the irony that surrounded him. In that room, for those long months, he'd devoted himself to realizing the greatest achievement of his life. At the expense of his job and his health, and very nearly his sanity and marriage as well, he'd pushed himself to his limits in order to make the Mirror work. Now that it finally did, he should have been headed for the fame and fortune he'd so desired, the time of his life. Instead, he'd arrived at the time of his death.

Nothing had gone according to plan, and yet in the end his goal would be met, though in a very different way from what he'd anticipated. His finest moment had indeed arrived, but it was not what he'd expected it to be. Seeing through time was an amazing feat, but it couldn't compare to sacrificing his own life to save the woman he loved. He'd never dreamed himself capable of so high an act.

The Mirror was a marvel, but it was, ultimately, just work after all. And though Harold could not deny he'd put work first through much of his life, in the end there could be no doubt as to where his true priorities lay. Too often he had lived to work instead of the other way around, but he would not die for work. He would die for love.

HALF-FULL

Take One

Like every other day that week, I woke up Thursday morning at a quarter to six, because that's when the neighbor's dog, Dolly, started barking. Annoying, little, yapping piece of Shih Tzu. Apparently Dolly's owner had started a new work shift, a much earlier one, and the furball's pee time had been adjusted accordingly.

"Shut up, mutt," I grumbled, careful to keep my voice low. The barking probably wasn't even enough to make the old man downstairs, my landlord, twitch in his sleep, but if I started screaming obscenities at the top of my lungs, he'd probably wake up to a heart attack. "How'd you like me to introduce you to the Anderson's Rottweiler?"

Not a very ladylike thought to start my day with, I know, but I really needed the sleep. And the truth is I've never claimed to be a lady, and I never will.

My next thought was even worse. I decided I'd probably be willing to eat the little ankle-biter myself for a cigarette. I was a day away from making it my first full week without one. I'd hoped it would be getting easier by then, but no such luck. If anything it was getting harder and harder all the time. I was on an unprecedented string of things not working out, and each new stroke of bad luck seemed to intensify my hunger for nicotine. Nothing could distract me for more than a few minutes from how much I wanted one. Every annoying thing made it worse, and the worse it got, the more annoying everything became. Especially waking up again to the grating voice of that squawking *rodent!*

"Shut up, shut up, shut up!"

In a single motion I threw off the covers and swung my legs over the side of the bed. If I just laid there and listened, I'd keep getting more and more aggravated until I was too revved up to have any chance of getting back to sleep. Which is exactly what I'd done each of the previous three mornings.

Despite the warmth of the spring morning, the floor felt cool beneath my feet. Still without opening my eyes, I danced my toes back and forth across the old hardwood slats, searching for my slippers, but they were nowhere to be found. Hadn't I been wearing them before I went to bed? I never went barefoot because the floor was constantly shedding splinters.

As I stood and shuffled away toward the bathroom, I habitually dragged my fingers across the top of the dresser. Incredibly, removing that one little thing from its normal spot made the whole room seem quite wrong. It occurred to me that maybe if I took the whole dresser out, and by doing so removed the place where the cigarettes were *supposed* to be, then I might not miss them so much. Even being as sleep deprived as I was, that was an insanely *out there* thought, and that I really considered it for a second gave me pause.

The bathroom light was sadly dim, but still bright enough to make me wince when it flickered to life. I glanced over to the mirror and found a zombie woman staring back.

"Better get it together, Cass."

I leaned in closer to study my reflection. I don't know why. Maybe because it was the only thing I could possibly do to make myself feel worse. I'd never been in danger of becoming a Victoria's Secret model, but I was at least *pretty*. At least I thought so. My mom always told me I was pretty. (Ugh, did I seriously just say that?!) Anyway, pretty or not, I was only thirty-six, and already the signs of aging were clearly written on my face. Shallow wrinkles creased the skin at the corners of my eyes and mouth, scars I'd earned by tanning too much in high school and smoking too much ever since.

I reached down deep, summoned up my best smile, and found that it looked totally fake, even to me. Wearing it also multiplied my wrinkles times three and showed off how much the smokes had stained my teeth. I couldn't maintain the effort anyway, so I let my natural irritation face fall back into place. At least it was genuine. Better.

Running my fingers through my shoulder-length hair, I spotted several new strands of gray. They had to be new because I'd ripped out all the old ones the week before. It wouldn't have been so bad if I was a blonde, but they stood out glaringly against my natural milk chocolate brown. They were like little neon signs flashing *old* all over my head. I struggled for a moment to isolate one, intent on weeding it out, but what was the point? If I kept plucking them all, I was going to end up bald instead of gray.

At least my green eyes, just like my mother's, were still as pale and clear and lovely as ever. They were always my best feature, and it seemed unusually kind of fate to have left them alone while everything else was getting soft and saggy and wrinkled. And gray.

Outside, Dolly's shrill voice finally, *mercifully,* fell silent, her doggy revelry punctuated by the sound of the neighbor's back door slamming shut. It still wasn't six o'clock, and my alarm wasn't set to go off until seven, which meant if I could manage to drift off again, then I could have a shot at another full hour of sleep. I needed it—bad. I'd been up late doing homework for my night class . . . *again.* We were getting around to the end of the semester, and Animal Anatomy and Physiology was proving to be all I could handle.

I told myself it'd be worth it in the end. I'd get it all done somehow and end up being Cassidy Glasco, Veterinarian Technician. And it would be a great job for me. I'd always loved animals (other than Dolly). I loved that they couldn't talk, and therefore couldn't lie, and therefore made superior companions to people, especially men.

Not that I'm bitter or anything.

"Back to bed, Cass," I ordered the woman in the mirror. "We'll worry about tomorrow when it gets here—in an hour. You don't need a cigarette." I added that last bit with a finger jabbed right into my reflected nose.

I flicked off the bathroom light on my way out, returning my little upstairs apartment to near perfect darkness, which was a bad choice. If I'd left the light on, I would have noticed my slippers were sitting there right outside the doorway, and if I'd taken a second to slip them on, then I wouldn't have caught a nasty splinter in my right heel halfway back to the bed.

Oh yeah, it hurt, but not half as bad as the funny bone shot I took on the edge of the dresser as I hopped/stumbled the rest of the way across the room. The dresser rocked, almost tipped over, and everything I had piled on top of it went sliding off and down to the floor. I listened to the crash as I collapsed onto the bed, was sure I heard something break, but couldn't think right then what all had been up there. All I could think of was the one thing that should have been there, but wasn't.

"I need a cigarette."

"What's going on up there?" called a husky voice from downstairs.

"Nothing, Mr. Linder," I shouted back. "Everything's fine. Sorry."

"I need quiet. I'm a light sleeper."

Yeah, bull! If he was such a light sleeper, then how come I could hear his snores half a house away, even while Dolly was barking her head off outside? What a crock of Shih Tzu.

I rolled from my back to my belly, then to my side, and then to my back again, and finally settled with my legs crossed at the ankle, which kept my injured heel suspended and marginally eased the throbbing pain there. I thought about hobbling back to the bathroom and working the splinter out right then. I thought about turning on the bedroom light, finding out exactly what had fallen to its death from the dresser, and cleaning up its remains. I thought about how much I'd like to skip work that day, and about how much I'd like to remove the vocal chords from my neighbor's dog, and about how much I'd like to smoke five cigarettes right in a row. I thought about all that crap at once, and I was still thinking about it when I drifted back to sleep.

When I woke up again, I did so more gently than the first time, arching my back, stretching, yawning, but keeping my lids pinched tight. I'd been having an uncharacteristically wonderful dream where Brad Pitt and George Clooney were fighting over my bar tab. I didn't want the afterimages to fade. *Why don't you pay the bill, Brad, and George, you can leave the tip.* (In my dreams, neither George nor Brad ever lies.)

It was all good until I realized how hard I was squinting against the light coming through the window. It was really bright. I mean like daylight bright.

"Oh, no. No, no, no, no, no."

As panic set in, I flew out of bed and sprinted into the bathroom, barely even noticing the pain in my foot or the clock radio that lay in pieces at the foot of the dresser. (I did, however, notice my slippers sitting there next to the doorway. *Grrrrr.*) I brushed my teeth in about ten seconds, started to brush my hair, but then paused, frozen in another stare down with the woman in the mirror. There was no need to hurry, I realized. It had to be way too late already.

As my energy level plummeted from redline to idle, I hobbled back into the bedroom, careful to avoid more floor splinters and shards of plastic from the broken radio. With no more sense of urgency, I unplugged my cell from its charger and powered it up. It was already ten after eleven, just as I'd suspected—way too late. I'd skimped on sleep for too many nights in a row, and my body had finally rebelled, refusing to stir when I needed it to, and now I'd lost the whole morning. And I'd missed my financial aid meeting at the college, putting the future of my continuing education in jeopardy. My day had just gone from sour to curdled.

By the time I got the splinter dug out of my heel and the mess in my bedroom cleaned up, another half an hour had slipped away, and it was almost time to head to work. I hadn't eaten a thing yet, and I hadn't had a sip of any caffeinated beverage, and my body was crying out for both. And, of course, a cigarette. On my way out, I grabbed an apple, a candy bar, and a Pepsi, and crammed them into my backpack next to my school stuff. My lunch of champions.

My apartment was the second floor of Mr. Linder's house, a space that had become inaccessible to him due to a bad back, a bad hip, and about five other failing body parts. Old age was not treating him well. He was perpetually grumpy and a chronic complainer, but a good man at heart, and his converted upstairs was a safe place I could (barely) afford to rent, which made it a rare find.

Near the foot of the outdoor staircase that led down from my kitchenette, my bike, a rusty yard sale pick from the previous summer, leaned quietly against a maple that had just begun to leaf out. A length of rusty chain and a padlock I'd bought at that same yard sale tethered them together. I usually rode the bike to my night class at the college, which was less than a mile away, another perk of renting from the old man. I even rode it to work a couple times when I had to, but that was a lot farther, and on busier roads. Instead of risking my life everyday peddling through traffic, I usually rode the bus to the mall. It made so many stops along the way that it was hardly faster, but it was certainly easier, and way safer. And though it was a luxury, and I was broke as a joke, I was willing to skimp on other things so I could (barely) afford it.

My stop was only two blocks away from the house, and I would have had just enough time to beat the bus there—if it hadn't been for the garbage. I remembered it right as I was stepping onto the sidewalk from the end of the driveway. Glancing back toward the house, I spotted the black bag sitting just outside the front door, right where it was every Thursday morning. Mr. Linder could get it that far, and then I carried it on out to the road. That was our routine.

A simple enough task, right? But not when you're having the kind of morning I was.

I didn't have much time to spare, but I had a little, and I should have used it. I should have taken my time. Instead, I charged back up to the house at full throttle, grabbed the bag at its tie like I meant to strangle it, and swung it over Mr. Linder's highly neglected flower garden. Midswing, the concrete gnome that lived in the garden caught the bag with the tip of his little mushroom umbrella, pierced its belly, and eviscerated it, spilling out a week's worth of the old man's garbage. A not quite empty TV dinner tray landed right on top of my foot, coating the toe of my shoe with congealed meatloaf gravy.

"Awesome."

Not bothering to knock first, I jerked open the front porch door and reached around to where I knew Mr. Linder kept the garbage bags. I ripped a fresh one off the roll, struggled for a moment to tease it open, and then started cramming all that nasty crap in there with my bare hands. That's how ticked I was. Usually it would have grossed me out way beyond tolerance, but right then I really didn't give a rip. All I knew was that the bus would be coming any second, and I couldn't miss it. I couldn't afford to be late for work. I couldn't afford to leave the mess and end up evicted from my apartment either. I couldn't win.

"What a disaster!" growled a familiar voice. I glanced up and saw Mr. Linder's gray, grizzled head protruding through the door. I didn't respond for fear I might say something *unladylike.*

"You have to be careful," he added. "Those are generic garbage bags, not the fancy ones. If you want the fancy ones, you can buy them yourself. I'm not paying . . ."

Shut up, shut up, shut up!

Even though I had my back to the road, I recognized the bus's unmistakable rumble as it passed by the end of the driveway. I was just wedging the last big piece of garbage, a sticky honeydew rind, into the new bag. There were still a few little scraps here and there, but I didn't have time to be that thorough. I threw my backpack over my shoulder, finagled the twisty tie into place as I hauled the fresh garbage bag out to the end of the driveway, dropped it, and sprinted away down the sidewalk.

"You've got to be more careful!" the old man hollered after me.

I was only half a block away when I heard the hiss of the bus's door sliding shut.

"Wait! Please wait!"

I was already huffing and puffing, but I spent my last reserves for one final burst of speed, testing the limits of my tarred up lungs, and all for nothing. The bus started pulling away without me, and had matched my speed by the time I reached out in a last chance effort to bang on the back door. I couldn't quite reach, and apparently no one, including the driver, noticed my frantic pursuit. Or maybe they all saw me, but no one gave a crap. Probably. Regardless, the bus didn't stop. I kept up for just a second, long enough to get a face full of black exhaust as it shifted into second gear.

Coughing and wheezing, I gave up and staggered over to the curb, where I plopped down on my butt and dropped my pounding head into my hands. I took a generous five seconds to recuperate, and then hauled myself up and headed back toward the house and my waiting bicycle.

Mr. Linder was still standing at the door and poked his head back out long enough to give me a little lecture about haste. *Thank you sooo much.* He was still talking as I rode away down the street. I ignored him, which was showing some serious restraint. I couldn't possibly have said anything nice.

It was a three mile ride to the mall, and I'd probably made it about a hundred feet when I heard the first, faint rumble of thunder.

"Perfect."

I made it to the mall alive, which was a wonder considering I could only see ten feet in front of me most of the way there on account of what I believe to have been the first ever southern Michigan monsoon. I still can't believe I managed to stay upright and not get creamed by some motorized commuter. I did get soaked, however, and chilled and about as aggravated as I'd ever been in my whole life. It sucked.

The rain died as I rolled into the parking lot, not that I gave a crap at that point. Not like I was going to air dry in the last thirty seconds of my ride. The shoe store where I worked was on the east side of the mall, and there was a bike rack not far from the nearest entrance. It was usually empty, and that day was no exception. At least the bike guaranteed me a good parking spot. Yeah, right. Like I wouldn't have preferred to park my car in the farthest spot out in the lot right in the middle of a gigantic puddle full of broken glass next to the grassy spot where all the dog walkers stop for puppy potty pit stops—IF ONLY I'D HAD A CAR TO PARK!

I was struggling with the padlock, which was as rusty as the bike and didn't open or close without a fight, when a soft voice spoke behind me.

"I don't think anyone would steal it anyway."

I turned, ready to lash out, and found a ragged-bearded man in the dirtiest clothes I'd ever seen. He was as drenched as I was, and was pushing a shopping cart full of discarded cans and bottles and what I supposed to be his every earthly possession. Beneath the beard his features were young, no more than thirty I guessed, though it was hard to judge.

"I don't mean it like an insult. I'm just saying, I don't think people steal things like that too often. But if you can't make the lock work, and you're worried about it, maybe I could keep an eye on it for you. I'd be happy to. Maybe you could pay me a little. Just whatever you could spare."

Just when I thought I couldn't possibly feel worse than I already did. Now, not only did I feel depressed about my own crappy life, I actually felt guilty about being depressed, because here was a dude whose life was crappier than mine. Now I felt like a whiner, too.

I unzipped my backpack, fished out my billfold, and opened it up to find . . . one five-dollar bill. That was it.

"Sorry, man," I apologized as I handed over the Lincoln. "That's all I got."

"That makes it a greater gift, not a lesser one," he responded. Pretty eloquent for a homeless dude.

"Yeah. No biggie." Not so eloquent of me. "And you really don't need to keep an eye on my bike. You're right, nobody'll mess with it. Piece of crap."

At that, the guy gave a little chuckle. He thanked me again, nodded, and then moved on, pushing his cart ahead of him. One of the front wheels wobbled back and forth, which seemed to make it tough to steer. It was just about enough to make me tear up. I almost never do—I am not the *sensitive* type, but right then, after everything else that morning, that stupid wheel seemed like the saddest thing I'd ever seen in my whole life. It almost got me, but I turned away just in time, took a deep breath, and got moving again.

Things went smoothly from there for at least . . . thirty seconds. Give or take.

I knew I was cutting it close for work on account of having had to ride my bike, and I knew I didn't dare show up late . . . *again.* I'd been late a couple times already, not because of any slacking on my part, but because the bus driver sucked and never had the guts to roll through on a yellow. And my boss was ridiculously hung up on punctuality, so much so that I thought another tardy really might cost me my job.

That's what I was thinking about as I was double-timing it toward the mall entrance. What I was not thinking about was what it takes to qualify as a decent human being, obviously. If I had been, then instead of moving to the far left door and hurrying through, I'd have gone to the right door, where this old lady was stuck in her power chair. She had the thing wedged halfway through the entrance and was ramming it back and forth, never moving more than an inch or two, and every other time she shifted this ultra annoying back-up alarm kept coming on. *Eeeeeee.*

Disgraceful as it is, I have to admit I had every intention of keeping right on going. I pretended not to notice her, which was a joke with that alarm going on and off, and hustled away down the hall . . . until she started calling out, and not just to anyone, but to me specifically. And it was *so* pitiful. She sounded like one of the geriatrics from those emergency help button commercials. *I'm stuck in my go-kart, and I can't get free!*

"Please, miss, can you help me?"

I almost kept going. I mean I was right on the edge, but apparently there was some small part of me that was still more decent than desperate, because I hit the brakes. Even if it made me late—even if I lost my job and then lost my apartment and had to move out to the parking lot with the shopping cart guy—I couldn't just ignore her when she was begging for help like that. I'm not *that* horrible of a person. Bad day or not, I'd have been crossing one of those lines you don't dare cross, because once you do, you might never get back on the right side of it again.

Not surprisingly, getting her unstuck turned out to be a gigantic pain in the butt. For one thing, those little scooters weigh a lot more than you think. I began to realize it when I tried and failed to just shove the thing over a bit, and then I really got it when the old lady kicked it into reverse without warning me and backed over my foot. I said something that would have made my mother cringe, but I'm pretty sure the old lady missed it. She seemed hard of hearing anyway, and that awful back-up alarm was going off again.

"I know it fits," she said after several minutes of struggling. "I've driven it through here before. Are you trying? It doesn't seem like you're even helping. Are you pushing it?"

She was the one who was pushing it, right to the limit! If she'd said one more word at that point, or so much as bumped my pinky toe with her back wheel, I'd have left her there for the next sucker that came along.

She finally came free. I don't even know how. I guess we just found the right angle with all the jockeying around. And away she went. The door caught me in the heel as it swung shut, hard. I swore again, but I'm pretty sure she still didn't hear it. I'm pretty sure I wished she had. She waved her wrinkled, little hand as she drove off, which I suppose was her token display of gratitude.

Oh, you are sooo welcome.

I found my boss, Ken Fowler, standing in front of the store with his hands on his hips, the same pose I used to find my dad in when I'd get home after curfew. That's just how I felt, too, like a kid who'd been caught breaking the rules, except this time it hadn't been my fault. The universe was conspiring against me.

"I'm sorry, Mr. Fowler. I missed the bus this morning and had to ride my bike, and then there was this old lady . . ."

He turned and headed into the store, not even giving me a chance to finish. He gathered up his things and left without saying a word, which I took to mean he was madder than I'd ever seen him. He'd always been able to yell at me before. Better, I supposed, that he say nothing than say I was fired. That's what I was expecting.

My first customer arrived just a minute later—in her power chair.

To prove I have some decency in me, I'll go ahead and *not* describe the old lady's feet. Yikes! And I had plenty of opportunity to study them as she tried on twenty pairs of shoes. And that's not me talking like a fisherman for the sake of the story. I counted. *Twenty!* Three pairs, her favorites, she tried on twice, asking me to retrieve them again *after* I'd put them away.

At least a dozen other customers stopped in and needed help while I was messing around with her, and that's a lot when I'm the only one working. We used to get scheduled two at a time on weekdays, but as business had fallen off I'd become a solo act. It sucked when more than one customer showed up at once, especially if one was *needy,* but at least I'd held onto my job while a couple others got the boot. Then again, for all I knew, my tardy that day had been the final straw. I might have been canned already and just not known it yet.

Needless to say, basically every customer that came in that day got lousy service and left unhappy. I figured odds were good at least one of them would call in the following morning and voice their complaints to Fowler. It would probably be the woman who kept complaining to me about the price of cigarettes. It was quite possibly the last thing in the world I wanted to talk about, and though I tried repeatedly to steer our conversation somewhere else, like to the shoes she was allegedly interested in buying, she just wouldn't let it go. The third time she brought it up I asked her to please stop talking. I even said *please.* I guess she took offense anyway, because she got up and walked out. "That girl sucks," she'd say to Fowler when she called the next day. He'd apologize to her, offer her a discount on her next visit, and then scratch my name off the schedule. That was my guess.

Believe it or not, the one customer who left clearly satisfied was the old lady. After tortuous hours of fitting, she picked the ugliest pair of clunky, white boats in the store and seemed pretty darn thrilled about it. No kidding, they didn't look that different than the box they came in. They weighed a ton, too, but as she said herself, she hardly walked anymore anyway, so what did it matter?

"Thank you, honey," she said on her way out. She wore her new shoes after paying for them and asked me to pitch her old ones, which looked similar, but smelled way, *way* worse. "I have such a time finding shoes."

No crap.

The steady stream of customers continued after the old lady left, and didn't let up through the rest of my shift. I never even got a chance to eat my lunch, and all the hours on my feet gradually advanced the pain in my wounded heel from an ache to agony. Of course it would be the day everybody and their brother decided to go shoe shopping.

The place finally emptied out a little before five, just in time for my relief. Fowler's daughter, just sixteen, had started filling in here and there over the winter, including the tail end of the days when I had class. She only wanted a few hours anyway, so it worked out. She was a good kid, but she was a cheerleader—all the time. *Super!* The not nice part of me felt like slapping her every time she giggled, which was about every ten seconds. Her name was Angel. Gag me with a pompom.

As I was boxing up a pair of black stilettos I wished I could afford for myself, the store phone rang. Usually I'd have gone flying over to it automatically, but instead I froze. Somehow I just knew it wasn't going to be a simple question about our hours or anything like that, and Angel was going to be showing up any minute. I'd already put up with all the crap I could handle for one shift, so I just let it ring until it quit. Whoever it was, they could call back in ten minutes and have a cheery conversation with the shoe heiress.

Whoever it was, they let the stupid thing ring about a dozen times before they finally gave up.

"Was that our phone?"

I looked up from the spikes, and there was Angel, right on time as always.

"No," I lied, which is something I almost never do because I suck at it. Every time I try, my face turns red and I make an expression that's halfway between embarrassment and constipation.

If Angel recognized my fib, and I can't imagine she didn't, then she must not've cared enough to make anything of it. She was probably just being nice. *Puke!*

"How's your day, Cassy?" she asked as she tucked one of her hundred designer purses behind the counter. I didn't bother answering or telling her for the umpteenth time I didn't like being called *Cassy*. "I'm having the best day ever. I hope you're having, like, the exact same day as me. Know what I mean?"

I'd spent the whole day being annoyed, but now, for the first time, I was scared. In fact, I was terrified. I grabbed my bag, didn't even think to clock out, and practically ran out the front of the store. By doing so, I may have saved Angel's life.

Stabbed to death with a four-inch heel. Wouldn't that have made a headline?!

Outside the mall, I found the shopping cart guy had returned and was watching dutifully over my bike like the most cleverly disguised undercover agent of all time. Chivalry lives!

It was probably my first truly nice thought of the day, and it was nearly enough to break me out of my funk. For a second.

"You're not going to believe what happened!" he practically shouted, rushing toward me. "I got a job!"

"You what?" I asked, backing up a step. "You mean like a real job, a paying job?"

"Nine-fifty an hour. This guy walked up to me right after you went inside . . ."

He wasn't done talking, but I was done listening. I was only making nine and a quarter at the shoe store, and even though it proves how horrible I am for admitting it, that's all I could think about. I should have been happy for the guy, and appreciative of him guarding my bike like he did, but I just couldn't. Another day maybe, but not right then.

I shouldered my bag, stepped up onto the pedals, and rode away without even congratulating him. Like the horrible person I am.

The pavement had dried by then, and so had I, but the rain started in again almost before I was out of the parking lot. I think it had been waiting for me.

The rain slowed gradually as I rode away from the mall, and then stopped altogether. So did I. I'd started out like it was the Tour de France, pedaling myself to the threshold of a pass out, but as my limited energy reserves burned away, I couldn't help but mellow. Being ticked takes energy. Being ticked at the whole world takes lots of energy. That it ended up being a bike day instead of a bus day turned out to be a blessing in disguise, because I spent a good portion of my frustration through my legs.

By the time the first island of blue sky appeared overhead, I was feeling *marginally* better, which is to say I was no longer ready to knock out the next person who looked at me funny. As the first rays of sunlight speared down through that break in the clouds, a thin rainbow formed ahead of me. It was a faint one, its arc of colors so pale I could almost have missed it, but the backdrop of dark sky made it especially striking. It was beautiful.

I eased my bike off the side of the road and stepped down into mud that oozed about an inch up the sides of my shoes. I barely noticed, and I didn't care at all.

I think I mentioned it before, but I am not particularly sensitive. In fact, I'm more like the opposite—most of the time. But as I stood there, transfixed by what was maybe the loveliest thing I'd ever seen, I had . . . a moment. I feel ridiculous admitting it, but considering the day I was having, I think I was entitled to one little mini-meltdown. All of a sudden I was thinking about all the stuff I usually don't let myself think about, like that I was thirty-six, getting gray hair (and wrinkles), living alone, working a crappy job that paid squat, and barely managing to pass (and pay for) one night class at a time at the community college. How I had ended up where I was, I had no idea. I was going nowhere, and nothing I did mattered to anyone. And my heel hurt. And I wanted a cigarette—*bad*. My life sucked.

In the span of about ten seconds, I'd gone from being ticked to being awed to being dejected, and it wasn't even my time of the month.

Soaked as I was, I didn't realize at first that I was crying. Only when the clouds closed up again, pinching away that fragile glimpse of blue sky, did I come back to my senses enough to notice the tears. I wiped them away as quickly as I could, terrified someone passing by might see me. I scanned across the sky, but my rainbow was gone. It didn't rain another drop the rest of my way home, but the dark clouds seemed to follow me. They hung so low in the sky I swear I could feel them weighing down against my shoulders.

What a day.

I had to ride back past the house on my way to the college, but I kept my eyes straight down the road as I went by. I didn't need the sight of my pitiful, little apartment prompting more thoughts about my pitiful, little life, and I didn't need a glimpse of those last few scraps of crap from the garbage bag reminding me of my crappy day.

At the last crossroad before campus I stepped down off the pedals to wait for the light to change. Traffic was light, and I thought about running the bike across where there was a break between cars, but decided against it. I was tight for time, but with the way things were going, why push my luck? I probably would've tripped over my own feet and ended up decorating the grill of somebody's SUV.

I started across when it was my turn, walking the bike beside me. I had to weave back and forth to avoid all the potholes turned pools. I was almost across, just a couple steps from the sidewalk, when I spotted a long, gray screw at the bottom of a particularly deep puddle. My first instinct was to reach down and grab it, but it was some seriously gross looking water. I was halfway bent over, hesitating, my hand poised within reach, when my backpack slipped off my shoulder. I barely managed to catch it before it splash-landed, but lost my hold on the bike in the process, and it banged down against the asphalt.

I imagined all the *motorists* having a good laugh at my expense, and my anger flared again. I glanced up at the nearest car, a silver sedan pulling through the intersection, but I couldn't see the driver's face. I could, however, see a gray puff of smoke spill out through a gap at the top of the window. *Grrrrr!*

I shrugged my bag back over my shoulder and dragged the bike the rest of the way to the sidewalk by its handlebars, not bothering to set it up on its wheels again first. I stood it up again when I was safely off the road, threw my leg over the seat, and was just about to ride away when . . . I stopped. I don't know why. I was suddenly thinking about the screw again. I mean really thinking about it, so hard it seemed like I couldn't think about anything else. That initial urge I'd felt to pick it up came back, but times twenty. It was weird.

I glanced back at the crossing sign, and it was flashing the countdown, 8 . . . 7 . . . 6 . . . There were a couple cars coming down the road toward the intersection, but they were still a ways off. I had time.

I set the bike down on its side, walked back out into the street, and reached right down into that nasty bacteria bath. I grabbed the screw, ignored the slime I felt underneath it, and hurried back to the sidewalk.

I studied the thing for a second before chucking it into the wooded lot behind me. It was a big one, a drywall screw I think, though I'm not really sure. One a lot like it had stabbed up into the tire of my grandpa's car when I was little. He'd lost control for a second and nearly collided with oncoming traffic. I'd been in the back seat, and I remember it being one of the scariest moments of my life. Maybe I'd spared somebody else from having the same thing happen to them. I decided to assume I had. It would keep my day from being a total failure.

So there I was, having my little heroine daydream, when the light changed. The two cars I'd seen coming reached the intersection a moment later, never even having had to slow down. The first one, a Mercedes that probably belonged to some Dean at the college, plowed right through that big puddle, and the resulting splash covered me from head to toe. Now granted, I was already wet from riding in the rain, but now I was also filthy, stinking, and almost certainly exposed to some infectious virus or parasite or . . . something. I was pretty sure a little went in my mouth.

I was frozen in place from shock and rage, which gave the second car, a minivan, the opportunity to hit me with a second coat from the same puddle. They were probably doing fifty miles an hour, but time seemed to slow right then, offering me a clear view of the freckle-faced boy who was pointing at me through the side window and laughing his little red head off.

"Oh, come on!" I don't even know who I was yelling at. Whoever.

I arrived at the college a little late, more than a little ticked off, completely soaked—again, and reeking of street slime. I only bothered struggling with that rusty, old padlock for about two seconds, and then I chucked it into the nearest garbage can. I had to restrain myself from spitting after it as I watched it disappear down through the lighter junk. *Good riddance!*

Even though I knew I'd probably miss the beginning of class, I decided to head to the vending machines first, which were in the lobby of the next building over. It was a little bit of a hike, but I was caffeine deficient and starting to get a headache because of it. Granted, there were plenty of good reasons for my having a headache at that point, but I'm sure the lack of caffeine was at least part of it. Anyway, I didn't think I was with it enough to sit through a lecture and retain anything without some chemical stimulation, so I made it my priority.

I was within view of the Pepsi machine, just starting to unzip my bag, when I remembered I didn't have any money. I'd given away my last five bucks to a guy with a better job than mine.

It's a good thing there were a bunch of other people around, because if there hadn't been any witnesses, I really think I'd have lost it big time right then. I don't know if I'd have been punching that Pepsi machine, or kicking it, or ramming my head against it, but I'd have been doing anything and everything I could to get some caffeine out of there without paying for it. No joke. But since there were so many sane people around, I held back. I scrounged through all the crap at the bottom of my bag and ended up finding three quarters. It couldn't buy me the pop I really needed, but it was just enough for a stale auto-coffee from the neighboring machine. It would have to do.

To my surprise and relief, the thing didn't eat my quarters. It actually dropped down the little paper cup *before* it started trickling java, and judging from the steam, it was even hot. Judging from its bitterness, it was also sugarless. I'd ordered double-sweet. That was the only way I drank it.

"You suck," I told the machine before turning my back to it.

The gray-haired lady next to me (who was pumping dollar bills in to the Pepsi machine) looked at me like . . . well, like I'd just been insulting a lifeless vending machine, like I was nuts. Imagine that. Thinking back, I realize she may simply have been taking note of my head to toe mud mask, but I didn't think of that then.

"Bad day, sweetheart?" she asked. Big mistake.

"You think I give a crap what you think of me? I don't. I don't give a crap what any of you think of me!" I upped my volume at the end there to make sure everyone would hear. Like I didn't already have their attention. "And who you calling sweetheart, lady? I'm almost forty years old. I ain't your sweetheart, or anybody else's."

She looked terrified, like she thought it might go catfight any second. Her last single was poised before the Pepsi machine's bill receiver, and I could see it quivering in her grip. For one awful moment, I was actually tempted to rip it out of her hand, jam it into the coffee machine, and try again for a double-sweet I could actually drink.

Instead, I spun away from her and made a beeline for the door, thinking I'd better get gone before any gun and badge men came looking for the crazy woman on campus.

And I took my stale, bitter auto-coffee with me. I'd spent my last seventy-five cents on it, and I was going to force it down even if it tasted like poison. Even if it was poison!

One last treat awaited me outside the entrance to the science building. Leaned up with his back against the bricks, just a step outside the door, was this tall, gangly looking dude with a shrub of blonde hippie hair and a red bandana stretched across his forehead. An unlit Marlboro dangled from his lips.

"Hey, babe, you got a light?" he asked when I was a couple steps away.

"Shut up, jerk," I answered, and then I reached over and swatted that cancer stick right out of his mouth. I can still barely believe I did it. I'm lucky I didn't hit him in the face by accident. If the cops weren't already on their way for me, they would be now, I was sure. I hurried through the door and didn't look back.

Strangely enough, I could hear the guy laughing behind me, like he thought it was hilarious.

I hustled down the hallway, anxious to get away from the man whose cigarette I'd just assaulted. The door at my lecture hall was already closed, as I knew it would be, and I could hear the professor's voice speaking inside. I tried to sneak in as quietly as I could, but only succeeded in prolonging the groan of the door's dry hinges and drawing the attention of every person in the room, including the professor. And I hated, *hated,* all of them looking at me.

Refusing to make eye contact with anyone, I slunk into the otherwise empty back row of seats. The professor, who'd paused momentarily in his lecture, started in again. At least he didn't call me out on being late.

I sipped at my auto-coffee, and it was so bad it nearly made me gag. I'm surprised I didn't choke on it, because that would have drawn everyone's attention again and further humiliated me, which would have been par for the course. As it was, only the girl sitting nearest me turned back my way, and judging from the look on her face it wasn't because she could hear me, but because she could smell me. My new fragrance: *eau de pothole*.

I was just putting pen to paper, ready to start scrawling notes, when I saw the door swing open again. So yeah, I'd been late, but somebody else was even later. At least I wasn't the caboose after all. Good. Or so I thought. Then I saw who it was.

In stepped the gangly smoker dude. Without a second's hesitation, he looked right back at me, smiled, and waved. I think I almost died of heart failure.

He started making his way toward me, and though I was petrified, I absently noticed the professor had continued with his lecture without a hitch. If fact, nobody else in the room seemed to be paying the guy any attention at all. Had the door even squeaked when he came in? I didn't think so.

Despite the friendly grin stretching across the guy's face, I expected the worst. I expected a slap, or a face full of my own coffee, or at the very least a public announcement of the kind of person he thought I was. Instead, he walked up and casually slid into the next chair over, right beside me.

"I bet you're trying to quit smoking, right?" he asked once he'd settled. His voice came out several notches above a whisper, but nobody turned their head to scowl at us. Weird. "That's my guess. I been there. It sucks. I hope you hold out better than I did."

I couldn't respond at first. I was shocked he wasn't ticked. He should have been. I would have been.

"I hope so, too," I finally managed. "I need to quit because of my job. Can't go outside for breaks anymore. They're too expensive anyway. Can't afford it."

"Right on. Good luck."

Right on? Who says that? Now that I was pretty sure I wasn't going to get beat up or anything, I spared enough attention to really look the guy over. Interesting. And a little creepy. The crazy hair and bandana were hard to miss, even at a glance, but I hadn't noticed the *'Beam me up!'* Star Trek shirt or the Indiana Jones lunch box.

"Are you in this class?" I asked. I was pretty sure I would've remembered him.

"Here I am," he answered.

Oookay. I wasn't really sure if that was a yes or a no.

I'm pretty sure I was about to apologize when the guy popped the lid of his lunch box and picked out a sweating can of Diet Mountain Dew. He cracked it open, and my mouth started watering like a dog whose owner just spelled out *t-r-e-a-t*. He took a ridiculously long first drink, swallowed audibly about seven times in a row, and then set the can on the table between us. His eyes moved up to mine as he wiped his mouth on the shoulder of his Trek tee.

"Want a sip? That coffee doesn't look very good."

I almost did it. Despite the fact I'd have been swapping germs with the weirdo, and despite the fact I generally thought of diet anything as gross, I almost went for it. That's how bad I needed a pop.

"It came out unsweetened," I answered noncommittally. I was still tempted. "I like extra sweet."

"Allow me," he said. Then he reached back into his lunch box, pulled out a turkey baster (for real!), and plunged the thing right down into my coffee cup. He gave it a couple good stirs, whispered something I couldn't quite make out, and then shook it dry behind his seat.

What—in—the—world??? Was this payback for the cigarette thing? Was he trying (and failing fantastically) to be funny? Was he seriously some kind of lunatic?

"Why did you do that? Why do you have a turkey baster?"

"Oh, sorry," he apologized, though he didn't look sorry. "I wasn't thinking. This is actually my wand, not a turkey baster. I mean it used to be a turkey baster, but I turned it into a wand. You can turn anything into a wand. Did you know that? Something ordinary looking like this is best in my opinion, because then people don't see you coming, if you know what I mean. When people see me with this, they probably think I'm a chef, not a wizard. Is that what you thought?"

I didn't tell him what I thought.

"Are you okay?" he asked when I hesitated to answer. "You look a little . . . unsettled."

The urge to get up and run out of the room was almost overpowering, but if I ducked out early after showing up late I figured the prof would probably tell me not to come back, so I faced forward, willed myself to concentrate on the lecture, and prayed with all my might the guy would just leave me alone.

"Am I making you uncomfortable?" He smiled as he asked this, like the idea was amusing to him. "Look, I know you don't meet a lot of wizards, but we're alright for the most part. We put our pants on one leg at a time and all that. I'm Marlon." He offered his hand to shake.

"Like *Merlin?*" I asked, allowing a nervous giggle to slip out with my words. I did not shake his hand.

"Like Brando," he corrected. "You know, the Godfather? Apocalypse Now? You've never heard of Marlon Brando? A Streetcar Named Desire? *Steeellaaa!*"

Yes, I'd heard of Marlon Brando. I did not, however, know who Stella was. I did know that whoever she was, the guy had practically shouted her name, and yet, unbelievably, everyone else in the room still seemed completely oblivious. Not one other student so much as turned their head, and the professor kept right on lecturing. "Any questions?" I heard him ask the class just then. Yeah, I had a few. Like, let me see, *had I lost my freakin' mind or what?!*

I decided to leave. Yeah, I might get kicked out of the class if I did, but my priorities were shifting fast. Seriously, who's worried about their GPA when they're in the midst of a psychotic break?

I stood, and so did everybody else, in almost perfect unison.

"It's our break time," explained Marlon, answering the question I hadn't asked. "I'd usually go out for a smoke, but I'll skip it if you'd like to continue our conversation."

"No, no," I blurted. "You go ahead. I'll be here when you get back." Yeah, right!

He seemed to find that hilarious, breaking into a fit of laughter that shook his afro like a bush in the breeze. Could he read my dishonesty as easily as he'd read my confusion? I couldn't help but think so, and it made me feel completely exposed.

"Why don't you sit back down and relax for a minute," he suggested as he slipped the baster back into his lunchbox. "You look flushed. Take a few deep breaths and sip your coffee. I bet it'll help."

I nodded in agreement and tried for a smile I'm not sure I quite managed. He chuckled again and then followed the crowd out of the room, taking his pop and lunchbox with him.

I sat back down after he'd gone, not because he'd suggested I should, but because I was feeling a little light headed. Passing out would go better from a sitting position. I found myself taking deep breaths, too, but again, not because he'd told me to. I just . . . needed to catch my breath. That's what I was thinking about when my hand, without my telling it to, reached down, took the coffee cup, and lifted it to my lips. I took a sip, and then another, and another. I had it half-drained before it occurred to me how good it was, how *sweet*.

It might seem like I'd have jumped out of my seat and gone chasing right after him, but I didn't. I did get up and make my way first out of the room and then down the hall toward the entrance where I'd seen him lounging before, but I took my time. I moved with deliberate steps, thinking about a dozen things at once, a couple of them doozies. Like could I really be losing my mind, and if I wasn't, then was I ready to totally rethink what was and wasn't possible? *Magic?* Just thinking the word made my headache double.

The slow walk gave me a few extra moments to consider things, but I don't think it would have mattered if I'd had an extra hour or a year. I stepped out the door, and there he was, standing in the exact same spot as before with another unlit cigarette hanging from his lips. I had absolutely no idea what to say.

Seeing me, he threw up his hands in a gesture of frustration. "Doesn't anybody carry a lighter anymore?"

It seemed strange for him to ask such an ordinary question.

I reached down to my right hip pocket, the one that had worn out first in every pair of pants I'd owned for almost twenty years because it's where my Zippo lived. I slipped it out and fired it up.

"Thanks," Marlon mumbled out the corner of his mouth.

He tried to blow the smoke from his first drag away from me, but the breeze blew it right back into my face. I can honestly say it smelled terrible, and yet somehow it still made me want one so bad it hurt. Try to figure that one out. The craving hit me so hard that for a second, I actually forgot why I'd gone out there. That's how powerful my addiction was. I was two minutes removed from the revelation of a lifetime, and all I could think about was how bad I needed a cigarette. Only for a second, though.

"You're still carrying your lighter," he said before I could start in. "That's a bad sign. Part of you is still open to the possibility you might not stay quit. You don't want to have to buy another lighter if you start again. Am I right?"

"How did you sweeten my coffee?" I asked instead of answering his question. "And if you're going to say it was magic, because you're a wizard, then why can't you light your own cigarette? Turkey baster wands can make sugar, but not fire?"

"Oh, I can do fire, too. It's not so much a matter of what I *can* do as it is what I'm *supposed* to do. We're really only supposed to use magic to help others, not ourselves, although I did conjure up some tee-pee for myself the other day in one of the men's rooms here on campus. You can get away with a little one like that once in a while—when it's a desperate situation."

"You desperately needed toilet paper?"

"Yes I did. Desperately."

"So what else can you do with your . . . *wand,* besides sweeten coffee and make toilet paper? And squirt broth? Could you wave it over me and make all this stinky mud disappear?"

Instead of answering right away, he threw his head back again and laughed like I'd just told him the funniest joke ever. "Sorry, I couldn't help myself. You really do stink. Yeah, I can do that if it's what you want. But I'd think it over first if I was you. I'm hardly your average guy, and if you're going to ask me for a favor, you might want to make it a little more . . . ambitious."

Not that I was really buying into this whole *wands and wizards* crap, but there was definitely something funny going on. I wasn't taking anything for granted.

"So are you like a genie?" I asked. "Do I get three wishes?"

"No, I'm not like a genie," he said, busting out into laughter again. I was really getting annoyed with how funny this guy seemed to think I was. "But I got stuff to do," he went on. "I'm finding that class kind of boring, so I think when I'm done with this smoke I'll head home. They're showing *The Wrath of Khan* on SyFy tonight."

He held his cigarette up so I could see it was already half-gone.

"If you really could grant me a wish, I don't know how I could possibly choose what to wish for. I can think of about a dozen things I'd love to change just about today. It's been one of the worst days I've ever had, and I would love to go back and change every bad choice I've made."

"Really? This was one of your *worst* days? I'd have guessed it was one of your best."

So much for his extraordinary perceptiveness.

"Does it look like I've had a great day?" I asked, waving my hands up and down over my grimy clothes.

This got him laughing again, and I had to fight back the urge to kick him in the shin.

"Yeah, alright," he agreed reluctantly. "I can do that."

"You can do . . . what?" I asked.

Ignoring me, Marlon flicked away the butt of his cigarette and sat down on the grass, crossing his legs meditation style. He set his Indiana Jones lunchbox down in front of him, popped it open, and brought his supposedly magical kitchen implement back out. He poured the rest of his Diet Mountain Dew into the box, about half a can, and started stirring it around with the tip of the baster. As he did so, he started mumbling something under his breath, too low for me to understand.

A wave of fear suddenly ran through me. Whatever this guy was capable of, I was an idiot for getting mixed up with it. He could definitely be dangerous. I glanced around, but the other students lounging about were caught up in their own conversations, oblivious to our little scene. My anxiety ramped up until the urge to run was intense, but I couldn't. I couldn't do anything. I was frozen.

"Okay, I think that should do it," he said as he rose back to his feet. He held up his *wand*, pointed it right at my face, and I could see it was now loaded with several inches of green soda. "Good luck."

And though I tried with all my willpower to duck away, I couldn't. I couldn't even blink—not until I felt the cold, sticky splash hit me right between the eyes.

My fear turned to outright hysteria when everything went dark. I was blind! I reached my hands to my face, rubbing furiously at my eyes, and found they were, somehow, dry. Then I noticed how quiet everything had become. I couldn't hear the other students talking anymore. In fact, the only thing I could hear was a dog barking. It was high pitched, a yipper. It sounded just like . . . *Dolly?*

Take Two

My senses began to register one by one, slowly, as if I was just waking up, which I wasn't. I was pretty sure I wasn't. The voice of the yipping dog, the only break in the silence, captured most of my attention, but I also became aware of the soft feel of fabric in my hands. My fingers were curled up into fists at my sides, and the fuzzy cloth bunched under them felt just like the blanket from my bed. Then I realized my eyes weren't as completely useless as I'd thought. I wasn't actually blind, I decided, but in a very dark place. I could just barely see the edges of a drawn window curtain. I unclenched one fist, waved my hand in front of my face, and yep, I could see it, too. And there, over my shoulder, plain as day, were the glowing red numbers of my clock radio atop my dresser.

Holey socks, that didn't just feel like my blanket—it was my blanket! And that was definitely Dolly out there barking her annoying, little head off. Holey socks!

"You're okay, Cass," I mumbled as I stepped down off the bed and headed toward the bathroom. "Everything's okay. Everything's fine. You're fine." My voice didn't sound fine, though. It sounded like it belonged to somebody who was freaking out big time.

I flipped on the light, planted my hands on the countertop, and stared at the zombie woman in the mirror. I looked . . . as crappy as I always looked in the morning. Except it wasn't morning, was it?

How could it be when it had just been evening like a minute earlier? Hadn't it?

"It's a memory lapse," I told my reflection in a panicky whisper. "You had a bad day. You took as much as you could, and then you blocked the rest out. You don't remember coming home from school and going to bed, but you obviously did. Here you are. You just don't remember. Unless . . ."

No! I wouldn't even let myself consider that. Not for a second!

What time was it anyway, I wondered? The numbers on the clock radio hadn't even registered with me when I'd glanced at them.

I flipped on the light as I stepped back into the bedroom, and what do you know, there were my slippers, right where I'd left them. Not wanting to catch another splinter, I stepped into them, but even as I did so it occurred to me the pain in my heel was gone. Could it have healed so well in a day? I didn't look because I wasn't sure I really wanted to know.

The clock radio read ten to six, the same time I'd gotten up . . . *yesterday?*

"That doesn't mean anything. Dolly's been waking you up the same time every morning, and it's the same today. Your memory's messed up, but that's it. Everything's okay."

Except it wasn't, obviously. This was the second time I'd looked at the radio, and I still hadn't caught on. When I finally did, when it finally hit me, I let out a scream—a big one. I'm talking a full blown Fay Wray giant gorilla screech.

I stumbled back to the opposite wall, trying to put as much distance between me and the radio as I could.

"You're broken!" I yelled at it, pointing an accusing finger that was shaking like a dashboard hula dancer on dirt road. "I broke you . . . *yesterday!*"

"What's going on up there?" called Mr. Linder from the first floor. "I need quiet. I'm a light sleeper."

Instead of answering, I tiptoed across the room to where I always left my cell to charge at night. I never took my eyes off the clock radio for fear it might . . . I have no idea. The phone was right where I expected it to be. I hardly breathed while it powered up, and then I stopped breathing altogether when its display finally popped into view.

It said it was Thursday. Again.

"Holey socks!"

I spent the next hour sitting on my bed, my feet dangling over the side, waiting for some other crazy thing to happen, but nothing did. I watched the time slip by with the shifting numbers on the clock radio, which showed no other signs of weirdness beyond its being miraculously unbroken.

As I sat there, my breathing slowed and my heart settled from my throat back down into my chest where it belonged. I considered the evidence. First there was the coffee, sweetened with a touch from Marlon's turkey baster, and there was my waking up in bed with no memory of getting there. Then there was the clock radio. Oh, and my heel—I'd checked, and there was, impossibly, not a trace of where the splinter had been. Could I have dreamed a whole day's worth of stuff while I was sleeping? Maybe, but not that day, not that stuff. My wildest dream wasn't half that creative.

My head felt like a pop bottle that had been shaken up like crazy and was ready to explode as soon as somebody cracked the lid.

"I'd love to go back and change every bad choice I made," I recited to the empty room, which was growing lighter by the second. That's what I'd wished for. Was it possible? How could it be? But then how could it not be if the radio wasn't broken and the phone said it was Thursday?

My thinking was interrupted by David Lee Roth, who was suddenly singing to me from the top of the dresser. "*I'm hot for teacher . . .*" It was seven o'clock. I'd set the alarm Wednesday night to make sure I was up in time for my financial aid meeting at the college, and this time it had worked.

This time, everything might work. It felt like a dangerous thought, but a seductive one, too. If I really was getting a do-over, then I wasn't off to a bad start with it. I'd already avoided stepping on a splinter and breaking my alarm, and now I was up in plenty of time to make my meeting.

I turned off the radio as I passed the dresser and resisted the urge to reach for my cigarettes. I was awake enough this time to know they wouldn't be there. And I wore my slippers. I squared up with the woman in the bathroom mirror again and found myself wondering if maybe she didn't look quite as haggard as before. Was I feeling a little better? It was sort of hard to gauge, but I thought so.

"Why not just go with it, Cass?" I asked. "Just go with it."

And I did. I took a shower, got dressed, downed a Pepsi and a toaster waffle, and headed out. I still felt super weirded out, but I was also nursing a little spark of hope. A do-over day. What people wouldn't give for the chance, right? And not just any day, but one of the worst days I'd ever had!

It took five minutes to ride over to the college, and five seconds to find out my meeting was canceled. A hand-written note on the door to the Student Services Court said all morning appointments would have to be rescheduled due to a computer network failure. I could have slept in after all, and it wouldn't have mattered.

It took fifteen minutes to ride back. I'd left the house full of adrenaline, enough to mask how far behind on sleep I still was, but after finding out I'd gotten up early for nothing, that extra boost disappeared in an instant. It was a pretty flat ride, really, but it felt distinctly uphill on the way home.

I tried to focus on the incredible potential of the remainder of the day ahead of me, but it was tough. It was easier to think about how much it sucked that I'd missed not only my meeting, but a chance to rest up as well.

There was something else, too, a twinge of unease that my incredible do-over day, if that's what it really was, wasn't starting out so great after all. Thursday on the first try had been one disaster after another, and even though it seemed like I should've been able to avoid every misstep on round two, it wasn't working out that way so far. Hmmm.

Back at the house, I tipped the bike over in the grass and dragged myself up the stairs. As soon as I was through the door, my eyes went right to the dresser, but it wasn't the clock radio that had my attention this time. Instead, I focused on the empty place next to it. I think the cravings must've been dampened earlier by my overwhelming dread and disorientation, but now the cigarettes were calling to me again, big time. I could sense their presence, just a half-mile away at the corner party store.

I patted my pants pocket and felt the shape of my lighter there. I didn't even remember having picked it up, and I hated finding it. I was afraid to let myself see it, so I just let it be. I lumbered across the room, kicked off my shoes, and hopped up onto the edge of the bed, where I intended to think over everything else that would happen over the course of the day and how I could make it all go right. The morning light pouring in through the window only reached halfway across my crumpled blanket, so I laid back to reach it. I only meant to stay there for a second.

I flew into motion as soon as I woke up, before even bothering to check the time. I knew I'd been asleep for a while. I knew I was in trouble. I glanced at the clock radio as I flew across the room, and its glowing red numbers confirmed it—I had three minutes to make the bus.

A monstrous splinter, twice as big as the first one, speared up into the arch of my foot halfway across the room, painfully reminding me that my shoes were still lying next to the bed. I one-foot hopped back and jammed them on, stifling a scream. The pain, unlike the splinter itself, wasn't twice as big. It was ten times as big!

I grabbed my bag as I hobbled through the kitchenette, but didn't think to grab any sort of lunch for later. All I was thinking was that I was going to miss the bus *again*, and that this Thursday wasn't turning out any better than the first one.

I almost bit it hurrying down the stairs, but somehow managed to stay on my feet, and then I hit the driveway running. It killed my foot, but I could already hear the bus rumbling up the road, so I pushed through the pain, and I made it. Barely.

As I climbed up inside, I noticed the driver's eyes go wide. I'm sure I looked like I was having a heart attack. I'm not sure I wasn't. It felt like it. But as we pulled away and the rain started to fall, I took a seat, settled down, and kept dry—all good things. I dared to hope I was finally on track.

Then I noticed the cigarettes. They were lying on the floor, practically at my feet. It was a half-full pack of the brand I wished were my regulars, but couldn't afford. I pulled my feet back, afraid even the tiniest contact might infect me with a willpower eating disease.

I looked around, thinking it might be best if I just moved to a new seat, but the bus was practically full, and I wasn't about to go settle in next to the lady with the crying baby or the guy in the Magnum P.I. shorts (who was no Tom Selleck). So I stared out the window and tried to focus on the rain, which was really coming down.

And it was working. I think it was. I'd put those stupid cigarettes right out of my mind.

My feet were starting to go numb from holding my legs tucked up under the seat, and as I shifted to a more comfortable position my bag slipped off my lap. I bent down to pick it up and came up with the cigarettes instead. I didn't *decide* to pick them up. It just happened. But then I couldn't put them down. I lifted the pack up to my nose, breathed in their scent, and decided they smelled terrible, which didn't make me want one any less.

I reached down to my pocket and felt the familiar shape of my lighter. Had those smokes been left there specifically for me, I wondered? It seemed like it. It seemed like fate was conspiring against me.

Right then I knew I was done. Unless the world ended in the next two minutes (and I knew it wouldn't—it hadn't on Thursday number one), then I was going to fire one of those suckers up as soon as I stepped off the bus. If I could wait that long.

And I did. I hopped out of my seat as the bus was turning into the mall parking lot and charged up the aisle. I forgot my bag initially and had to go back for it, and then I lost my footing and fell over right into the shorty-shorts guy, who blatantly touched my butt as he helped me up. (Tom Selleck? Shoot, he wasn't even Tom Arnold!) It would have earned him a slap another day, but I didn't even bother to cuss him out. That's how bad I wanted off the bus.

The rain hadn't stopped yet, but it had slowed enough that I could smoke in it, and that's all I cared about. I slipped one between my lips as I stepped off the bus, turned my back to the wind, and lit up. It tasted awful, and I immediately hated myself for doing it. As soon as I'd burned it down to a nub I lit another. The second one was half-gone by the time I was nearing the mall entrance closest to the shoe store. I stared down at my feet as I walked, hiding my face from the rain, so I didn't even see him coming until he was right beside me, and because I was so intent on how much I sucked for caving, I hadn't thought to expect him.

"You know those cause cancer?"

He startled me for a second, but only a second, and then I realized who it was. The bus had kept me dry, but it hadn't got me to the mall much faster than my bike had, and there was homeless dude, right where I should've known he'd be.

"*Yes*, I know these cause cancer," I shot back, venting all my addict guilt right into his face, "and *no,* you can't have my last five bucks." And then I stormed away like a pouting child who just got sent to her room.

"I don't want your money," the man called after me. "I was just offering a little friendly advice, trying to add a couple years to your life. Jerk!"

That put a hitch in my stride, but I wasn't about to go back and apologize, and I wasn't about to part with my last five bucks, either. Especially since I'd realized by then I'd left the house lunchless. I'd need that five bucks soon, and soon he wouldn't. He was going to be making nine-fifty before he knew it.

Unlike the homeless guy, the old lady in the power chair did not take me by surprise. I found her stuck right where I'd found her before. And what did I do? I steered myself to the door furthest over from her, kept my eyes forward, and pretended I didn't see her. Even when she called out to me, even when she practically begged for my help, I just kept on walking.

Did this prove I was a horrible person? Yep. Obviously it did. Tough crap. That's what I thought about it. Someone else would be along to help her in a minute, and she wasn't going to starve to death in the mean time, and I wasn't going to risk losing my job playing the Good Samaritan. Mr. Fowler had been so mad when I'd shown up late that he hadn't even acknowledged me. I'd made the wrong choice before, and it had cost me. But not this time.

Or so I thought.

I was feeling lousy as I approached the store, which is how you expect addicted, horrible people to feel, but I was also feeling confident I'd made the right choice. Getting in your good deed for the day was fine, but your job was your job, and there couldn't be any comparing the importance of the two. Work was what paid the bills and kept my whole life moving forward. The hard and simple truth was that for the time being, money had to be my priority, not jackknifed geriatrics. I'd made the right choice. I was almost sure.

So then why was Fowler still standing out there in front of the store with his hands on hips, looking ticked? I picked up my pace when I spotted him, which increased the throbbing in my splintered foot, but a quick glance down at my phone confirmed I was going to be right on time. What the heck?

"What's wrong, Mr. Fowler?" I asked, pulling up a few steps short of him. I could practically feel the anger radiating out from him, and I was honestly afraid to get any closer than that.

He didn't answer. He tromped back into the store, grabbed his stuff, and left, just like he had before. He didn't seem any different at all.

I wish I could say the same of my first customer of the day. The old lady showed up in her go-cart not more than a few minutes later than she had before, but in a very different state of mind.

"Can I help you?" I asked, filling my voice with all the eager clerk enthusiasm I could muster. My only hope was that she wouldn't recognize me. No such luck.

"*You!*" she hissed. She pointed one crooked finger at me, and I swear it was like she cast a spell with it or something. My stomach twisted, and an instant headache bloomed behind my eyes. She sneered at me so hard she actually bared her dentures. Oh yeah, she was ticked.

"Look, I'm very sorry, Ma'am, but I couldn't afford to be late for work, and I knew getting you unstuck wasn't going to be easy. I knew—"

"Oh you *knew*, did you?" She started forward again, quickly closing the distance between us. "You young people these days think you know everything. Let me tell you what I know, honey: I know what goes around comes around."

Seriously? Was that a threat? Because that's what it sounded like.

And then I had my answer. She rammed me. She hit the gas and ran her stupid go-kart right into my shins, and holey socks did it hurt!

"I can't believe you just did that," I sputtered.

"Believe it, honey. What goes around comes around. Now go fetch me something in a size ten, plain white or beige with a good arch. Actually, you might as well grab a couple pair. I like to try a few before I choose."

No kidding. I think she made me cram her nasty feet into about twice as many granny boats as before, just out of spite, and she was way less patient when I had other customers to help. The whole time my headache kept ramping up until I was miserable with it. I wasn't sure whether another cigarette would make it better or worse, but I knew I was going to find out as soon as I could.

The rest of my work shift played out exactly as I knew it would, which sucked, but I couldn't see any obvious way to make it go any better. It was busy like crazy, and I had all I could do to keep up, just like before. My head pounded and my foot throbbed. The phone rang right when I expected it to, and I ignored it again. Then Angel showed up, all cheery and annoying. I lied to her about the phone ringing, and refrained from calling her something awful when she called me *Cassy*.

Shopping cart guy was hanging out near the mall exit, which I also expected, but I was surprised to find him in a crappy mood.

"It's *you,*" he practically snarled when he caught sight of me. "The *smoker*. Still guarding that last five bucks with your life? Maybe you should spend it on breath mints. Or whitening tooth paste."

"You're pretty crabby for a guy with a great new job, aren't you?" I shot back as I hurried past.

"New job? Why would I need a new job? I love being the mall greeter. It's what I always wanted. Now if I could just find a nice girl like you to share my cart with, I'd have it all. Hah!"

He was shouting by the time he finished, and the louder he got, the faster I walked. I glanced over my shoulder every few steps to make sure he wasn't coming after me. Why was he so mad, so different from before? What the heck?

I went for a cigarette as soon as I reached the bus stop, and was surprised to see how bad it shook in my hand. Sheesh, the guy had really unnerved me.

That cigarette tasted awful. The next one, which I lit up immediately after flicking away the first one's spent butt, was even worse. Before

I was done with the second one, the rain started up again, right on time like everything else. I remembered the rain clearly enough—it would have been hard to forget, but I didn't remember the cold chill that came with it. I suppose I'd been pedaling the bike before, and that probably kept my temp up, but it seemed like more than that. My first Thursday of the week had turned into a seriously bad day, but this one wasn't going any better. Despite the fact I knew where all the crap was along my way, I kept on stepping in it anyway, and this time it didn't just feel bad, it felt . . . *wrong*.

The bus ride home was quicker than the ride to work, and Moron P.I. with his grabby hands was nowhere to be seen, for which I was grateful. However, I also missed the rainbow. I looked for it when I noticed the rain easing off, but my tinted window didn't offer much of a view. I couldn't even spot that little island of blue sky, though I knew it was out there somewhere.

Bummer. It really had been a beautiful rainbow.

The bus was still three blocks down the road when I spotted the flashing lights, but even from that distance I thought I could tell they were at my house. My first thought was that it was going to be the police waiting to arrest me for unlawful rudeness to a homeless dude and gross old person negligence. (That's gross negligence, not gross old person. Actually, having seen her feet, it could have been either.) They were going to lock me up for being a horrible person—that's what I thought. And I deserved it. I was *guilty!*

As I stepped off the bus, I realized what I'd at first thought to be a police car was actually an ambulance. *Oh, no.* I didn't know what to expect as I jogged down the sidewalk toward the house, but I knew it wasn't going to be good. How could it be?

An EMT slammed the back doors of the ambulance closed just before I could get a peek inside.

"What happened?" I gasped at him as he hurried to the driver's side door. "Who's in there?"

"It's the guy who lives here," he answered. "Are you family?"

"No, but I'm—"

I swallowed down the rest of what I was going to say as he slammed the door in my face. A second later, they pulled out and sped away, presumably toward the hospital. At least they didn't fire up the siren, which I hoped meant it wasn't anything life threatening.

"You're Cassidy, right?" someone called from behind me. I turned to find the neighbor, Dolly's owner, headed toward me. "You're renting the second floor from Mr. Linder?"

"Yeah, that's me. What happened? Is he okay?"

"Threw his back out. I saw him go down as I was getting home from work. He was taking the garbage out to the end of the driveway, and about halfway there he hunched forward and fell on his face. The ambulance guy said he probably slipped a disc. He hit his head when he landed, got a little cut over his eye and a nasty goose egg."

I might as well have pushed him down myself. It wouldn't have been any more my fault if I had. The neighbor kept on talking, but I couldn't concentrate on what he was saying. I think he actually might have been apologizing for Dolly's barking, but I'm not sure. It didn't matter. My stomach was gurgling, and I was getting that sour prevomit taste in my mouth.

I turned away and walked off without excusing myself, which was yet another act of rudeness for the day, but it was better than the alternative, which was opening my mouth to say something and puking on him. I'm positive I would have.

I made it up about four steps, heading for my apartment, intending to lock myself away where I hopefully couldn't do any more damage, when I suddenly froze. *Epiphany.* I was feeling guilty about Mr. Linder's accident to a degree I'd rarely experienced, and adding that to the canceled meeting, the sliver, the cigarettes, the shopping cart guy, the old lady, and even the rainbow I'd missed, which I felt strangely bad about—I couldn't take anymore. But maybe I didn't have to. I'd blown it big time, turned a bad day into a catastrophe, but I'd had my shot, my do-over day. Couldn't I have another? I'd *wanted* a second chance, and I'd got it. Now I *needed* a third. I had to find Marlon!

It took me forever to coax open the padlock and free my bike from the maple tree, probably because I was hurrying and shaking and frantic. As soon as it came loose, I threw the lock and the chain aside and hurried away. Adrenaline sped me along for a ways, but adrenaline can only take you so far. In my case, it took me about halfway to the college, at which point my legs turned into lead and I was forced to ease off the accelerator or risk blowing my engine. For all I knew, arriving early wouldn't do any good anyway. I knew how to find the wizard, right where and when I'd found him before.

I stepped down off the pedals at the last intersection before campus. Again. Instead of waiting for the light to change, I rode across through the first break in traffic. I almost tipped when I swerved to miss the big puddle, but I made it.

I didn't even think about the screw until I was a good fifty yards away. When I did remember it, it wasn't like it just popped into my head—it was like it *exploded* in my head. The image of it flashed before my eyes in perfect detail, the sharp edge of every gray thread as clear and precise as if I was standing over it again, only a reach away. My pulse jumped like someone had just injected a syringe of espresso right into my heart. The urge to go back for it was intense.

"You can get it later," I whispered to myself. "This day's already shot, but next time you can do it all right." It made sense, but I still couldn't make myself move. I looked down at my fingers and saw the color had drained from them as I strangled the handlebars.

A loud splash drew my attention back to the intersection. It was the Mercedes, plowing through the puddle and sending up the wave of stinking grossness that had doused me. Prying one fist free from the bike, I absently grabbed a handful of the front of my shirt and inspected it. It looked as clean as when I'd put it on. It felt dry and comfortable, and very, very *wrong*.

Then came the awful squealing of rubber on asphalt. I turned back in time to see the minivan sliding sideways off the side of the road. I couldn't see the boy in the backseat, but I could picture his face just as clearly as I could picture the screw. The van made it all the way to the edge of the woods, having hardly even slowed, and the sound it made when the tree stopped it was . . . indescribable. I'm not going to try, anyway. I can't.

I couldn't move. I couldn't breathe. I couldn't do anything.

Other cars were stopping, their drivers and passengers emptying out and hurrying to try and help. Who knew if they could? Who knew what they'd find?

Following their lead, I hurried away to try and help as well—in the opposite direction. There was no way I could ride the bike shaking the way I was, so I dropped it and took off running toward the school. I was sobbing, completely out of control, and my headache had reached skull-splitting intensity. I tried closing my eyes against the pain, but the image of the screw immediately reappeared. The sound of the crash echoed in my ears, and I hated it almost as much as I hated myself for causing it. Because I had, hadn't I? I'd had the chance to prevent it, and I'd let that chance slip by. *Guilty.*

I vaguely noticed people staring at me as I made my way across the parking lot at the college. A few called out, asking if I was okay, if I needed help. I didn't acknowledge them. I needed help, yes, more than I'd ever needed it in my life, but they couldn't give me the help I needed. I prayed someone could.

I rounded the corner of the science building, exhausted almost to the point of collapse, and there, looking for a light for his dangling Marlboro, was the answer to my prayer.

"It didn't work," I sputtered through my sobs. I grabbed two handfuls of his Star Trek shirt and shook him as I shouted in his face. His shocked expression barely registered with me. "I tried to make things better, but instead they went worse. Everything turned out so much worse. I have to try again. I have to make it right. Please. *Please!*"

"Do I know you?"

It was probably the only thing he could have said to shut me up on the spot. He didn't know me because today was the first day we'd met. This was Thursday number one for him, just like it was for everybody else. The realization hit me hard enough to buckle my knees.

I let go of his shirt and stumbled back a step, to his obvious relief. I forced myself to take a deep breath, which moved me one incremental step toward composure. My sobbing settled down to regular crying.

"I'm sorry," I managed in a lower voice. "I know you don't remember me, but we have met before. I need your help."

He looked a little more confused than afraid now, which was an improvement. He opened his mouth to speak, but instead of responding to me, he mouthed the words *I don't know her* to a pretty blonde girl who was passing by right then.

I stepped toward the blonde, placing myself back into Marlon's line of sight, and said, "Please. It's very important, and you're the only one who can help me."

"With anatomy and phys?"

"No, with today. This whole day's gone horribly wrong, and you have to help me fix it. I know you can. You helped me once already, or tried to, but nothing went the way I meant for it to, and now Mr. Linder's at the hospital, and there was a car accident because of the screw I didn't pick up, and—"

Marlon held up in hands in the universal *whoa* gesture. My tears were coming faster again, and my voice had turned back into blubbering. He probably couldn't even understand me.

"Here," he said, slipping the bandana from his head and offering it to me. My breathing was so ragged I had a hard time filling my lungs enough to blow my nose.

"Thank you," I said, offering the bandana back. He didn't take it.

"Actually, I only meant for you to dry your cheeks with it. But no worries, I've got lots of those. Go ahead and keep that one, in case you need it again."

"Oh, sorry," I apologized.

"Like I said, no worries. Now how exactly did I help you before? When did we meet?"

I didn't answer until I had my breathing back under control, which took a minute. To his credit, Marlon waited patiently.

"We met right here, today, although it seems to me like it was yesterday. It was a different today. You used your turkey baster to help me—"

"You care if we go inside and find a better place to talk?" he asked, cutting me off.

Now I had his attention.

The classrooms were always locked when they weren't in use, and the first one I tried was no exception.

"I tried that one already," I said when Marlon stepped up to the same door. I was hardly surprised when it opened right up for him. How much of an obstacle was a locked door to a guy who could turn back time?

"Hey, look at that. It must've just been jammed or something." He smiled innocently as he said this, but dropped the act when he saw my reaction. "Or maybe it was locked. Alright, Cassidy, let's talk."

We stepped into the empty room and shut the door behind us. The voices of the students passing by outside dropped back to a low murmur.

"I don't remember you from today or yesterday," Marlon offered in a flat, emotionless voice, "and I almost never show my turkey baster to people I've just met."

"Then how did you know my name was Cassidy?" I asked. My question seemed to throw him for a second. Aha! Busted.

"You just introduced yourself to me outside," he answered.

I was pretty upset, granted, but I was also pretty sure I hadn't said my name.

"Look, you said you needed my help, right?"

There was no arguing that. I'd never needed help more in my life. I started my story with him sitting next to me in class, intentionally skipping over the little cigarette incident outside the building. I told him about our conversation, and my coffee, and finally about the magical Mountain Dew and my do-over day. I then quickly recapped the events of my second Thursday, finishing with the terrible car accident. I was worked up again by that point, tears and all.

"Sounds like things got worse instead of better," he noted so casually it made me want to scream.

"You think?!" I forced myself to dial it down, took another deep breath. "Please, I really think the people in the van were hurt bad. At least. I can't stand the thought that it was my fault. And poor Mr. Linder's back. Please, help me."

Marlon regarded me coolly for a few seconds, and then said, "My granddad always told me to be careful what I fished for." This was not the response I'd been hoping for.

"What you *wished* for?" I asked, thinking he'd misspoken. "Is that what you meant?"

"No, I don't remember him ever saying that. He was big into fishing. About everything he said had something to do with fish. He used to tie his own flies and—"

"Please, Marlon," I butted in. "*Please.*"

He stared down at me, saying nothing. All of a sudden he looked way less goofy and way more . . . formidable. I don't know why it didn't really hit me until right then, but a man capable of defying physics and cheating time might be capable of . . . anything? Who knew? My next words, as well as my breath, caught in my throat. It felt like the tears trickling down my cheeks froze solid.

"So exactly what is it you want me to do, Cassidy?" he asked at last. Even his voice seemed different now, edgy and dangerous.

It took a few seconds to find my voice again, but I finally managed to whisper, "If I could go back one more time, I'd try to make things right, not for me, but for everybody else, all the people who were affected by the choices I made."

"That's what you want to fish for?" He smiled as he said this, but it was a cold smile, humorless. "Take a second. Think it over. Be sure."

I did. I took several seconds in fact, but my mind didn't change. The echo of the van's collision was still ringing in my ears. If I could prevent it, if there was any chance at all, then there was really no choice to make. "I'm sure."

"Okay. Are you ready?"

"Right now?" I asked. I took another deep breath and clenched my teeth when I was done blowing it back out. I silently promised myself that if I got another do-over day, I'd do it right. I'd remember it wasn't just *my* day. I'd remember how far-reaching the consequences of my choices could be. I was ready. "Yeah, alright. Crack open that soda and let's get to it."

A little half-smile crept back onto his face, and this time he looked honestly amused. "Because it really was the soda that did the trick. You're a pretty funny chick, Cassidy. And a good person. Don't forget that." His half-smile bloomed into a full one, he winked, and then he disappeared.

Take Three

Dolly's doggy voice was the sweetest sound I'd ever heard. Because of her barking, I didn't even have to wait for my eyes to adjust to the darkness to know it had worked. I was back.

I catapulted out of bed, so fast I got a wicked head rush that forced me right back down. I sat there until everything settled, and then I sat there for a few more minutes after that, thinking and thanking and readying myself for the day.

Thursday. It was going to be a good day, and not because I was going to *make it* be good, but because I was going to *let it* be good. Because it had been good to start with—I just hadn't realized. Someone had, though. *I'd have guessed today was one of your best.* Marlon had said that just before he'd sent me back the first time. It had sounded like such a stupid thing to say, but how true it had turned out to be. After all, by picking up that screw I'd prevented a terrible accident, maybe even saved a life. Could a shoe saleswoman hope for a better day than that?

I stood back up, more patiently this time, and started oh so carefully across the dark room. I had a busy day ahead of me, lots to do, but haste right then would only lead to a sliver, I knew. I made it to my slippers unscathed. They were right where I knew they'd be.

I showered, dressed, and ate my breakfast, Pepsi and toaster waffle, without hurry or delay. I had to keep moving, but I had time. I beat the clock radio to the punch, switching if off while it was still quiet, and I never even thought about the empty spot on the dresser where my cigarettes used to spend the night. That is, not until I caught myself slipping the Zippo into my pocket. I gave it a hard look, polished it affectionately on the sleeve of my shirt, and then told it I was sorry but I didn't need it anymore. Its days of riding around in my pocket were over. I had it aimed at the garbage basket, poised for sayonara, but then a better idea came to me. With my financial aid meeting canceled, I had time for an unscheduled errand before work.

My errand took even less time than I'd expected, though it also took a little more credit card flexing than I'd hoped. Oh well, it was money well spent. And even though it looked goofy to me, and I didn't really get it, I had the feeling *he* would love it. I hoped so. I slipped it into my bag and put it out of my mind.

I got back to the house with just enough time to pack my lunch (yes, my same sad lunch) and take out the garbage. I double-bagged the trash, which seemed to do the trick. The yard stayed crap-free, and I kept my hands out of Mr. Linder's leftovers.

Even though I could have caught the bus, I decided to ride the bike anyway. There weren't going to be many open seats, I knew, and I didn't want to put myself within striking distance of those lost cigarettes. I wasn't anxious to see shorty-shorts again either. So I loaded up my backpack, threw it over my shoulders, and saddled up my rusty steed. I pedaled away beneath the flimsy shelter of a rain poncho I'd bought at the zoo about a decade earlier. I'd thought of it just as I was ready to leave the house, found it right away in the top dresser drawer, the first place I looked.

I still got a little wet on my way to the mall, but I didn't get soaked like before. I took my time when it was coming down the hardest, which kept it out of my face for the most part and kept the back tire from rooster tailing. I was a little bit ahead of schedule anyway, and that wouldn't do. I needed to be right on time.

And I was.

"Hey, I'll give you five bucks if you keep an eye on my bike," I called out as soon as I saw the homeless dude headed my way. After fighting the padlock free for the last time back at the house, I'd added it to the double-bagged garbage. Who needed the hassle? And seriously, no one was going to steal that bike, no matter where I left it.

"Okay," the guy agreed after a moment's hesitation. "But I doubt anybody'd mess with it anyway." Right on cue.

"Yeah, you're probably right. Anyway, I appreciate it. Thanks, man." I handed him the Lincoln, my last five dollars, and walked away. I couldn't help but wonder what kind of mood I'd find him in later on. Despite being on my third Thursday, I couldn't predict that bit, which was odd. Well, he was five bucks better off than he'd been, and I had to keep moving toward the next check on my list, so . . . good enough.

I was glad my timing had worked out right with the cart guy, but I was also hoping that by slipping away a little quicker I might beat the old lady to the mall entrance. Maybe if I was already holding the door open when she got there . . . But no, I rounded the corner and there she was, stuck like a lab trying to crawl through the cat door.

"Let me give you a hand there, Ma'am," I offered generously. It was so much easier to be generous now that I knew what to do, right? Wrong! For some strange reason, I did not know what to do. I thought I remembered just the right combination of angles and pressure that had finally freed her before, but it just wouldn't work. And she kept turning on that awful back-up alarm, which honestly bothered me just as much as before. *Eeeeee.* She finally wiggled through again, somehow, but I don't think we shaved a single second off our time. Go figure.

I found Mr. Fowler just like I'd found him both times before, silent and seething.

"Sorry if I'm a little late, Mr. Fowler," I apologized even though I knew there was no point. "There was this old lady in one of those power chair things . . ."

But he was already off to retrieve his stuff, and then he was out of there, done for the day, *see-ya*. I snapped my jaws shut as soon as he turned away from me, trapping the rest of my explanation behind an impassable tooth dam. Nothing I was going to say was going to help, so better just to let it go. If I still had a job the next day, great, and if I didn't, oh well. I'd just have to go find another one. The world would continue to turn.

After stowing my bag behind the check-out counter I headed into the store room and started gathering up jumbo old lady shoes. I was wet from my thighs down and possibly pink-slipped, but I was also caffeinated and generally optimistic about the day. Bring it on, grandma!

I'm tempted to say my shift went great just to keep the positive vibe going here, but that would be a serious, steaming pile of crap. The old lady, though nice once again and appreciative of my help, still insisted on trying on a ton of shoes before ultimately deciding on the very first pair I showed her. Whatcha gonna do? I did manage to shorten the stay of a few of the other customers by bringing their favorites first, and I saved a little time by neglecting, just a bit, the customers I knew weren't going to buy anything anyway. So I streamlined my efforts. Sue me.

When the phone rang later that afternoon, I answered it. "Loving Laces." Had I mentioned the name of the store already? It was Angel's idea, of course. Her dad had given her the honor when he'd first opened the place. Gag me with a shoehorn!

"Hey, Cassidy, it's Ken." Mr. Fowler had invited me to call him Ken more than once, but I could never quite get used to it. He seemed like a *mister* to me. "I wanted to apologize for earlier. I thought we had a major problem with the money, and I was upset. It had nothing to do with you, so . . . sorry."

"No big deal. Did you want me to recount the drawer or anything?"

"No, no need. It turned out to be just a screw up in my sheets. The money's fine. I'm just a lousy book keeper. Has it been a good day?"

What a loaded question that was!

"It's been steady," I answered. "Sales are good."

"Good. You have any customers right now?"

"Nope. We're empty at the moment." Right as I said that Angel came fluttering in. I waved, and she beamed at me with the candlepower of a small solar flare.

"Then you've got a second. Good. I had a phone call from my great aunt a minute ago. She was in the store this afternoon, and she wanted me to know how well you took care of her. She also said you helped her with her power chair on your way in. It was awfully nice to hear. So look, I know there's been more for you to take care of since I had to cut the staff back, but it has helped us get back ahead of our bills. In fact, I think I can afford to bump you up a notch on the pay scale. And I think I should. How 'bout another seventy-five cents an hour?"

"That would be . . . awesome. Thanks, Mr. Fowler." Now I was beaming, and I could tell by the look on her face over there that Angel thought it was because of her. *Please.*

"Ken is fine, Cassidy. And you're welcome. When Angel gets there, tell her I'm baking lasagna tonight, okay?"

"Yeah, sure. Will do. Have a good night."

A raise! Bam! *Cha-ching.*

"How's your day, Cassy?"

"It's good," I answered quickly. "That was your dad on the phone—lasagna tonight."

"That is so super awesome!" You'd have thought I just told her someone found a cure for split ends. "Lasagna's like my all-time favorite." Of course it was.

I did my best to smile and nod and pretend like I cared as she went on to elaborate on the wonderfulness of her day, but I hardly heard a word of it. I was thinking about my phone conversation with her dad. Specifically, I was thinking about how it might have gone differently if I'd picked up on Thursday number two. He'd probably been calling to chew me out that time, and then to fire me. Great aunt whatever her name was had surely given him an earful about my failings as a saleswoman and a human being.

His great aunt. Seriously, how perfect was that?

Homeless dude was still guarding my bike outside the mall, and lo and behold he had big news.

"I got a job!"

I didn't get that at all, how he did, and then he didn't, and now he did again, but whatever. I was happy for him, and I told him so.

I slipped back into my stylish plastic poncho before riding off, and I didn't even mind when it started raining again almost immediately. In fact, it kind of made me stoked because it reminded me what was coming. This time there was the anticipation to go with it, and I'm not kidding, it was even better than before. Best. Rainbow. Ever. It was so beautiful it triggered my tear ducts again, and left me feeling bad for those poor suckers on the bus that weren't getting to see it.

There were no emergency responders at the house when I rode by, no garbage scraps in the yard. All was well on the home front. I risked going one-handed on the handlebar long enough for a fist pump, and I didn't tip the bike in the process—another minor miracle.

I continued on toward the college, checking my cell repeatedly to make sure I had plenty of time, which I did. When I reached the last intersection before campus I stepped down off the bike, waited for the light to change, and then went straight for the notorious puddle. I didn't even hesitate this time, but plunged my hand right down into that slimy crud, and as I did my bag slipped off my shoulder—again. I caught it just short of the muddy water—again, but lost my grip on the bike by doing so, and down it went—again. Talk about a slow learner. Sheesh!

I picked up the screw and the bike and my bag and dragged it all over to the streetside. I cocked my arm, ready to chuck the murderous bit of hardware back out into the woods, but then I hesitated. I brought it back down to eye level, rolled it back and forth a few times across my slimy-gross fingers. What a harmless looking little thing it was, but how deceiving looks could be! Just like how crappy this day had seemed the first time through.

On an impulse, I jammed the screw into my pocket. I'd keep it, I decided, as a souvenir from a really good day, and as a reminder of what made a day good.

I glanced down the road and immediately spotted the Mercedes and the minivan, cruising toward the intersection from maybe a quarter mile away. The urge to backpedal out of there was strong, but I fought it off, stood my ground. I closed my eyes and mouth, took a deep breath, and waited. It felt like I had to wait quite a while, longer than I should have, but I'm sure it was just my anticipation making it seem that way, stretching the time. It was like listening to the lit fuse sizzle on a firecracker I couldn't see. I knew it was going to go off any moment. And then, finally, it did.

It was still cold, still gross, but at least it didn't take me by surprise, and I managed to stay tight lipped through both rounds and avoid drinking any, which was huge. Plus, I had my poncho on, and it protected me from the worst of it. What a great investment that thing had turned out to be for three bucks. I opened my eyes as soon as I knew it was safe, in time to catch a glimpse of that little punk redhead having a conniption in the back of the minivan, just like he was supposed to be.

"You ungrateful brat," I hollered after him. Then more softly, to myself, I added, "I probably just saved your life."

I arrived at the college a little late, a lot stinky, half-soaked, and filled with a deep sense of satisfaction that was like nothing I'd ever experienced. I was momentarily startled to find Marlon absent from the entrance to the science building, but then I remembered I'd made one other stop first. I was ahead of schedule. Instead of simply waiting for him, I decided to go ahead and run that little errand, just for the fun. Because isn't it fun to have someone magically sweeten your coffee with an enchanted turkey baster? Heck yeah, it is. Take my word for it.

I walked my muddy, stinking self in to the vending area, but when I reached into my bag to dig out the spare change I knew was hiding in there, I found Marlon's gift instead. The engraver had done a nice job with it. Even if it looked weird to me, I was confident it would be the right kind of weird for him.

"Bad day, sweetheart?" asked the gray-haired lady standing next to me.

"Actually it's been a really good day," I answered, which seemed to confuse her. "I got splashed by a car that ran through a mud puddle, but it's no big deal. I'll dry."

"Those things happen, don't they?" she said. "Gotta roll with the punches. That's what my husband always used to say. He boxed when he was young. It's kind of my motto now: *roll with the punches.*"

I hadn't really taken a good look at her before, but she had a funny smile, higher on one side than the other. I got the feeling she'd be fun to know.

"That's my motto, too," I responded. "I've never had a motto before, but now that's it. I just decided."

The high side of her smile lifted a little higher yet, and she said, "I'd like to buy you a Pepsi, sweetheart. Would that be okay?"

"I'd love one. Thank you."

I took my first big slug of it right there in front of her, and it was, beyond doubt, the most delicious Pepsi I'd ever tasted. She looked genuinely pleased to see how much I enjoyed it. Awesome.

By the time I got back to the science building, Pepsi in hand, Marlon was at his post, Marlboro poised for firing.

"Hey, babe, you got a light?"

"As a matter of fact," I offered with a smile, and then I handed him my Zippo.

His face lit up when he saw it like it was his birthday and everybody had just jumped out from behind the furniture and yelled *surprise!*

"Is that the crest of the Klingon Empire?" he practically shouted at me.

"Yeah. I guess it is." The truth is I couldn't remember what the engraver had called it. Lucky for me he was a Trekkie as well as an engraver. He'd sketched out the design on paper for me, promised any fellow Trekkie would love it, and I'd taken him at his word. What else could I do? Like I knew about any of that crap. But now that I saw the look on Marlon's face, I knew I'd scored a hit. *Right on.*

"Right on," Marlon said, echoing my thoughts again. Okay, that could not be coincidence.

He thumbed open the Zippo like a pro, flicked it to life, but I stopped him just as he was about to light up.

"Actually, I'm trying to quit. Could you wait a sec until I'm out of range?"

"But what about this?" He held up the lighter.

"I don't need it anymore. Keep it."

"Whaaat? For real?" he asked, shifting his eyes back and forth between me and the lighter. "Thanks, babe. That is too groovy."

"That's me," I agreed as I headed in for class. "I'm a groovy kind of chick."

"Peace out, Cassidy."

I just caught that last bit as the door was swinging closed behind me, and this time I knew, I *knew,* I had not said my name. I spun back around, but he was gone. I thought about asking the other students who were lounging around if they'd seen which way he'd gone, but they wouldn't have. I was pretty sure.

I had trouble concentrating that night in class, and understandably, right? When our break time came around I took my Pepsi, which was still half-full, and walked outside to stretch my legs. The sun was setting, and the sky was almost clear, stained a beautiful rusty red in the west. I was glad to see the rain had moved on because I'd left my poncho inside. There was still no sign of Marlon, but there was this suit and tie guy who gave me the funniest look as I stepped out the door. He walked on for a second, but then glanced back and gave me the same funny look again. A nervous feeling rose up inside me when he started back my way. I was in uncharted territory, the part of Thursday I hadn't rehearsed.

"Excuse me, miss," he said hesitantly. "Didn't I see you at the mall today?"

Now it was my turn to hesitate. I tried to remember if he was one of the no-buy customers I'd neglected. I didn't think so.

"Yeah, I was there. I work at the shoe store."

"I thought so, but I wasn't sure. You were wearing one of those disposable rain jacket things, a poncho. With little pink zebras on it. You were pretty well hidden under there."

"Yeah, that was the point," I said as my fakey smile slid into place. "The rain showed up while I was riding my bike to work."

And yes, the poncho really was safari Barbie style. I saw no need to share that particular detail before.

"Those things happen, don't they?" he said. Whoa, was that an echo? "My name is Logan Fordson. I work here at the college. I saw you helping out that young man on your way into the mall today, and I was . . . impressed. It's so easy to just look the other way in situations like that, and most people do. Most of the time I do, but today you inspired me to be better. After you went inside I offered him a job, a position on our grounds staff, and he accepted. I have a good feeling about him, and I have a good feeling for having taken a chance on him. I just thought you might like to know, and I wanted to say . . . thanks."

"You're welcome." Hmmm? Had I ever said those words before and really meant them? Not that I could recall, but this time I did. I said them again just to see if it would give me the same good feeling a second time. It did. "You're both welcome."

He nodded and offered his hand, which I accepted.

"I guess we both got in our good deed for the day," he said as we shook.

"Actually, I got in several," I amended. "It's been a good day."

Printed in the United States
By Bookmasters